NINE YEARS GONE

SHELLY CRUZ

Jennifer

NINE YEARS GONE

Love is a
Sacrifice. ♡ *[signature]*

Para mi media naranja. Te amo. Te adoro, tu eres…

CHAPTER ONE

The Last Time

MARIALENA

"WHAT TIME ARE YOU leaving for Mohegan?" I ask Massimo as I'm stretching my arm into the upper cabinet in search of the coffee beans.

His trip to the Mohegan Sun Casino in Connecticut with the guys is today—a prequel to his bachelor weekend next month. One of his buddies, Dom, is a car collector, and several of the guys usually drive down for the car show and auction.

"At 4:30 p.m. I'm picking Benny up at noon. We're

gonna grab lunch at Umberto's before driving south," he responds, yawning while sitting at the kitchen counter. Galleria Umberto's is a long-time lunch-only place in Boston's North End best known for its Sicilian-style pizza and arancini.

"Mmm, I'm wicked jealous. You know I love their food."

"What about the rest of the guys? They're not having lunch?" I ask as I'm filling the kettle with water. After placing it on the stovetop, I set the timer to ensure it doesn't boil.

I scoop coffee beans into the grinder, place the lid on but don't press down as I'm waiting for his response. I glance over the top of my glasses and stare at Massimo. He's beautiful, especially at this time of day, just woken with sleep in his dark eyes, jet-black hair thick and messy.

My heart pangs because this is the last morning he'll sit across from me as I'm making coffee. Jesus, what I'm about to do is gonna shatter him. But I can't think about that right now—not with him inches away from me.

"They're both working. We'll pick up Dom from his office, and the others will meet us at Mohegan later tonight," he tells me as he's scrubbing his hands over his sexy morning stubble.

I press down on the coffee grinder and pour the grounds into the French press. As I wait for the kettle to finish, I strut over to Massimo. He's perched on the stool on the other side of the kitchen counter, and I step into him so I can be closer.

He welcomes me by widening his legs and wrapping his arms around my thick waist. Gazing up at me, he purses his lips, something he does on the regular. It's his way of silently asking for a kiss, and no matter how many times he does it, my belly flutters.

I smirk, take my glasses off, and drop them on the counter, leaning down to kiss him. His lips are warm and soft. As I do, he squeezes his arms around me and pulls me down into his lap, deepening the kiss. "Intoxicating" is the only way I can describe his kisses, his touch, his scent, everything about him.

I break away from our kiss and say, "I'm opening today, so I have to leave by 10:30 a.m." I hate that I have to work today; I'd rather stay home so I can savor him for our last few hours together. But, if I don't go to work, he'll know something is up. My arms tighten around him, taking in his strength—committing it to memory.

His fingers draw circles on my lower back. "Okay, now stop talking." He resumes kissing me, deep and slow, where we spend a few minutes loving on each other.

The timer beeps and interrupts our morning make out session. Reluctantly, I pull back and replace my glasses, touching my right hand over my swollen lips while sliding off his lap.

He smacks my ass, and with a mischievous grin says, "You know exactly how to get me all worked up, don't you?"

"I have no idea what you're talking about." I sashay away from him, knowing he's ogling my big ass because I'm still in my tank and panties. He's right, though, because I'm as worked up as he is. I remove the kettle from the stove, pour water into the French press, and let the coffee brew as I get our mugs ready for us to have breakfast.

After I finish the breakfast cleanup, I head to our bedroom to shower and get ready for work. I expect to find Massimo in the shower or packing. Instead, when I step into the bedroom, he's sitting on the antique trunk at the foot of the bed, naked, reclining back, stroking himself. It stops me in my tracks, although it shouldn't because this is typical Massimo—always ready for sex, want and need at the forefront of his voracious sexual appetite. *Fuck, I'm gonna miss it, in all its thick glory.*

I lean against the entryway and watch him as I'm licking my lips from the longing he creates in me. "Hard at work?"

His eyes, dark and hooded with desire, bore into mine when he says in a low, husky voice, "Come over here. You're leaving soon, and I won't get to be inside you until next week."

My heart squeezes because I know this is the last time I'll see him.

The last time I'll feel him inside of me.

The last time he'll make love to me.

I push off the doorjamb and remove my frames, placing them on the dresser to my right. I stride across the room until I'm standing in front of him.

He puts his hands on my curvy hips and squeezes before moving them over my buttocks. The pressure of his hands heats me. I peer down at him and lick my lips, my curls cascading around my face. We gaze into each other's eyes as he's caressing my rounded cheeks.

The love in his eyes burns at their edges, the embers searing me. Can he see right through me? See the sadness seeping from my pores, itching to escape? If he could, he would call me out on it because the significance of what's about to happen is too great not to.

"Take this off," he commands, tugging at the bottom of my tank top.

I do as he asks, tossing it onto the bed. He runs his hands over my belly, cupping one breast in each hand, squeezing, rubbing, tasting. I moan in response and lift my hands to run them through his ink-black hair, tugging at it. With his desire-laden eyes, he watches me and guides my body down to straddle him. I remain up on my knees so he can position himself beneath me. His fingers are hot, scorching me. He runs them along my skin before sliding my panties to the side, allowing him to enter me. As he fills me, my head falls back from the pleasure, and we get lost in each other.

A couple of hours later, I'm dressed and gathering my things to leave. I work the bar at Massimo's family restaurant in the Financial District, which he owns with his brother, Rocco, and sister, Stella.

Trattoria Lorenzo Restaurant & Bar is located in the heart of the city and is known for its authentic Italian food, with a full bar to complement it. Last year it won the "Best of Boston" award because the chef hails from Italy, and the signature drinks are the best in the city—but maybe I'm a little biased. When the offices start emptying, the bar is full, buzzing with conversation, great music, and flowing drinks.

"Call me later," I tell him as I'm lacing up my boots. I stand and turn toward the door, ready to leave. Massimo rises from his place on the couch and struts across the living room until he's inches from me. I prop my glasses onto my head, and he embraces me, softly kissing my temples.

"I love you," he whispers, resting his forehead on mine.

I lift my eyes to meet his, green to dark brown, his six-foot-three frame towering over my five-foot-eleven one. "I love you too, more than you'll ever know," I respond. As I say the words, tears well in my eyes, and a tear trickles down my right cheek.

"Hey, what's the matter? Why the tears?" he asks, lifting his hands to frame my face, his thumb touching the beauty mark that graces my left cheek, drying the tear away.

"You know how I get with road trips since Benny's accident, anxious and nervous," I say while nodding my head to avoid his eyes as the lie slips from my lips. *Fuck, this is so hard.* For all the times I thought about this moment, now that it's here and he's staring down at me, it's not like anything I'd imagined. It's a million times worse.

He murmurs, "Lena, look at me." His fingers force

me to look up. "You always get anxious but tears? That's new," he adds in a curious tone.

"I'm just gonna miss you is all." My eyes flitter down away from his as I whisper the words. *Fuck, he's gonna notice I'm being evasive.*

I take a deep breath and lift my eyes, connecting with his again. With more confidence and a smile, I say, "I'll be fine. You'll be home before I know it, and then I'll think back at how stupid I'm being. Call me later?" I ask while snuggling into his arms, pressing my nose to his neck to take in his scent, hiding my eyes from his.

He pulls back from me, his hands cupping my face again, and stares at me for a few seconds, his eyes assessing mine. "Okay. I will, babe. Now go, before you're late." He swipes his lips to mine. I hug him, squeezing him tight one last time before leaving the apartment. I close the door behind me, tears dripping from my eyes as I descend the stairs.

As usual, the lunch rush has the bar full, and it keeps me busy. Today, I am thankful for the full house, the loud voices, and the chatty customers because it keeps my mind from thinking about what I am about to do.

I'm dragging today, not my usual upbeat self, who's on the ball while working the bar. Although I wish I had spent the day at home with Massimo, taking in every last minute with him, it's better that I'm at work. With me here, he doesn't suspect anything is amiss.

There are a few familiar faces I see scattered across the bar and in the dining room. Most men wear suits and ties; women wear their business suits or dresses. The lunch crowd is quite different than the happy hour or dinner crowd. Customers at lunch are usually more formal with each other—negotiating business deals over homemade *tagliatelle alla boscaiola*. On occasion, you get a couple who wants to sit in a back corner to hide away from prying eyes. Makes you wonder what they're up to. The patrons that stand out the most are the tourists sprinkled into the business crowd. They often walk over from the Old State House or the Custom House Tower, Boston's original skyscraper, both a few blocks away. The tourists stick out like sore thumbs. They dress in their comfy sneakers, don backpacks or fanny packs, carry folded-up maps, and usually have a camera hanging from their necks.

"Lena, I still need two glasses of Chardonnay and a ginger ale for table six," Beth, one of the waitresses, calls out from the end of the bar.

"Be right there," I call back. She must be annoyed

with me today; it's the third time I've made her wait. I've been in a daze all shift, slow getting orders out and in attending to customers. I haven't been able to focus on anything.

The rest of the lunch rush passes in a blur, and once it's quiet with only two customers remaining, I begin cleaning up when Shannon, the other bartender, arrives. She's a Southie girl, thick Boston accent, long flaming red hair, and milky white skin.

"Hi, Shannon. What's up, girl?" I ask as she's tying the apron around her waist.

"Same shit, different day, Lena. You know how it is," she responds in a flat tone with a scrunched nose.

"Can you cover my lunch shift tomorrow?" I ask her. "I have to go to the doctor and forgot to take the day off," I tell her as I'm loading dirty glasses into the dishwasher behind the bar.

"Sure, I can use the extra cash. Is everything okay?"

"Yes, just my annual checkup with the gynecologist. Exciting, I know. Thanks, Shannon," I say, grinning at her before I finish cleaning up.

The end of the shift drags. I'm anxious to leave, get home, and start packing. I keep glancing at the clock on the computer only to see the minutes crawling. It feels like time has stood still when all I want is to leave.

My phone vibrates in my apron pocket, and when

I grab it, I see Massimo's name across the cracked screen. I hurry to the end of the bar to get some privacy when I press the green answer button, placing the phone to my ear. "Hi," I answer in a hushed voice.

"Hey, babe, how's work?" he asks.

"Super busy as usual, you know how Thursdays are."

"Yeah, I feel you. Don't miss it, not gonna lie."

"I wish you were feeling me; I could use a little of your loving right about now," I murmur into the phone in a soft voice, closing my eyes to memories of earlier that morning. I hear him grunt and take a deep breath in response.

"Lena," he declares in a stern, raspy tone. I know he's not alone, which means he won't say what's on his mind.

"Massimo," I begin, but his name hangs on the tip of my tongue. There are so many things I want to tell him; my mind races with thoughts. Instead, I swallow the words, and "Have a safe drive" falls from my lips.

"Thanks, babe. Listen, we just picked up Dom. I love you. Everything is gonna be okay," he says, reassuring me.

"I know, love you too. Call me later. I don't care what time it is, okay?" I respond.

"You got it. Bye, soon-to-be Mrs. DeLorenzo," he

says in a playful tone. His words sting like a mother-fucker—I'll never be Mrs. DeLorenzo.

When my shift ends, I hail a cab to take me home because it's pouring rain. After giving the cabbie my address, I stick my hand inside my pockabook in search of my phone to call my best friend, Luci. Luci is that friend we all have, the one we all need, the one that calls you out on your bullshit when you most need it.

We have been friends most of our lives. I remember when she started the school year in the middle of third grade. The desk next to mine was empty, and Ms. Stewart assigned her that seat. The desk fascinated Luci because the top lifted, and she could put her things inside of it. I said hello to her, and when she spoke, she had a thick accent. I later learned she had moved here from Italy with her family. Talking to her now, you'd never know she didn't speak a lick of English when she moved here. We've been best friends ever since.

She answers my call on the third ring. "What up, bitch?"

"I'm in a cab headed home, just finished my shift. Are you still coming over later?"

"Sorry, Lena, I can't. I'm actually driving into the

city right now because I picked up a shift."

"Standing me up, huh?"

"Don't be mad. We can hang out another night." Little does she know that won't be happening. I'm going to miss Luci so much. Since we've been friends, we've seen each other nearly every day of our lives. She's going to be so upset when she finds out I ghosted, but keeping her out of the loop is the best decision for her.

"It's fine. I was looking forward to hanging out with you, sharing a bottle of wine, but no biggie." The lies keep coming, and I'm surprised how easy the words spill from my mouth. Maybe it's better this way. Who knows? She probably would've known something was up with me and foiled my plans.

"Smooch you," she says.

"Smooch you back." I hit End and toss the phone back in my purse. Back when we were in college, Luci and I were at a party, both a little buzzed, and instead of saying "love you," she said "smooch you." It stuck.

Once inside our apartment, I stop and take in the view of the place. We live in an amazing two-bedroom apartment on beautiful Marlborough Street in the Back Bay. Its exposed brick and open space are what I fell in love with the minute I saw it. As a young girl, I always wanted to live in one of these buildings. Now here I am, living in my dream apartment with the man I love, and I am walking away. I am gonna miss it. Miss him.

After removing my boots, I stride across the room and sit on the couch, giving myself a few minutes to take in the magnitude of what I'm about to do. I'm overwhelmed by sadness, yet I know it has to be done. I'm leaving behind everything and everyone, and it causes the tears to flow. Deep sobs fall from me as I lay my head back on the couch, my feelings inundating me.

When I wake up, it's dark. I lift my head and rub my eyes. The grogginess of my unexpected nap is heavy, and it takes me a couple of minutes to snap out of it. I rise from the couch and shuffle across the room to turn the light on, the sudden light too bright for my still sleepy eyes. It's almost 8:00 p.m. I haven't heard from Massimo yet, which means he'll probably call me soon.

After I finish eating the sandwich I prepared, I grab my suitcases out of the second bedroom closet, rolling them into our bedroom to lay them open on the floor. I spend the next few hours filling them with my clothes, shoes, jackets, and my favorite blanket and pillow—my life in three suitcases full of stuff—what a sad sight. I lose my balance and need to steady myself with the wall, taking a deep breath to calm my nerves.

This is all way harder than I'd imagined when concocting the plan.

I'm in the bathroom brushing my teeth when my phone rings. Not wanting to miss the call, I scurry into the bedroom to grab the phone off my nightstand. Massimo's name flashes across the screen. "Hello, hang on," I say, slightly muffled because I'm brushing my teeth. I rush back to the bathroom to avoid toothpaste falling from my mouth. Once at the sink, I put the phone down to rinse quickly.

"Sorry, was brushing my teeth. How was the drive?" I ask as I turn the bathroom light off and pad over to our bed.

As I pull back the sheets and climb into bed, Massimo tells me about the drive and their plans for the weekend. I lie on my left side, moving the phone to my right ear, and hug Massimo's pillow, inhaling his scent as I listen to his voice. "I miss you," I interrupt him mid-sentence.

"Me too," he responds.

We chat for a little while when I hear one of his buddies say, "Hey, let's go. The casino is waiting for us."

"Hey, babe, we're going down to the casino. Get some sleep, okay?"

"Okay, be safe. Good night," I say, tears sliding

down my cheeks. "Love you," I mutter, squeezing my eyes shut.

"Love you more," he responds, and the line goes quiet.

That's the last time I would hear his voice for nine years.

CHAPTER TWO

Still Interested?

MARIALENA

THE OLD-FASHIONED GLASS SITS on the rubber mat as I pour a double shot of Jack into it. Once finished, I lift it and place it onto a cocktail napkin just as Massimo slides into the stool at the other side of it.

"I almost thought you weren't gonna make it today," I say, biting my bottom lip.

Massimo has been coming here every Thursday since the first night he came in late last year, but he's usually early, before the dinner rush. It's nearly 11:00

p.m., so I'm surprised to see him here this late but really happy he chose to still come by.

I've been bartending at the Florentine Cafe for a year and a half. I started working here during my last year of undergrad because the place where I used to wait tables had closed. Tracy, the manager from that restaurant, started working here, and she knew I always wanted to bartend. When there was an opening, she offered it to me.

The Florentine is an Italian restaurant in Boston's North End, Boston's oldest neighborhood that's a thriving community of locally owned shops, restaurants, bakeries, churches, and schools. It's often referred to as the Little Italy of Boston because of its long and storied connection to Italy and its culture. Although it's a restaurant, the bar scene here is formidable, especially since we're one of the few places that stay open late every night.

"You miss me?" he asks before sipping his whiskey.

"Maybe," I tease.

"I haven't missed a week yet. Wasn't about to start now." His stare is intense, and my heart thunders in my chest at his words.

"Good to know I can count on you."

He's smirking, his tongue running along his teeth,

before sipping his whiskey again.

"You can always count on me." His words make me blush.

"Is that right?"

He nods yes, our gazes lingering on one another.

"It's quiet in here tonight," he says, looking around the restaurant.

"It's quiet now. It was busy earlier since we had nice weather. Probably not many warm nights left, so Tracy opened up the windows. Why you here so late tonight?"

"Tomorrow is our grand opening. We were putting the finishing touches on everything."

"Well, that's exciting. You've been talking about it for months; I'll have to go check it out soon."

"I'd like that." Happiness spreads across his face.

"Lena," Marcus, my friend who's working the bar with me tonight, calls for me. Marcus was here when I joined the team, and we instantly hit it off. We're on the bar together four nights a week, which means he's basically my work husband. Almost every Friday and Saturday night we hang out after work, whether it's grabbing food at one of the late-night spots or having drinks somewhere. We like to wind down after a busy night and scope out cute guys together.

"I'll be right back," I tell Massimo.

I stride toward Marcus, who's at the computer. He's slightly taller than me, with a short buzz cut and light brown skin. I look up at him and ask, "What's up?"

"I see your delicious man is here tonight," he whispers, wiggling his eyebrows.

"No suh! He isn't my man, not yet at least." I wink.

"Oh yeah? You finally gonna go out with him?"

"Yeah, I think I'm ready to say yes. But he doesn't know that yet," I add, leaning into the shelf to my left. "It's been two months since Stefano left me; I think it's time I move on."

"Girl, Stefano was an asshole. The best thing that ever happened to you was him leaving. Good riddance! Besides, that fine piece of ass—" he points to Massimo, who's behind me "—is feening for you."

Once Marcus and I became closer, it was no secret that Marcus hated Stefano. They tolerated each other because of me. Marcus and Luci hit it off right away over their mutual hate of Stefano.

Massimo has asked me out a few times in the past, but each time he did, I rejected his invitations because I was still in a relationship with Stefano. Eventually, he stopped asking, although he didn't stop coming into the bar every week. When Massimo found out I was single again, he told me to let him know when I was ready to date a real man.

"You didn't call me over here to remind me how fine he is."

"Since I'm closing tonight, I'm gonna take a smoke break and go to the bathroom before you leave," he tells me.

"Okay. Any of your customers need anything?"

"No, I just checked in with all of them. You're good." He walks toward Massimo and out from behind the bar, and I follow him but stop when I reach Massimo's seat.

"Marcus is closing tonight, so when he gets back, I'm done for the night." I nudge my glasses up to adjust them.

Massimo's eyes widen, and a grin spreads across his face revealing his canine teeth slightly raised and larger than the others. "In that case, give me my check. I'll leave with you."

"Night, Tracy," I say, exiting the front door with Massimo behind me. Once outside, I stop, and Massimo stops beside me.

"Where'd you park?" he asks as he's putting on his leather jacket.

Fall in Boston is unpredictable. Some days are

warm, and others are downright cold, more akin to winter than fall. Tonight is one of the nicer nights, high 50s and clear skies. It's beautiful out, chilly air but not cold and no wind—no doubt the Berkeley Weather Beacon in Copley is steady and blue right now.

"I was lucky today and found a spot a few blocks away." Parking is one thing that frustrates me about working in the North End. Street parking is hard to come by because I have to find an available visitor's spot. Most of the street parking in this neighborhood is residential and requires a resident's sticker. I usually have to drive around for at least fifteen minutes in hopes of finding a spot. Taking the T, the Subway system in Boston, when I work nights isn't possible because I usually finish after the last train, and I don't like taking the Kenmore bus home that late.

"I'll walk with you," he says, placing his hand on my lower back while guiding me toward North Square.

The North End isn't just the oldest neighborhood in Boston; it's steeped in history. Among the narrow streets and hidden alleyways, you'll find several stops along the city's Freedom Trail, a 2.5-mile walking path marked by a red line painted on sidewalks that spans the city to highlight locations significant to U.S. History.

North Square is home to Paul Revere's House, and

the streets in this triangular area are paved with the original setts, more commonly called cobblestones, and the street lamps resemble gaslights. The small square is quaint and busy during the day when it's filled with tourists and parked trucks whose drivers are unloading deliveries to various restaurants. But at this time of night, it's quiet.

I'm nervous—the butterflies in my stomach swirl in anticipation. Before speaking, the back of my left hand nudges my glasses up the bridge of my nose. "I have a question for you."

"What's that?" he responds.

"Are you still interested in going out sometime?"

He stops and spins toward me. "Is that a rhetorical question?" He rewards me with a beaming grin that reaches his eyes.

"Things change; life happens. The answer could be no." I shrug, adjusting the frames on my face and looking away.

Stretching his right hand out, his fingers graze the underside of my jawline. "Have I ever told you I love this beauty mark here?" His thumb swipes across my left cheek left to right and back again, over the beauty mark that sits in the middle. His pointing it out makes me squirm. I've tried to wear makeup to cover it up, but I was never happy with how it looked, so I gave up trying. Every time I look in the mirror, it glares back at me like a big hairy mole. In reality, it isn't that big. We're always our own worst critics.

"No, you haven't," I say sheepishly. The touch of his fingers burns my skin.

"Lena, I'm gonna kiss you now." My name falls from his lips as he's leaning toward me, his mouth landing on mine. I close my eyes. His bottom lip is plump and soft. When he moves, his tongue teases my lips, prying them open, and I comply. Massimo pushes his hands into my hair as our tongues tangle.

When our kiss ends, my glasses have skin imprints from his nose, and I remove them. "I'll take that as a yes," I say, blushingly, grabbing the bottom of my T-shirt in an attempt to wipe my glasses. I'll have to clean them better when I'm in my car.

"The answer is always yes."

Heat rises to my cheeks, and his proximity dizzies me. I take a step back.

"Sorry about your glasses," he says.

"It's okay. I'll get over it, but only because you're a good kisser."

"There's more where that came from, but we'll save it for another time." He winks at me and continues walking.

"This is me," I say when we reach my car, a white

two-door Honda Civic. It's a hand-me-down from my mom that she gave me a few months ago when she wanted to buy a new one for herself. The car I had after high school died last year. Stefano didn't want me to get a new one; he said he'd drive me everywhere I needed to go. I now realize it was just another way for him to control me. When my *mami* offered, I jumped on the opportunity because I was tired of not having a car and relying on Stefano or taking the T.

"When can I see you again?" he asks.

"I work all weekend, but if you're free next week, we can hang out. What about Tuesday?"

"I'll make it work. What's your number so I can call you?" I open my pockabook and look for a pen. I find an old receipt at the bottom to write on. When I look up, Massimo has his cell phone in his hand—waiting for me. "I'll save it on my phone," he says.

"617-555-1212."

He punches my number into his phone and hits send, and I can feel my phone vibrating inside my bag. "I'll save your number later," I tell him. "Thank you for walking me." I toss the pen back into my purse and stick my hand in, searching for my car keys. After I unlock the door, I lob my bag onto the passenger seat.

"Good night, Lena." Massimo brushes his lips to mine and smiles as he's waiting for me to get into my car.

I bring my fingers up and rest them on my lips. "Good night, Massimo."

A FEW DAYS LATER

"What are you reading?" Luci asks, sitting at the opposite end of the couch.

Luci's hair is a mahogany red, the kind of red that only comes in a box. She's always coloring her hair and experimenting with bold cuts. Right now, it's short, but it falls just above her shoulders, which accentuates her heart-shaped face. The strands are wispy, giving it a fresh, unkempt look.

"*Memoirs of a Geisha*, finally. I've been wanting to read it forever and kept putting it off." I'm lying on our couch with my knees up to rest the book against my legs.

We share a sweet two-bedroom apartment in Brighton's Oak Square. We wanted a place in the city, but the rent was extremely expensive, so we decided this neighborhood would be perfect. Considering Newton is a few miles away, we can visit our families easier, and we're still close to the city for work. Our apartment

26

is on the first floor of a house, has parking, and has a yard for us to sit in when it's not bitter cold outside.

"Let me know when you finish it. It's such a great book."

"I will. I'm going to the laundromat tomorrow. If there is anything you want me to wash for you, toss it into my basket," I say, closing my book. It's the one thing I don't like about this place; we don't have a washer and dryer, and doing laundry at the laundromat is like torture. It's my least favorite thing to do in a place I hate being.

"I'm off tomorrow; I'll go with you. I haven't done laundry in a couple of weeks, and it's piling up."

"I'm going early because I want to get it out of the way. And by early, I mean 11ish."

"What time is your date tonight?" Luci asks.

"He called me last night, said he'd pick me up at 6:30 p.m." I glimpse the time on the DVD player next to the TV. I already showered because I had to wash my hair, so I have time before I need to get ready.

"Where are you guys going?"

I shrug. "I don't know. He just told me it's casual. We're definitely eating something somewhere because he knows I love food." I laugh.

"I won't hold my breath on doing laundry tomor-row. Who knows? Maybe you go home with him and spend the night." Luci wiggles her eyebrows.

"I like him a lot! But I don't know about sleeping with him on our first date."

"Well, you've known him for a while. Doesn't that change things?"

"I don't really know him, though. Yeah, he's been coming to the bar for a year, but we don't know much about each other, just the superficial stuff. What if I sleep with him tonight and then ruin it?"

"Why would you ruin it?"

"We go out, sleep together, and that's it. It's done, and he won't want to see me anymore. Or, maybe he's actually a jerk like Stefano was. I rushed into that relationship, and look how well that turned out."

"Lena," she says while grasping my wrist. "This guy isn't Stefano! Remember that. I mean, I don't know him, but from what you've told me about your encounters at work, he seems nice. Besides, he's been going to see you every week for a year. That's gotta count for something. And at least you know he's consistent."

"I guess. It's been two months since Stefano left me. You think it's too soon to start dating?"

"Uh, no! I've been telling you to start dating since that asshole left, but you never listen."

"This is true. I'm too stubborn for my own good."

"Glad you own it."

Despite having seen Massimo more times than I can remember since meeting him, I'm nervous as I get dressed. I try on four different shirts and settle on the purple V-neck top with three-quarter-length sleeves, my favorite jeans, and my Dr. Martens boots.

"Luci, can I borrow your lipstick? That mauve-colored one you have?" I yell as I'm heading toward her bedroom. Her door is open, and I go into her room. She's inside her closet searching through her clothes.

"Yeah, it's there in the basket on my makeup table."

"Found it," I say and grab the tube. "I'm taking it with me. I need to buy one already; I always forget."

"Is he here?"

"No, not yet." I look at my watch. "He'll probably be here in a few minutes." I open the lipstick tube and use Luci's mirror to put some on, starting first with my cupid's bow. When I finish swiping it onto my lips, I smack them together to spread the color and, with my finger, remove some from the area below my lip. My hair is down, and because I washed it this morning, the ringlets are fresh and bouncy all around my head.

"You look sexy! You're definitely getting laid tonight, and I'm jealous!"

"We'll see," I say, trying to convince myself more than Luci. "What are your plans tonight?"

"Going to my mom's for dinner, to hang out with her and my sister."

"Nice, tell them I say hi and bring home leftovers, please. I love your mom's cooking!"

"I will. Have fun, and make sure to use condoms." She winks.

"You're too much," I say, laughing as I leave her bedroom and walk toward the front of the house. Luci's right, though. Yesterday I bought some condoms to have in my bag, just in case. Nothing worse than getting hot and heavy with a guy then not having condoms—talk about a buzzkill! Never know how things will go tonight. I sit on the couch so I can look out the front window and see when he gets here.

Moments later, he pulls into the driveway, and I watch as he exits his Jeep, strutting toward the house. He walks with such confidence; it's so sexy. I rise from where I'm sitting and hurry to meet him.

"Hi," I say as I open the door.

"Hey, you." He greets me in his usual manner by leaning in and kissing me on the cheek, except this time, it's different. In the past, it was a quick cheek-to-cheek kiss, the greeting most acquaintances use. Now, he places his lips to my cheek and lets them linger for a few moments. They're warm and soft. When he steps back, he gives me his megawatt smile. It makes my stomach flutter in anticipation.

"You ready?" he asks.

"Yeah." I grab my leather jacket from the coatrack and pockabook off the table, and follow him, closing the door behind me.

We walk out to his Jeep Wrangler, side by side, him with his left hand on my lower back. I climb into the Jeep. It's a hardtop, and inside it's black on black—suits him well because he's always dressed in all black.

When he starts driving, he asks, "Do you like to shoot pool?"

"Yeah, it's been a while, but I like it."

"Good, get ready to be schooled," he says, chuckling.

At that moment, the Backstreet Boys song "I Want It That Way" starts playing on the radio. "I love this song," I say and look over at him. He's stretching his hand out to change the station but stops before doing so and scrunches his face. The lyrics begin, and I start singing along. Massimo keeps stealing glances at me as I belt out in song.

When it ends, he turns the volume down and asks, "You sing like that for all the boys?"

"Nah, just the ones I like," I tease while staring at his profile. His nose is long and straight, and he purses his lips as he drives, his brow slightly furrowed in concentration. "What kind of music do you like?" I ask him.

"Mostly rock. Classic, 80s, heavy metal, but I listen to a little bit of everything. Some rap, hip-hop, dance classics, Italian music. Except country—can't really get into country music."

"And boy bands."

"Yeah, those too." He laughs.

"Where we going?"

"Jillian's. Figured we could grab a bite, shoot some pool, maybe play some video games or something. You good with that?"

"Sounds fun. Haven't been there in a while."

CHAPTER THREE

Cue Ball

MASSIMO

DRIVE INTO THE parking lot and pay the guy at the booth. Once we're parked, I unbuckle my seatbelt and shift toward Lena. "Hey, before we get out, come here." I reach for her hand and tug her toward me.

She unbuckles her seatbelt and scoots closer to me. Her long curls are cascading down her back, over her shoulders, framing her face. I reach up and push the ringlets to the side, caressing the beauty mark in the middle of her left cheek, causing her eyes to flicker.

The first day I saw her, I was awestruck by her beauty, the small mole accentuating her olive skin. Last week before I kissed her, I told her how much I loved her beauty mark, and she squirmed, trying to hide that my pointing it out to her made her uncomfortable.

"You're beautiful." I lean in to kiss her but stop halfway and use both hands to remove the frames off of her face, placing them onto the dashboard. Her pouty lips are covered in lipstick, accentuating them. I cup her jawline in my hands and lick my lips before pressing mine to hers. She whimpers when I gently tug on her bottom lip and suck on it. My tongue darts out, delving into her mouth. She opens for me—our tongues meeting and stroking each other.

Lena separates from me and bites her bottom lip. She lifts her hand and rubs her fingers across my mouth. "Your lips are so soft," she whispers. "And those canines…I liked feeling them with my tongue," she says and licks her lips. The things I'd like her to do with that tongue—thoughts of her using it—make my dick twitch. "They give you character."

"Character, huh?"

"Yeah, a little mischief and a whole lotta sexy!"

Lena extends her hand out and, with her thumb, removes lipstick from around my mouth, and says, "Now you don't have lipstick on your face." Her touch makes me hard, but I need to take it down a notch if we're gonna get out. Otherwise, my hard-on will be bulging, and it'll be uncomfortable to walk.

"Thank you." I shift in my seat to ease the pressure between my legs.

"Come on, let's go. I need to kick your ass in pool. Show you how it's done," she says and throws her head back in laughter. She grabs her glasses and puts them back on, and uses the visor mirror to remove the lipstick from the area around her mouth.

"Is that right? It's on, let's go."

We climb the stairs up to the third-floor entrance and stop for the bouncer working the door, asking for our IDs. I reach for my wallet and hand the guy mine. Lena is digging through her pockabook, looking for hers. When she finds her wallet, she pulls her license out and gives it to him. He looks at it and hands it back, and I snatch it before Lena can grab it. The bouncer stamps both of our hands, and we enter.

"You probably make a mug shot look good," I say.

"A mug shot?" she asks, raising one of her eyebrows in confusion.

"These license pictures are usually terrible. I call them mug shots. Yours is good though, but you're not wearing your glasses in your picture."

"Yeah, I didn't really need them when I had that license issued, so I didn't wear them."

"Marialena Lopez. How come you go by Lena?"

"Because, like you, most people mispronounce my name. Been like that my whole life, so when I was young, I had everyone call me Lena. It stuck. It's easier that way, and now it's grown on me." She shrugs, takes the license from my hand, and puts it back into her wallet.

"I'm sorry. I didn't mean to upset you." *Great, I'm already fucking it up!*

"I'm not upset. I'm used to it." She fidgets with her frames to adjust them on her nose.

"So, how do you pronounce your name?"

"You have to roll your R—Marialena." I love the way it sounds rolling off her tongue.

"Beautiful, just like you, but I definitely can't roll my Rs like that, so Lena it is."

"Show me yours." Lena extends her hand, palm facing up. I hand her my license, and she draws it close to her face. "You're right; yours looks like a mug shot. Considering you'll be thirty in a few months, not bad for an old man." She chuckles, handing it back to me. I bring my hand up to my heart, feigning being hurt by her words, but can't hold back my laughter.

"Old man! We'll see about that."

She winks at me and says, "I'm sure we will." She's flirting, and her sultry voice is such a turn-on. *Fuck, I want to make her scream my name in that voice.*

"Lopez, I like that name. Where are you from?"

"I was born here, but my mom is from Uruguay, and my dad is Puerto Rican. They lived in Puerto Rico after getting married and moved to Newton a couple of years before I was born. I'm the only one of my siblings born here. The rest were born in Puerto Rico."

"Next in line, please," the guy behind the counter calls.

"One table, please." I hand him my license, which he puts into a slot behind him and then slides a pool ball tray across the counter.

"Table seventeen. It's along the right side."

"Thanks." I pick up the tray, and we walk toward the back. Jillian's is a large open space. There's a round bar in the middle of the room surrounded by couches and tables. Video game and pinball machines flank each side of the bar, and several rows of pool tables are in front of us. There are large TV screens all around, all of them showing some sporting event.

The place isn't busy tonight. The few people you see are in small groups, everyone casually dressed in jeans, baseball hats, and T-shirts or hoodies.

"This is us." I point to the table and place the ball

tray on it, turning to remove two pool cues from the rack on the wall. "Ready, Lopez?"

"I was born ready."

"Confident, I like that." I begin to rack the balls so we can start playing, but I want to know more about this woman. I've seen her every week for almost a year, but our conversations have always been nothing but small talk. We've never wandered into the personal, and I didn't push because she had that boyfriend. But now, I want to be all sorts of personal with her.

"You said you have siblings. How many do you have?"

"There's six of us. Three girls, three boys."

"Oh, wow, that's a big family."

"Yeah, both of my parents come from big families too. My mother has nine brothers and sisters, and my father has twelve."

"Whewwww." I whistle. "My parents each have big families too. Made for big family events with lots of food."

"All the food is usually my favorite part." She laughs. "Speaking of, are there menus around here? We should order something to eat before we start playing. I'm starving." She wanders to one of the high-top tables behind me, drops her bag on the chair, and grabs two menus off the table.

I meander over and hover behind her to look at the same menu she is. Lena asks, "See anything you like?"

I inhale her unique scent before responding, "Yes." Having her so close gives me goose bumps. I want to pull her hair and kiss her.

"I definitely want fries. Maybe I'll just get a chicken sandwich," she says. "What about you?"

She has no idea that I wasn't talking about items on the menu. I'm so turned on by her right now, I need to step away, or I'm gonna have a hard-on all night. "I'll just get a cheeseburger." I take a few steps back toward the pool table.

At that moment, a server arrives. "Hi, I'm Cindy. I'll be your waitress tonight. You guys ready to order?"

"Grey Goose and soda with two limes for me, and a double shot of Jack, neat, for him. Two waters, a chicken sandwich with cheese and fries, no mayo, and a cheeseburger and fries," Lena says.

"How do you want that burger?" the waitress asks.

"Medium," I say.

"Anything else?" asks the server.

"No, that's all," I say. The waitress nods and walks off.

I look at Lena and ask, "Taking charge, are you?"

"Habit." She shrugs and picks up the pool cue, begins chalking the tip.

"How'd the opening go this weekend?" she asks.

"Lunch on Friday was crazy busy. Our computer system had some glitch, and we couldn't get it to work, so we had to handwrite orders. It was a fucking nightmare, but we survived. Thankfully, we called support, and they got it fixed by late afternoon. Other than that, it went well."

I saunter over to the pool table, pick up my cue, and remove the rack from the balls. "Ladies first."

Lena bends over and places the cue ball into place—setting herself up to break. Her long curls are falling over her shoulders, brushing the table, and the swell of her breasts peek out from her blouse. She glances up over her glasses, meets my eyes, and sticks her tongue out before looking back down and breaking.

"I had fun tonight," Lena says as she's zipping up her jacket.

We shot a few rounds of pool before heading over to play Skee-ball and then the pinball machines. I liked seeing her relaxed, laughing, and being competitive.

"Me too," I say, extending my hand in search of hers. When Lena feels my hand prying her fingers open, she glances up at me, and I ask, "This okay?"

She doesn't respond. Instead, she spreads her fingers wide, curling them around mine. Her hand is hot, and she starts rubbing her thumb back and forth in my palm as we stroll in silence to the car.

I wonder what she's thinking about. Is she debating whether she wants to go back to her place or mine? Deciding whether or not she's ready to have sex with me? Despite being candid and confident, she's also reserved, so I'm not certain. What I do know for sure is that I'm not ready to call it a night.

Although it's a Tuesday night, the street around us is busy. Lansdowne Street is known for its bars and nightclubs, and every night of the week, something is going on in at least one of the joints. I can hear the muffled music wafting from the establishments; people fill the street and are dressed up for a night out. Women are wearing short skirts and heels so high, I don't know how they can walk in them.

I like that Lena wore boots out on our date instead of heels, not that she needs heels because she's so tall. She looks sexy as fuck in those jeans; they hug those curves of hers, curves that I can't wait to grab hold of. And her ass, it's perky, and the round globes have me fantasizing about all the dirty things I want to do with her.

"What are you thinking about?" she asks, interrupting my dirty thoughts.

"I like that you didn't wear heels." I feel like I was caught red-handed.

"That's what you're thinking about?" She raises her eyebrow in disbelief.

"Well, I see all these women in heels, and I wonder how the hell they walk in them. They seem so uncomfortable."

"Heels are pretty uncomfortable. I rarely wear them."

"I'm not ready for our night to end," I say, glancing over at her. She meets my gaze and graces me with a lopsided smile.

"Me neither," she whispers back. We stand there for a few minutes, people passing us by as we take each other in.

"Let's get outta here," I say, grasping her hand in mine.

When we get to the Jeep, I unlock the passenger door so Lena can climb in. "Do you work tomorrow?" I ask.

"No, I don't work Wednesdays." She tugs on the seatbelt, and I grab it from her to finish snapping it into place. After I do, I stop before her, brushing my nose to hers, then softly kiss her lips.

"Do you want to come back to my place?" I ask,

pushing the hair from her face and dragging the pad of my thumb along her jawline. She nods.

"Is that a yes?"

"Yes."

I kiss her with fervor, eager to taste her, and tug on her hair to tilt her head back so I can kiss her jawline. Her scent drives me wild. She smells like coconut, and I want to devour her. I pull back, and her eyes open, but I can't quite read them. If I had to guess, I'd say they scream, "Make love to me." The right side of her mouth curls up, and she takes her glasses off to wipe them clean.

I walk around to the driver's side, excitement and anticipation coursing through my veins, hop in, and turn the ignition. Before putting the car in reverse, I grab the Stone Temple Pilots CD from my visor case and pop it into the CD player, and "Down" starts playing.

"This music okay?" I ask.

"It's a little intense, but you can leave it. Maybe it'll give me some insight into you." She grins and extends her hand, placing it on my leg, making my dick twitch again.

As we're crossing the lobby of the Lincoln Wharf Apartments where I live, I say hello to Peter, the concierge.

"This is a nice building," Lena says.

"It's all right. A friend of my father owns the unit I live in, which is how I ended up moving here. I like it enough." I press the elevator call button.

"What floor are you on?" she asks as we're waiting.

"Fourth."

Once inside the elevator, I press the "4" button and face Lena. She's standing in the corner, so I grab both of her hands and lift them, lacing her fingers with mine while our hands suspend between us. There may be silence, but our eyes speak to each other. Not sure if she can read mine, but hopefully, she can see that they're screaming, "Yes, I'll make love to you." Her emerald gaze is soft, turned up in line with the slight grin that graces her full lips. She looks like I feel—relaxed and content to be here in this moment with each other.

The elevator dings, and the door opens. I exit but don't let go of Lena's left hand as we walk down the hall stopping at apartment number 409. I insert the key and unlock it, opening the door with my foot. As soon as we step in, I kick off my shoes and place them on the dark red mat to my left, and Lena follows suit.

CHAPTER FOUR

Black & White

MARIALENA

"**M**AKE YOURSELF COMFORTABLE. I'm gonna put on some music," he says.

There's one step at the end of the foyer that leads into a large living room. Two large sliding doors sit along the far wall and open up to a balcony overlooking Boston Harbor. You can see part of the city's skyline and some scattered lights over the dark water. The view during the day must be incredible.

He's at the stereo equipment by the entertainment center along the left wall, and I sit on the couch's left arm. The floors are hardwood and the furniture is all black—sofa, coffee table, end tables, entertainment center, dining table, and chairs—such a masculine vibe.

Various Helmut Newton photographs adorn the walls—all black and white in identical thick black frames. To my left on the wall between the kitchen and the foyer hangs "Heather Looking Through a Keyhole." On each side of the entertainment center there is a picture of Linda Evangelista standing on a city street with short hair, one with her leaning into the camera and another where she's casually smoking a cigarette, both reminiscent of Sophia Loren. On the wall to my right, and to the left of the sliding doors, are two photographs side by side with a couple in each picture: "Woman into Man" and "Fashion Study, Paris, 1975." To the right of the sliding door is "Kiss," and behind me, over the wall alongside the dining table is a picture of a woman leaning over a round table, a man's hand unzipping her dress.

"I hope you like Tom Petty," Massimo says. He walks to the small bar set up in the corner, just outside the galley kitchen to my left.

"Who doesn't like Tom Petty?" I respond, my eyes pulling away from the photos and back to him.

"I think most people do. You want a drink? I don't have Grey Goose but I have Absolut, is that okay?"

"Yes, and yes. Thank you."

Massimo lifts the bottle of Absolut from the table and takes it into the kitchen.

"I love Helmut Newton photography. You have some really nice ones. The black and white suits you," I tell him.

"Black and white photography is my favorite; it leaves an element of mystery. There's room for interpretation when you're looking at it. What color is the dress or the woman's hair? Kinda like beauty is in the eye of the beholder. And life is never black and white, ya know?" I hear ice clink as he drops it into a glass.

The more I learn about this man, the more I like him. I stand from my spot on the armrest and pad over to the kitchen's entryway, leaning on the doorjamb. "I do. It's one of the same reasons I love black and white photography too. Back in high school, I studied it for two years and spent hours in the darkroom. I wanted to go to the Mass College of Art for photography, but my parents quickly crushed that idea. They said they didn't want me to be a starving artist, and I should study something that'll help me in life."

"What did you study instead?" Massimo asks as he's grabbing a soda bottle out of the fridge. When he twists the cap off, it makes the signature hissing sound of the pressure releasing.

"At first, my major was Psychology because I

47

didn't know what to study. After taking a Women's Literature class, I picked up English as a second major."

"Did you like it?" he asks while pouring soda water into the glass.

I shrug. "I guess, although I don't know what I'll do with it yet, which is why I started bartending until I figure out what I want to do with my life."

He hands me the drink he just prepared for me. "Sorry, I don't have any limes."

"I'll survive. Thanks." I take a sip and return to the living room.

Massimo grabs a glass from the counter and goes back to the bar table to pour himself a Jack. When he's done, he strides over to the couch, sits, and pats the empty space next to him. "Sit."

Doing as he asks, I sit next to him, lifting my legs onto the couch, tucking them to my left. "What about you? Did you go to school?" I ask.

"Nah, wasn't for me. My father wanted me to go work with him in landscaping, but I chose to go work at my uncle's restaurant instead, which is how I got involved in the restaurant business." He sips at his whiskey.

"How old were you when you started working there?"

"I was sixteen and worked as a busboy on Friday

and Saturday nights. When I turned eighteen, I started waiting on tables and learning about the business, eventually bartending and helping my uncle with the ordering and inventory. By the time I was twenty-four, I was the assistant manager and started thinking about opening up my own place. I approached my brother and sister, and that's how our idea took flight."

"What's your idea?"

"We want to have several restaurants around the city. They'd all serve Italian food but will have different specialties. The one we just opened is traditional Italian, with food and wine from all over the country. Our next one, whenever we're ready to open it, will be in the North End but will have a menu and wine list focused on the Roman kitchen since that's where our parents are from."

"That's awesome." I swirl the liquid in my glass before drinking some more. "Do you speak Italian?" I ask him.

"Not as much as I'd like to. My parents barely taught us growing up, although I wish they had. Took a few years of it in high school, but you know how that goes."

"How come they didn't speak it at home?"

"They wanted us to fit in, be American. They thought that by speaking Italian at home, we wouldn't blend in."

"A lot of parents from that generation thought that way. I know a bunch of people who've told me the same thing you just did."

"What about you? Do you speak Spanish?" he asks.

"Yes. My parents were the opposite. We weren't allowed to speak English at my house. My parents would ignore us if we spoke English to them. Literally, if you asked a question in English, they would stare at you or walk away from you as if you'd said nothing. It was really annoying."

"Bet you're glad they did though, because now you're fluent, right?"

"I am," I say, nodding in unison with my words.

"Say something in Spanish for me." He puts his drink down on the coffee table and reaches for me, starts drawing circles with his fingers just above my knee.

"Um, what do you want me to say?" The nerves pool in my belly, and I give my glasses a nudge with my left hand.

"Anything, whatever you feel comfortable saying."

I look into his eyes and say, *"Me gustas mucho y tengo ganas de besarte."*

"I have no idea what that means, but it sounds sexy as fuck." His hand moves from my leg up to my lips, and he drags his thumb firmly across my bottom lip. I open my mouth and pull his thumb in, swirling my tongue around his finger.

"Jesus, Lena." He takes the drink from my hands, puts it onto the coffee table, and then lifts my frames off, dropping them next to my glass. He draws me closer to him, and his lips crash into mine. He tastes like whiskey, and his breath is hot. I push my hands into his hair, tugging at its ends. Its thick, ink-black strands are a stark contrast to my olive skin.

I separate from him, resting my forehead against his, and close my eyes, inhaling his unique scent. Before our date, I told myself that I wouldn't sleep with Massimo tonight, but I'm drawn to him like a moth to a flame.

My body tingles all over, craving him—to touch, taste, and feel him. In the background, Tom Petty's "Runnin' Down a Dream" is playing. The melody of the music mixed with the vodka I've been drinking all night awakens the brave woman within me.

I rise, extending my hand to his. He looks up at me; his eyes are dark, lust burning at their rims, and he stands as well. I walk toward the hall to the left of the foyer, where the bedroom is, holding Massimo's hand behind me as he follows.

In the hallway, there is another Helmut Newton

photo hanging on the wall, a woman ascending a grand staircase with a black dress. The scoop back hangs low, revealing her entire back, the slit of the dress exposing the entirety of her left leg. The picture screams, "Follow me," as you stare at the woman's beauty.

When we're at the door to his bedroom, I enter but stop because it's dark. Massimo steps around me to turn on the lamp on the nightstand. He struts back to me and guides me to the foot of the bed. His hands caress my arms, across my hips, landing at the hem of my shirt. I want him to remove it but am also self-conscious about my belly.

Instead, I reach for his shirt and tug on it, wanting to help him lift it off. His chest is firm; short, dark hair covers his pecs and meets in the center, with a trail that goes right down the middle of his abs, disappearing into his pants. His belly is flat, but there isn't a six-pack there, which is how I'd imagined him considering his arms are toned, and his T-shirts are always snug around his biceps.

I place kisses along his chest from right to left, ending on the tattoo covering his left bicep. Black ink covers his upper left arm—a laurel wreath that meets at the top then circles down with a black rose in the middle.

Before I can ask about his ink, he says, "Lena, let me see how beautiful you are." His hands lift my head so I can meet his eyes. I reach up and rest my wrists around his neck, and I kiss him.

I want to taste him, let him ignite the passion simmering inside me so that I don't think so much about getting undressed. He returns my kisses, his lips soft and pliant. My hands explore his torso, fingers swirling over his skin.

Massimo's hands are on my breasts, rubbing and teasing them. The burning sensation in between my legs intensifies with each touch and kiss, stoking the fire within me. It's giving me the courage to peel my shirt off, tossing it on the bed. Feelings of doubt linger, causing me to cross my arms over my front.

"Are you shy?"

"A little." I nod.

He places a finger at my chin, raising my eyes to his. "You shouldn't be. You're so beautiful." Massimo lifts his hands and brushes his fingers along my clavicle and down the center of my chest. When his hands meet my arms, he uncrosses them so that they fall to my sides. He cups my breasts and runs his thumbs over the swell spilling over my bra. His lips find the beauty mark on my cheek and linger there before placing a trail of kisses down my jawline, my neck, my chest until he's kneeling with his mouth at my waistband.

I thread my hands into his hair. "Massimo, please."

I swallow hard; the flutters are a firestorm of fury, want, and need.

"Please what, Lena? Tell me what you want."

"You."

"You already have me. You'll need to be more specific." My skin burns in the wake of his kisses.

"To feel."

He pops the button of my jeans open, pulling the zipper, and shimmies them down my legs until they're lying on the floor. Once he removes them, he tugs my socks off, one at a time, and runs his fingers along the underside of each foot, causing a shiver to run up each leg when he does.

I feel exposed, standing in my panties and bra with Massimo at my feet.

Consuming me with his eyes.

Exploring me with his hands.

Tasting me with his tongue.

I close my eyes, and take a deep breath, reminding myself that this is Massimo, not my past.

My eyes open and I push my bra straps down. He smiles, exposing his canine teeth—teeth I want him to bite me with.

"Are you ready for me to remove these?" he asks, snapping the elastic of my panties. I nod in approval, and he slides them off me. When he removes them, he brings them up to his face, inhaling their scent, my scent, and tosses them to the side. Heat rises to my cheeks at his gesture.

Massimo stands and guides me to the bed where I sit leaning back on my elbows, watching him. He unbuckles his jeans, letting them drop to the floor, and pulls down his white briefs. His erection springs free, standing at attention, and he strokes himself as he stares at me. It's thick and beautiful, the tip glistening with his arousal. Before climbing onto the bed, he opens the nightstand drawer, grabs a condom, and tosses it to my left.

He kisses the area below my belly button, moves to my left hip, and gently bites the skin before moving to my other hip and doing the same. He runs his tongue up my torso until he lands at my bra, taking the bra's fabric in his teeth. At that, I rise and unclasp the back of it, removing it, letting my breasts free from their confines. My nipples are engorged from the arousal he's awoken within me, and he takes one in his mouth, bites and sucks on it, then moves over to my other breast to do the same.

"Your curves, they're fucking beautiful. You're delicious, and I want to devour you." He's licking and tasting my skin as he travels toward my mouth, where he begins to kiss me greedily. His kisses are intense like he's worried that if he stops, he won't be able to start again.

Massimo pulls back from me, extending his hand to grab the condom he tossed onto the bed and rips it open. I watch as he squeezes the tip of it between his forefinger and thumb. Before rolling it down his swollen length, he gives me a fleeting look and smirks. Once in place, he straddles and hovers over me. His kisses are ravenous. His fingers find my folds, begin rubbing, and I mewl in response to his touch.

"You're nice and wet for me, Lena." His gaze is intense as he guides himself to my entrance, sliding into me. "Fuck, you're wicked tight," he says, unable to control his eyes from rolling up.

He enters me, stretching me with a slight sting as he does. "Massimo, ahhh," I moan.

He stops, brushes his fingers across my cheek, and asks, "Am I hurting you?"

"No. You feel so good, just slowly, please."

"Slow, like this?" He glides in, inch by inch, and his stare is so intense that I close my eyes. My body is an inferno of heat that blazes with each of Massimo's measured strokes.

"Lena, open your eyes, sweetheart. I want to see you, watch as you come undone for me."

I open my eyes to his, glowing with need and desire.

My legs adjust, and I bend them to place my feet on the bed so that I can raise my hips to meet his thrusts. I grip his waist, pulling him deeper into me and the throbbing begins to intensify. Massimo's thrusts are steady; each one fills me and drags with each outstroke. My body is overwhelmed with the physical sensation of feeling him buried inside of me. His eyes glisten, and my breathing is heavy as the tingling at my apex strengthens. Pleasure consumes me as I climb to my peak and spiral into orgasm, struggling to keep my eyes open.

"Is that what you wanted to feel, sweetheart?" Massimo continues his rhythm as the orgasm rocks through me. He lowers his head, takes my left nipple in his mouth, and sucks on it while he drags his length in and out of me. Sweat beads at his forehead, and I lift my hands to squeeze his buttocks, to intensify his plunges. He lifts his head back up, his eyes meeting mine again.

"Massimo," I say. My hips move with his, my hands gripping him until he's fully seated within me. I run my nails up his back, and that causes him to come undone, pleasure blazing from his eyes as they roll up.

"Ohhhh, Lena." His orgasm hits him like a wave that crests; he rides it with slow, measured strokes. He continues to move gently, grinding his hips in a circular motion, kissing my nose, my lips, my jawline. Our breathing is heavy.

Massimo's body collapses and he lies on top of me. Our bodies are slick with sweat; the salty smell of sex fills the room around us.

"Are you okay?" he asks, lifting his head.

"No. I'm way better than okay. My body feels like Jell-O right now," I say, smiling.

"Mmm, I'd eat that Jell-O." He grins, kissing the underside of my jaw.

"I bet you would."

Massimo lifts his body away from mine and pulls out of me. A rush of cold air hits me when he does. I watch him walk out of the room as he's removing the condom. I find the corner of the sheet and drag it up, covering myself.

When he returns from the bathroom, he kneels on the bed, crawling across it, and hovering over me. "What did you say to me earlier in Spanish?"

I lick my lips, and while touching his mouth, I say, "I like you a lot and want to kiss you."

"I think I can accommodate that. You think this old man can handle it?"

"I don't know. Let's see." I giggle and bite my bottom lip.

He leans in to kiss me again.

The smell of coffee wafts through the air, and when I look to my left, the bed is empty. Massimo must be in the other room because I hear him talking to someone.

I stretch. My legs are sore after having sex several times last night. It's the kind of sore I could get used to. As I remember our night, my skin tingles. Massimo was able to draw my orgasm from me several times. He knew when to be gentle and when not to be. He played my body like a fine-tuned guitar.

I pull the covers back and reach for my glasses on the nightstand. I'm wearing Massimo's T-shirt, which I slept in last night. It smells like the cologne he was wearing. I pad my way to the bathroom just outside his bedroom door. As I'm in there, I hear him yell, "Fuck, Stella, I don't know but just deal with it! I'll be there later."

Stella, who's that? And why is he so upset with her? Ugh, is he in a relationship with someone? Great, just what I need. I leave the bathroom and head to the kitchen where Massimo is standing by the stove shirt-less and barefoot. His shorts hang low, exposing his deep V.

"Good morning," I say.

"Hi, beautiful." He kisses me.

I fix my frames to sit squarely on the bridge of my nose and ask, "Is everything okay?"

"Yeah, why wouldn't it be?"

"I heard you talking to someone. You sounded upset."

"Oh, yeah. I was on the phone with my sister. She's having some issues at the restaurant, but nothing that can't wait. I'll deal with it later."

His sister, phew! What a relief. I was beginning to think I was played last night. Glad I was wrong. "You got any coffee?"

"Yeah, I just brewed it. Mugs are in that cabinet," he says, pointing to the back-right corner farthest away from me.

"Thanks." I walk over to the cabinet, opening it to grab a mug. "Do you need one too?" I ask him.

"Yeah, thanks. Cream is in the fridge, and the sugar is in the cabinet next to the fridge."

"I drink my coffee black but can prepare yours. How do you like it?"

"I like it many different ways." He wiggles his eyebrows.

"I remember," I say, biting my lip.

He stops what he's doing and stares at me, licking his lips before responding, "Two sugars and just a little bit of cream."

I pour our coffee into the mugs and prepare his. When I sip it, it's weak, tastes like dirty water, and I scrunch my nose.

"Is my coffee terrible?"

"Kinda," I say, nodding. "It's not strong at all."

"I can make another pot."

"Nah, I'm good. I can have some more when I get home. I'm a coffee snob, so it's nothing personal."

"Okay. Now I know, next time I'll let you make the coffee."

"Next time?" I ask, happy to hear him say those words.

CHAPTER FIVE

A Man Like That

MARIALENA

THE RAIN IS HEAVY as we're driving west down Storrow Drive toward my apartment. The radio is playing softly, and we're both quiet, listening to the Red Hot Chili Peppers sing "Californication."

"You ever been to California?" he asks.

"Not yet. It's on my list."

"It's beautiful. I'll take you someday. You'll love it."

"How presumptuous of you." I try to keep my tone serious but am not doing a very good job at it.

"Not presumptuous because I know you and I are

just getting started." His words are confident, yet he's not arrogant. Last night he was polite yet assertive, gentle yet firm. His mannerisms complement each other. Before yesterday, I had never fully experienced the facets of his personality. When he would sit at the bar, he was friendly and flirtatious yet reserved. I always wondered what he'd be like behind closed doors, and so far, I really like what I'm seeing.

"You know?" I ask, raising an eyebrow. He responds with a nod and a sexy lopsided grin.

When he drives up to my house, I'm gathering my things to say goodbye and make a run for the front when Massimo says, "Hang on, I have an umbrella. I'll walk you."

"You don't have to. It's okay if I get a little wet."

"I like you nice and wet too." He winks, before continuing, "But I want to. I'm not ready to let you go just yet." I can feel the heat rise to my cheeks at his remark. Good thing he's turning to get out of the Jeep.

He meets me at the passenger door, and I exit, where Massimo wraps his arm around me so we can both be under the umbrella.

Once at the front door, underneath the shelter of the balcony's roof, he tosses the umbrella to the floor and steps into me, grasping onto my hips.

"I had such an amazing time last night and this

morning. I'm not ready for our date to end." His voice is low and husky. He squeezes my hips and kisses my beauty mark.

"Me too," is all I can manage to say. His proximity makes it hard to think clearly.

"This is gonna sound crazy, but I'm gonna say it anyway," he says with a crooked grin. "I know you're off tonight and then work for the next few nights. What do you think about hanging out again later? I don't think I can wait until next week to see you, and I can't just go to the bar tomorrow like I always have. Things are different now, and it'll be near impossible for me to sit there and just watch you work and pretend that small talk will be enough. Not after last night and this morning."

"You're right. It sounds crazy." His face falls when he hears my words. "But I like crazy, so yes."

He's grinning again, rubbing his thumbs back and forth over my cheeks. "Want to come back to my place? We can order takeout and watch a movie."

"Only if we can watch *Rocky*."

"Get outta here. You like *Rocky*?"

Nodding, I say, "It's one of my favorites. I love them all. If you don't like *Rocky*, I don't know if this—" I gesture my hand between the two of us "—will work out."

"Like it? I can basically quote all the movies. 'Together we fill gaps,'" he says, with a big toothy smile.

I'm ecstatic over the quote he chose. "You're so cheesy!"

"Oh yeah? Come here. I'll show you how cheesy I am." He starts kissing me as if it's the last time he'll ever see me, and I respond in kind.

"You guys gonna stand outside and make out all day?" Luci asks, interrupting us. I look over at her, and she's leaning against the doorjamb, still in her sweatpants and T-shirt.

"Hi, Luci. This is Massimo." I gesture to him, and he's already extending his hand and leaning in to give her a cheek-to-cheek kiss. I remove my glasses using my shirt to wipe them clean before putting them back on.

"Hi, Luci. It's good to finally meet you."

"You too, although I feel like I already know you, Lena talks about you all the time."

I could kill her! I can't believe she just said that to him. Of course, Massimo loves it because he's grinning from ear to ear.

"That's good to hear. Here I thought I was barely a thought in Lena's mind."

"You're right, Lena. He's cute."

I shake my head and laugh. How embarrassing yet

typical.

"Yeah, I think so too," I respond.

"I'll let you two get back to your make out session. It was nice to finally meet you, Massimo. I'm sure I'll be seeing you again." She smirks before going back inside, closing the front door behind her. I can see her walking toward the kitchen through the door's glass pane.

"She loves to do stuff like that to me."

"You know you love her for it."

"I do. She keeps it real. So, what time do you want to meet later?"

"Whenever. Just let me know, and I'll come pick you up."

"You don't have to. I'll drive to you."

"Are you sure? I don't mind." He steps closer to me, pushing back the curls falling over my eyes.

"Yeah, I'm sure."

"Okay. Call me when you're on your way." He gives me one last peck, grabs the umbrella, and sprints to the car.

I watch him back out of the driveway and then go inside. As soon as I close the door, I hear Luci say, "Holy shit, Lena! You weren't fucking lying when you said he was hot. Damn, that man is f-i-n-e FINE!"

"You have no idea! He's so... I don't even know

how to explain him. He's sexy and sweet and an incredible kisser!" My fingers trace my lips as I say the words, remembering the feeling. I sigh and head to the cabinet to pull down the coffee to make a pot of espresso in the Bialetti coffee maker.

"And?"

"And what?"

"How was he in bed?"

I stop what I'm doing to look at her, leaning into the kitchen counter. "So good. So. Fucking. Good! I don't think I've ever had an orgasm like that." I grab the coffee maker and twist it open to fill it with water, and place the coffee basket back in.

"Ugh!" she sighs. "I need to get laid so I can have that look on my face too."

"You do, especially by a man like that. He must've given me at least five orgasms, between last night and this morning."

"Damn, girl, look at you as you talk about him. You're glowing."

Turning back to finish making coffee, with a spoon, I scoop some coffee grounds into the coffee maker, twist it closed, and put it onto the stovetop. "I really like him, Luce—like a lot! I know it was just our first date, but it didn't feel like it. He was funny, sweet, flirtatious, asked a lot of questions as if he's genuinely interested in getting to know me. Most guys I dated in the past loved talking about themselves."

"Before interrupting you, I was being creepy and watching you guys through the door and the way he stares at you. That man is in love!"

"No, he isn't!" I open the cabinet door, grab two espresso cups, and place them onto the counter.

"Oh, he totally is. Mark my words."

"Is it crazy of me to think I could see myself falling for him too?"

"Yes and no. I mean, yesterday was your first date, but you've known him for a while, so not really. When are you seeing him again?"

"Later tonight."

"Already?"

"I know. I feel like I'm rushing, but I can't help it. It was his idea, though. Said he couldn't wait until my days off next week to see me." I gnaw on my bottom lip as thoughts of Massimo swirl.

The aroma of the coffee brewing hits my nose. I turn the stove off, grab a spoon to stir it, and pour some in each of our cups, handing Luci hers before sitting.

"Follow your gut; it never steers you wrong. You'll be fine. You already learned that mistake the hard way, so I know this time you won't ignore it."

"Seriously. Had I followed my gut instinct, I

would've broken up with Stefano long before things ended the way they did."

"Let's not ruin a great morning, enough about that jerk. Are you still doing laundry today?" she asks.

"Ugh, yeah. If I don't, I won't have clothes for work this weekend. When I'm done drinking coffee, I'll go change, and we can head out. After we get everything into the washer, we can have lunch next door while we wait."

"Hi, beautiful." Massimo answers my call on the second ring.

Luci and I did laundry and had lunch. After putting my clothes away, I showered and got dressed, then called my parents and one of my sisters to chitchat. I didn't want to call him too early and sound eager, but it was torture waiting for time to pass.

"Hi. Whatcha doing?" I ask in a breathy voice.

"Just got in from visiting my parents. I haven't seen them since Sunday, and my mother gets worried if she hasn't seen one of us for more than two days. Old school, ya know?"

"You have a good relationship with her?"

"Very good. I either see her or talk to her every day.

She gives great advice and always knows what I need. Usually before I do."

"That's awesome."

"It is, especially since I don't have one with my father." His candidness surprises me, considering we've only been on one date.

"I'm sorry. It's never easy when relationships with parents are strained."

"It's fine. Anyway, I don't want to talk about my father. Are you still coming over?" *Wow, that change of tone was like night and day.*

"I am. What should I bring? A bottle of wine?"

"Just bring all your sexiness. I got everything else covered."

"I think I can handle that. I'll leave now."

"When you get here, pull into the lot and give the guard my unit number. He'll direct you to the visitors' spots."

When I exit the elevator and turn toward Massimo's unit, he's in the hall waiting for me. He's barefoot, jeans hanging low and a T-shirt that's too short for him, giving me a peek at the skin between the top of his jeans and the hem of his shirt. His hair is unruly and sticking up in all directions. As soon as I get close to him, he kisses me.

At first, his kisses are soft, his lips caressing mine. But then his tongue penetrates my mouth and swirls over and around fervently, his hands grasping onto me with possessiveness.

I pull away and look around, afraid that one of his neighbors may interrupt us. "Hi," I say. My fingers linger on my lips, my breathing heavy.

"I missed you," he confesses.

"I see that," I respond, biting my lower lip while smirking.

"Come inside." He holds the door open for me, and I step in, slipping my booties off and placing them on the mat to my left.

When I enter the living area, I see the table set. There is a bottle of red wine in the middle of it next to a vase of red roses in full bloom, the cupped petals perfectly symmetrical. I place my pockabook onto the end table, opening it in search of a cloth to wipe my glasses. Once they're clean, I drop it back in my bag.

"Everything looks nice, and these flowers are gorgeous."

"For you."

"Thank you, that was sweet. Want me to pour us some wine?"

"That would be good. Then I can call the restaurant to order. One of my guys will bring it to us."

"Great. I eat pretty much everything—except no veal and no swordfish."

"Okay. I'll order a few things to share. A caprese salad, and *bucatini all' amatriciana*. Do you prefer *involtini di pollo* or grilled lamb?"

"Let's do the chicken." I pad over to the dining table to open the bottle of wine while Massimo calls in the order. I pour, swirl, sniff, and sip it. It's delicious.

When he's finished, he saunters over, and I hand him his glass.

The melody of the music streaming through the speakers is hauntingly beautiful, and I ask, "What are we listening to?"

"Andrea Bocelli's 'Aria: The Opera Album.' It's one of my mother's favorites, and it grew on me."

"I'd never take you as a guy who likes opera."

"I'd never take you as a girl who likes *Rocky*."

I purse my lips and nod before turning toward the balcony's sliding doors. "Can I open it, go outside?" My hand is resting on the handle.

He strides toward me, stands flush at my back, and murmurs, "The answer is always yes," softly at my ear. It sends shivers down my spine. With his left hand, he covers mine with his, unlocks the door, and slides it to the right, opening it.

It's the tail end of the day; the sky is changing colors as the sun sets behind the city skyline. It's so peaceful out here. I rest my arms on the railing, taking in the deep oranges across the horizon and hiding behind the tall buildings. "What an amazing view." The city's skyscrapers fill the sky to the right, with the Boston Harbor extending wide across. In the distance to my left, Logan Airport's control tower stands tall. "Do you come out here often?"

"No. I work too much."

I glance at him. "But you must take a day off at least once a week, no?"

He shrugs. "Not really. I took last night and tonight off to be with you but haven't had a full day off in months. Between the restaurant and helping my parents, I'm always busy. It's good to have my head occupied though, keeps me out of trouble."

"You're definitely trouble. It's written all over here." I lift my hand to touch his face, swiping my thumb across his right cheek. I begin leaning into him, wanting to taste him and press my lips to his, jutting my tongue out in search of his, and he complies. Our tongues twist and swirl, deepening our kiss, but his phone ringing interrupts us.

"Sorry," he says, his breathing heavy. "It might be

our dinner. Otherwise, I wouldn't even have the phone on me." He checks his phone and then answers it. When he hangs up, he says, "I'm going to meet Kevin downstairs and bring everything up."

"Do you want me to help you?"

"No, I'm good. You relax. I'll be right back," he says and jogs out toward the door. I linger on the balcony, taking in the last few minutes of dusk, enjoying the brisk air. My fingers rub my swollen lips, remembering his kisses. I would give anything to have an apartment as sweet as this one. I'd sit out on this balcony every day, the weather permitting; enjoy my coffee; and read my books. It's heaven. If things continue as they've been, I may be able to do just that. I really like him and hope we're not rushing only to realize he's too good to be true. I'm not ready to have my heart broken again, and I know he would shatter it.

"I'm back." I hear him say.

Massimo pulls the DVDs from the entertainment center and drops them onto the coffee table, and we sit on the couch to relax.

"Oh, you have all five movies."

"My brother and I used to watch these movies all

the time growing up. We'd love catching them on TV back in the day."

"Ah, the good ole days."

"Which one do you want to watch?"

"All of them, but let's start with the first." At that, he rewards me with a crescent-shaped smile.

"Yo, Lena, let's do this." He winks and gets up to put in the movie.

CHAPTER SIX

Noche Buena

MARIALENA

TWO MONTHS LATER

"BABE, WHAT SHOULD WE do for Christmas this year? It'll be our first together," Massimo asks.

"What do you usually do?" I respond.

"I'm with my parents on Christmas Eve and Christmas Day. What about you?"

"Christmas Eve, or *Noche Buena* as we call it, is the big night for my family," I begin telling him. "We celebrate that night more than Christmas Day. We usually go to my *Tio* Ramon's house for *Noche Buena*; his house is known as the party house. Christmas Day, we go to my parents' house to open gifts and have an early dinner. We keep it chill."

"Do you want to do the twenty-fourth with your family, and we can have Christmas Day with mine?"

"Sounds like a plan."

I load the car with the gifts I have for my aunts, uncles, and cousins. My mom is making the potato salad to take, and she asked me to make *coquito*. Earlier this week, when I was making it, Massimo came over to hang out. He was curious about the drink since he'd never seen it. Puerto Rican egg nog was the easiest way for me to explain it. Coconut milk, sweetened condensed milk, evaporated milk, egg yolks, rum, and cinnamon. It's my father's recipe. I hope everyone likes it as much as they like my dad's, although his is undoubtedly better than mine.

When he backs out of my driveway, Massimo asks, "Where in Cambridge are we going so I know which way to go?"

"Broadway, near Kendall Square. I usually take the Pike and get off at the Allston-Brighton exit." I'm searching the radio for some music and stop when I hear *NSYNC singing "It's Gonna Be Me" and crank up the volume. As he's driving, Massimo is stealing glimpses to watch me sing along, trying to hide his smirk.

When the song ends, he turns the volume down and says, "You and your boy bands." He chuckles.

"You jealous?"

"Nah." His hand lands on my leg and he runs it up toward my apex. "This is all mine."

I bite my lip at his gesture and my heart pounds in my chest.

"Are you ready for the Puerto Rican house party?" I ask.

"What should I expect?" he responds, glancing over at me before switching lanes to get off at the exit.

"There's gonna be a ton of people there. *Tio* Ramon is my father's brother. All of my aunts and uncles from the area go over, plus most of my cousins and my cousins' kids. You'll see. It's a serious house party with a lot of people, loud music, dancing, drinking, and tons of food, which is my favorite part."

"Of course, it is. It's one of the things I love about you; you enjoy food as much as I do." He lifts his hand, brushes his fingers across my cheek. My heart skips a beat at his admission.

"Oh, and my dad and uncles sing old school Puerto

Rican folk songs with their instruments."

That catches his attention, and his eyes widen when he asks, "What kind of instruments?"

"My father plays the *güiro*, which is this long wooden percussion instrument. It's open on one end and has notches cut into one side. It's played by rubbing tines along the notches to make a ratchet, scratching like sound—*tsch, tsch, tsch, tsch*—like that. My *tio* Ramon plays the *cuatro*, which is a small guitar with five strings. And, depending on the night, one of my other uncles plays the conga drum. My father is the one who likes to sing the most."

"Wow, that's pretty cool. I can't wait to hear that."

"I think so too, although as a kid I hated it because I thought it was so boring."

We make the rounds saying hello to all the family, and I introduce Massimo to everyone. My aunts all fawn over him, saying he's so handsome, squeezing his cheeks, touching his arms, "*Que guapo, guao*" or "*Que lindo nene*." It's a little embarrassing, but he's such a good sport about it.

"You seem to be a big hit with my aunts."

"I'm a charmer—what can I say?" His shoulders

shake in quiet laughter. We stop when we see my parents in the far corner of the kitchen, my father with a beer in hand, and my mother sitting and talking to one of my aunts.

"Hello, Mr. Lopez," Massimo says, extending his hand to greet my father. "It's good to see you again."

Last month we had Thanksgiving at my house, which is when he met my parents and siblings for the first time. I was more nervous than he was about it, worried that they'd grill him or make him feel uncomfortable. But I worried for nothing because Massimo immediately felt comfortable, fit right in with my family, and spent most of the night talking with my brother and father about cars and football.

"Please, call me Hugo. Good to see you too," my father responds and hugs me, pressing a kiss to my temple. "*Hola*, Nena."

"Hi, *Papi*," I say, before bending to kiss my mother. "Hi, *Mami*." Massimo is right behind me doing the same.

"Hi, Mrs. Lopez."

"*Nene, mi nombre es Blanca*. You call me that, okay?" she declares, more than asks, and places her palm on his cheek, patting it gently.

"Okay, Mrs.—I mean Blanca." He smiles at her, and my heart constricts seeing his interaction with my mother. My parents asking to be called by their first names is their way of letting Massimo know that they like him. I had introduced Stefano to them, but they didn't warm up to him as they have with Massimo. It's funny how we see things so clearly in hindsight.

"Okay, let's go eat," I say. "I wait for this night every year because all my aunts make their best dishes, and I overeat—like a lot! It's all so good, so I hope you're hungry."

There are so many food choices that I make sure to load up both of our plates with my favorites, *arroz con gandules, pernil, yuca con mojo, maduros*. Before sitting, I grab a *malta* from the fridge, and we sit down with one of my cousins, Felix. We don't see each other often, mostly at the family events throughout the year and always on *Noche Buena*. Turns out Felix and Massimo have some friends in common because Felix is a DJ around the city, and Massimo is well-known in the restaurant/club circuit.

When we finish eating, we go into the cellar, where it's an open space for everyone to dance. It looks the same as when I was growing up. The walls are wood paneling from floor to ceiling, the floor is a dark gray concrete, and there's a wooden bar in the back-right corner. The congo drums are along the back wall, and there are a few folding tables and chairs opened up around the perimeter. In a few hours, nearly everyone will be down here singing and dancing, and it'll be as packed as any nightclub.

We gravitate to the left side of the room where it's less crowded. From here, I can point everyone out as a way for him to know who everyone is. One of my cousins is to our right with her three kids settling a fight between them, the youngest of the kids crying over whatever happened.

"Do you want kids?" Massimo asks me.

I look at him, adjusting the frames on my face. "Um, yeah, I do."

"Doesn't sound very convincing," he responds, raising an eyebrow.

"You just caught me off guard is all. I wasn't expecting that question."

"With so many kids around, it just popped in my head. Figured I'd ask." He shrugs before pushing back the curls falling over my left eye.

I continue scanning the room. "That's Felix's wife in the orange shirt," I say, pointing across the room to my left. "And their two daughters, the youngest one is adopted. She became part of the family when she was six because her parents were drug addicts."

"She's lucky she found a family. Adoption isn't for everyone."

"What's that mean?"

"Not everyone is open to adopting a strange kid into their family."

I give my glasses another nudge. "That sounds kinda heartless."

"I'm not trying to sound that way. Just saying that it's not for everyone."

"Would you adopt if you had the opportunity?"

"No."

"Why not?"

"Because I want my own biological kids."

"Nena." My father interrupts us, and I'm glad for it. That conversation with Massimo was awkward and uncomfortable, and we're not in the place to have that discussion. "*Vamos a bailar.*"

Felix is at the DJ table he set up and Los Hermanos Rosario's "*La Dueña del Swing*" starts playing, which is one of my dad's favorite songs. He grasps my hand and starts pulling me toward the center of the floor to dance, something he's done since I was little. I learned to dance with him from a young age by placing my feet on his while he carried me around the dance floor. As I grew, we would always dance merengue and salsa at all of the family parties.

"I'll be back," I say to Massimo. "Watch and learn so we can dance later."

My father and I dance among the others—aunts, uncles, cousins, friends, all crowded together, shaking our hips as we spin and twirl. I see Massimo off to the side, watching us with mischief in his eyes. No doubt he's enjoying watching me shimmy my hips. When the song finishes, I go see Felix and ask him to play Marc Anthony's "*Nadie Como Ella*" before walking over to Massimo.

"You and your dad dance really well."

"He's my favorite dance partner," I admit.

"Daddy's girl," he says, rubbing his thumb across my beauty mark. "I can see it all over his face."

"Yeah, my brothers and sisters rag on me all the time. Tell me that because I'm the baby, I have it easy, and my parents treat me differently." I shrug.

When the Marc Anthony song begins playing, I grab his hand. "Come on. I asked Felix to play this so we can dance. It's a good song for you to learn how to salsa."

"I can't watch you shake those hips if we dance," he whispers into my ear.

"No, but you can get away with having your hands all over me in the presence of my entire family."

"When you say it like that, I'm down, but go easy on me because I've never danced to this music."

Dancing with Massimo is more like counting steps,

which is expected, considering it's his first time. But it doesn't matter—he's indulging me, smiling, and moving energetically to the beat of the music. And if he's uncomfortable, he hides it well. Besides, he's enjoying being handsy with me.

"I'm terrible at this salsa thing," he says, laughing.

"Yeah, you are. But it's okay; you'll learn the more you do it." I look into his eyes, hoping he can see that mine are telling him I want him to stick around.

CHAPTER SEVEN

Loyalty

MASSIMO

TWO MONTHS LATER

"HAVE YOU THOUGHT ANY more about coming to work at my place?" I ask Lena as we back out of her driveway. We spent the night here last night because we were at her brother's house in Newton until late. We're driving into the city to my apartment so I can get dressed because we're going out to dinner later for my birthday, which was earlier this week. Stella and Lena wanted to do something more elaborate since I turned thirty, but I asked them to please not make a big deal of it. We compromised and decided to have dinner with my parents, siblings, and some of the guys.

"I think it would be weird," she proclaims. "You'd be my boss. I don't know how I feel about that."

"Well, yes, but it wouldn't be like that. You know we're starting to talk about opening the second restaurant. Hopefully, by the end of this year, we can find a location for it and have it open next summer. I want you to be the bar manager for both."

"I'd still be working for you."

"Technically, yes, but I see it more as you'd be working with me. I want you to run both of them with me. Create signature drinks, train staff. That kind of stuff."

"I do like the idea of that. But I've also been thinking about my future. Do I really want to bartend for the long haul?"

"What are you thinking about doing?"

"Not sure, really. As a kid, I always thought I'd be a lawyer. Some days I think I want to go back to school. Other days, not so much," she says, turning away from me, staring out the window as she twirls one of her ringlets with her left hand.

"That's incredible, Lena. I can see you doing that. Then we'd have a lawyer in the family." She glances over at me and raises an eyebrow at my proclamation.

Lena is observant and intuitive, reserved yet feisty, passionate, and persistent. I can totally see her being a lawyer.

"Tell me more about why you're thinking about law school."

"I remember growing up, my parents needed a lawyer, and he came to the house. I was twelve, and I had to translate for them to help them understand. I was so entranced by him. He sounded really smart. I asked him if he liked being a lawyer, and he told me he did. When I asked him why, he said he learned something new every day because the law lives and breathes, which makes it ever-changing. I never forgot that. Ever since then, law school is an idea that has lived in the back of my mind." Lena's eyes are upturned to match her grin.

"I never would've thought of the law like that. That's a pretty cool way to see it."

"That's why it stuck with me. Anyway, I'd have to take the LSAT and apply, so we'll see." She lifts her shoulder in uncertainty. "I have to be mentally prepared to do it, really want it; otherwise, I'll be miserable."

"Think about it. If you decide to work with me and eventually go to law school, we'll make it work. You know I'll support you."

"You just want the pleasure of saying you're my

boss." She smacks my leg and giggles.

"I do like to boss you around!" I wink at her and grasp her hand, curling my fingers with hers.

"Happy Birthday, Massimo!" Everyone says in unison after I blow out the candles on the cake.

Dinner is at my friend's restaurant in the North End. He recently hired a pastry chef from Italy, who has been getting praise for the outstanding desserts offered. The cake he made for me was ridiculously good, with layered strawberries and cream. Later tonight, we're going to a club because Lena and Stella said they feel like going dancing. I'm not much into clubs anymore, but I have a hard time saying no to my girls.

When we're ready to leave the restaurant, Rocco drives our parents home even though it's just a few blocks away. It's twenty-two degrees outside and windy, so Lena and Stella stay behind while I get the Jeep. We'll pick Rocco up and drive over to Element, the city's hottest nightclub. Dom, Nick, Benny, and his girl will meet us at the club.

Rocco's friend is the manager at Element, thankfully, because the line stretches down the block when we arrive. It's shocking to see some of the women waiting in line with no jackets, short skirts, and open shoes as if it were the middle of summer.

Once inside, we check our coats and take the stairs up to the fourth floor, which is the main floor of the club. Element is actually a restaurant and club, with the first three floors being dining rooms and the top two being the nightclub. The fifth floor overlooks the fourth-floor bar and dance area, so the space up there tends to be more crowded. The DJ booth is perched in a private balcony overlooking the entire club. Tonight, she has the crowd going wild with electronic music pumping through the speakers.

The place is packed, bodies one next to the other as we shoulder our way through the throngs of people toward the bar. As I part the crowd, I have Lena's hand grasped firmly in mine; behind her are Stella and Rocco. Lena is looking around for Luci, who said she was meeting us here after she finished work. Since Luci bartends at a few different places around the city, she rarely gets to come out with us, so I was surprised to hear she would be here.

She'll be meeting my friends for the first time, although she's met Stella a few times already when Stella has hung out with Lena. Dom and Nick are already at the bar when we get there, and Benny and his girl are off to the side in their own world, dancing.

I'm waiting for the bartender to take my order when I hear Lena greet Luci behind me. Lena's face lights up now that Luci is here. I order us lemon drop shots because Lena doesn't like to mix her alcohol, and she'll only do shots if they're vodka based.

I gesture for Benny to come over so I can hand out the drinks. "Thank you all for celebrating thirty with me. I wouldn't want to be with anyone else. Salute!" We raise our glasses and shoot them back.

Lena takes the opportunity to introduce Luci to the guys. Although I can't really hear what they're saying over the loud music, I can see it written all over Dom's face that he's into Luci. She's a beautiful girl, so it's no surprise. He's gonna be disappointed to find out she's dating someone.

"Come on, old man. Let's dance and see those moves," Lena says, grasping my hand and pulling me toward the dance floor.

She looks sexy as fuck tonight. She's wearing a black skirt that hugs all her curves and falls above her knees with black tights and knee-high boots. Her red scoop-neck top lets me see the swell of her breasts, and it makes me hard. She has no idea how sexy she is. She's modest in comparison to how most women dress, rarely showing skin. But that's one of the things I love about her. My imagination runs wild thinking about what's underneath her clothes, even though I already know—and it's all mine!

The electric beats cause our bodies to move in unison, her back to my front, and I grasp onto her rounded hips, squeezing and hugging her so she can feel my hard-on. I push her curls back from her shoulder, exposing her sweat-sheened neck, and drop kisses there, inhaling her coconut scent. Lena lifts her hands, wrapping them around my neck, pulling my face toward hers in search of my lips. When our mouths collide, she turns into me, deepening our kiss.

Lena brings her lips to my ear and whispers, "Happy Birthday, Massimo. I'll give you the rest of your gift later when we're home, and it's just you and me." Her breath is hot, her voice sultry, and I feel my dick straining inside my jeans. She's rubbing her nose against mine and licking her lips that are covered in dark red lipstick. Lipstick that accentuates her full lips and makes me want to fuck her mouth.

"The only gift I ever want."

"Don't I know it," she responds before eagerly kissing me. Her lips are fiery, and she shoves her tongue into my mouth, caressing my teeth.

She breaks away from me, saying, "I'm gonna go to the bathroom—gotta pee, and my glasses are all dirty."

"Okay. Take Luci or Stella with you," I say, my breathing still heavy. We start making our way back toward where the others are still by the bar, drinking and swaying to the music, the bulge in my jeans making it uncomfortable to walk. Thankfully it's dark and crowded in here. Dom and Luci are off to the side, trying to have a conversation, so Lena grabs Stella and heads toward the bathroom.

I order a tall glass of ice water from the bartender. No more drinks for me since I have to drive later. At that moment, Rocco squeezes in next to me and starts telling me that he was talking to his friend about our next restaurant and what they were discussing. He set a meeting for us for next week where we can sit down to talk business without all the noise around us.

"Will you order me another drink?" Stella asks.

"Where's Lena?" I respond, glancing over Stella's shoulder.

"She stopped back there to talk to someone," she answers, pointing toward the bathroom.

I push past her and rush toward the bathroom when I spot her talking to Stefano. His hand is grasping her left arm firmly, and she's trying to push it off of her. From this angle, I can't tell if she looks scared or upset.

I keep forcing my way through the crowd to get closer, and when I reach her, I clench his wrist, shoving it away from her. "Get your fucking hands off her!"

"Massimo, it's okay. I'm handling it," Lena says, laying her hand on my arm in an attempt to calm me down.

"So it's true, you are with this tool. I had heard you two were dating but didn't actually think you'd go out with him," he says to Lena while looking at me.

"Stefano, I see you haven't changed. You're still an asshole. Come on, Massimo, let's go," Lena says, as she's pulling my arm, but I'm not moving. I want to rip this douchebag's face off for putting his hands on my girl and for talking smack.

"That's right! Let your girl save you. You've always been a pussy," he says, a sneer rolling off his tongue. Rage overtakes me, and I yank my arm away from Lena. She must pick up on my anger because before I know it, she's standing between Stefano and me.

"Lena, move!"

"No. Massimo, let's go." Her arms stretch out to rest on my chest. Her eyes are searching for mine, but my blood is boiling, and all I see is my fist breaking this asshole's nose. "I want to go home. Let's leave."

"Lena, fucking move. NOW!"

She flinches.

"Okay. I am moving," she says, taking a step back, "but I'm walking to the door and leaving. So, you better come with me because I'm going home."

She's stoic in her words, but all I want to do is punch Stefano's face in. She stares into my eyes before turning her back to me and leaving. *Fuck!*

When I look back to where Stefano is standing, he's no longer there, and the people around me are all staring.

"What happened?" Stella asks, approaching me from behind.

Without looking at her, I respond, "Go get Luci, tell her we're leaving." I shove my way through the crowd, and when I get to the stairs, I take them down two at a time. Lena is on the stairs on the second floor, waiting for me, and her eyes are turbulent behind her wire frames.

"What the fuck was that?" I growl.

"Why are you yelling at me?" She moves to the side to let a group of women pass us as they're ascending the stairs.

"You're defending that douchebag now?"

"What? No, of course not!" Her head shakes. "I was handling the situation before you came over and caused a scene."

"Caused a scene? You haven't seen anything, sweetheart. I wanted to fucking destroy him!"

"I know, which is exactly why I did it."

"I can't believe you defended him. What were you thinking?"

"Are you listening to yourself? I didn't defend him! I stopped you from getting into a fight."

Her words infuriate me even more. "Exactly! You defended him. I see where your loyalty fucking stands." I push my way past her and start taking the last flight of stairs down before stopping to say, "I'm fucking out. Go home with Luci."

"Massimo, wait!"

But I ignore her, take the rest of the stairs down, and head straight for the door. The bitter cold shocks me yet feels refreshing. I have so much rage coursing through my veins right now that the cold air helps me breathe. I left my jacket inside, but Lena has the coat check tickets anyway.

I sprint to get to my Jeep, stick the key in the ignition, turn it on, and peel out of the spot.

While driving, my phone rings, and I see Lena's name. I hit ignore. Seconds later, my phone rings again, and this time it's Rocco. "What?"

"What the fuck Mass? Where'd you go?"

"I left. Make sure Lena leaves with Luci."

"What? Why?"

"Just do what I ask! I'll talk to you tomorrow." I hit End and toss the phone onto the passenger seat.

Last night I barely slept because I was too enraged over what occurred at Element. Add Lena not being with me, and it made for a long, miserable fucking night. But I know myself, and when I'm angry like that, I need to be alone to cool off. Otherwise, I'll say and do things I'll later regret.

I drove for hours last night, blaring music to silence the rage. It's the first time Lena has seen me get so upset. She's never experienced any of my anger issues. Let's hope it doesn't scare her away.

I know it's early, but I need to see her, make sure we're okay. I didn't call her to let her know I was on my way because I don't want to give her time to think about what she wants to say when she sees me. I need to see the look on her face to gauge what she's feeling and thinking.

When I drive up to Lena's house, I park behind Luci's car. I hope she's awake because it's early, just a few minutes shy of 8:00 a.m. I knock on the door and wait. I'm about to start knocking again when I see Lena walking down the hall until she opens the door. Her green eyes are puffy and red, with dark circles underneath them.

"Hi, babe," I say.

She reaches out and pulls me into her, hugging me tightly. "I was so worried about you. I called you all night, and you didn't answer once. I thought something happened to you."

"Yeah, I probably should've let you know I was fine. Sorry about that."

She lets me in before closing the door. We go into the living room, and she sits on the couch cross-legged.

"What you did last night, that can't happen again," she says, adjusting her frames.

"I know I should've answered your call."

"That's not what I'm talking about, although that too," she corrects me. "If I hadn't stood in between you and Stefano, you would've punched him, or worse."

"I know! You should've let me!"

"Don't you see? You can't do that. It's exactly what he wanted, to goad you. That's the type of guy he is, always looking to start a fight, hit someone. He would've pressed charges against you, just to cause trouble and hurt us."

"Did he hit you when you were together?"

She shakes her head. "He came close—pushed me a few times, grabbed my arms really hard but never hit me."

Motherfucker! Lena's words cause my blood to boil. I should kill him. When I found out she was dating him, it took everything I had to not say anything to her about the type of guy I know he is. Being from the neighborhood, we all know he's a douchebag that treats his women terribly. Not surprising for a guy who disrespects his mother. But I couldn't be the one who told Lena all these things because then it would look like I tried to break them up so I could hook up with her. She might not have gone out with me if I had. I knew their relationship wouldn't last. It was just a matter of when it would end. And so I bided my time. Had I known he had gotten physical with her, things would've been very different.

I need to touch her and feel her energy, so I shift my body closer to hers, resting my hand on her leg. "You shouldn't have stood between the both of us. You could've been hurt."

She places her hand over mine. "You would never hurt me, which is exactly why I did it. How could you ever think I was defending him? I was protecting you from yourself. My loyalty is yours. You scared me last night. I've never seen you so upset like that. Your eyes glossed over, and it's like you couldn't see me. If I'm being honest, there was a moment when I was scared, when you screamed at me to move."

Her words cause feelings of shame and guilt to creep in. This woman, who I love, was scared of me. I would never, could never hurt her; I only want to protect her. I scoot even closer to her, gliding my thumb across her beauty mark. "I'm sorry."

With both of her hands, she grasps mine in hers, kissing them. She starts at the fingertips, moving up to the back of my hand before turning over to my palm.

"Please don't do that again. You caused a scene unnecessarily. If you and I have an issue, then we have an issue. I don't want to argue or make it known to the entire world that we're having problems. Outside forces weaken relationships. What happens between you and me, is for us to deal with. You good with that?"

Just two minutes ago, this woman told me I scared her, yet she already forgives me. I probably don't deserve her. "Yeah, I'm good with that."

"As for leaving, if you need time because we're arguing, I'll give you all the time you need. I get it. When things get heated, it's best to cool off before we discuss it, but please just tell me you need it, so I don't worry about you."

"I don't deserve you."

"Why would you say that?"

"Because I'm an asshole."

"You can be, but you're my asshole." She stands from where she's sitting and doesn't let go of my hand, pulling me toward her bedroom.

CHAPTER EIGHT

Shattered

MASSIMO

IT'S JUST AFTER 6:30 A.M. when I'm walking through the front door and easing it closed because I don't want to wake her. I'm exhausted after playing the tables till late then driving home. I haven't spoken to Lena since Thursday night; her phone kept going to voicemail. I'm mostly annoyed because she does that all the time but never for this long. It's been more than twenty-four hours since I've spoken with her, and I started worrying, which is why I decided to drive home early. I kick off my shoes and pad down the hall.

When I stop in front of our bedroom, the door is slightly open—weird because Lena always sleeps with it closed. I still remember the first night we spent here. We had just moved in together after dating for a year. I had come into the bedroom when she was already in bed reading. When I left the door open behind me, she demanded that I close it because she was scared of sleeping with it open. At that moment, I didn't understand her fear, but I'd do anything for that woman, so I closed it without question.

I nudge the door open, reaching my hand to the right to flick the light switch on. The bed is empty and neatly made. *What the fuck?!* I stride across the bedroom and into the bathroom, flicking that light on as well. Nothing here either.

I stick my hand in my pocket and pull out my phone, flipping it open to dial Lena's number. It goes straight to voicemail again. Now I'm panicking. *Where the fuck is she? Did something happen to her?* In a few quick steps, I'm inside our walk-in closet. When I flip the light switch, it's like someone drove a knife deep into my heart. My step falters. Our closet is half empty. Most of her stuff is gone. The shock of what I am seeing has me frozen in place.

It's early, but I flip my phone open again and dial Lena's mother anyway. If anyone knows where Lena is, it's her mom. "Hello," she answers in a sleepy voice on the fourth ring.

"Hi, Blanca," I begin, "sorry to call you this early, but is Lena at your house?" I ask desperately.

"Hello, Massimo. No, Marialena is no here," she says, still trying to wake from sleep.

"I just got home, and the apartment is empty. Lena isn't here," my voice hitches. "She's taken all of her stuff with her. I think she left me." That last line barely falls from my lips.

"I'm sorry, Massimo, I don't know where she is. She called me yesterday, but she no give any details, no tell me anything. I call her now and tell her to call you," she says, her tone worried despite the thick accent.

"Thank you," I force the words from my lips and end the call. Next, I dial Luci, but her phone goes straight to voicemail. No surprise there since she bartends at one of the nightclubs on Lansdowne Street on the weekend and probably fell asleep a couple of hours ago. I flip the phone closed and toss it onto the bed. Rage mixed with concern courses through my veins and I punch the wall in anger then pace back and forth and let myself fall onto our bed, tears burning in my eyes.

How did we get here? I don't understand what's

happening. A few days ago, we sat on this trunk, and we didn't just have sex or make love. We worshipped each other, and her body spoke to me as it always did. We were like two pieces of a puzzle, fit perfectly together. There is no way this is happening to me right now; it's the fucking *Twilight Zone*.

I abruptly stand and storm out of our bedroom and into the guest bedroom/office across the hall. Most items in this room are untouched: the computer, the pile of papers sitting to the left of the monitor, Lena's LSAT study guides for the exam she was scheduled to take later this year, my guitar propped up against the amp. I hurry out of this room and sprint down the hall into the kitchen.

There in the middle of the empty kitchen counter is Lena's phone, its cracked screen prominent. I extend my hand across the bar to grab it, and it's powered off—no wonder it keeps going straight to voicemail. When I lift it, I see her engagement ring and a folded piece of paper underneath. I drop the phone back onto the counter, move her ring to the side, and greedily grab the note.

Massimo,

Writing this is the hardest thing I've

ever done. I love you, and because of my love for you, I'm walking away. You deserve so much more than I can give you. By the time you read this, I will have left Boston. Don't bother looking for me. I left so you can live out your dream. Thank you for loving me.

~ Lena

Reading the words knocks the wind out of me and causes me to stumble. I need the kitchen counter to hold me up. The only thing Lena's handwritten note does is confuse me more. What the fuck does it mean? I reread it over and over again to see if I missed anything. No matter how many times I read the words, I am unable to comprehend them. There is nothing but heartache scribbled there.

Our wedding is in two months, and we planned on starting a family together, so this makes no sense to me. I drop the scrap of paper onto the counter, lean forward, resting my hands along the edge of the countertop. My head drops, and I squeeze my eyes shut, letting out a long breath. "Fuck!" I scream out to the emptiness in the kitchen, in my home, and in my heart.

It's early when I get to the restaurant. The kitchen staff won't start arriving for another hour. After deactivating the alarm and locking the front door, I stride across the dining room to the back stairwell and take the flight of stairs down to the cellar and into the office.

Lena was supposed to work yesterday, and I need to know if she came in. I open the file cabinet where we keep the weekly reports and pull out Friday's folder, but her name is nowhere within any of the documents. I toss the folder onto the table to my left, groaning in frustration.

I pull a chair out from the table and sit, resting my arms on my thighs and hanging my head. I'm at a loss and feel like I am suffocating right now—more questions than answers, confusion clouding my thoughts, pain constricting my heart.

How long has Lena been planning her escape? More importantly, why? How could I not see this coming? Am I that blind when it comes to her?

"Hey, what are you doing here?" my brother asks as he takes the last steps down into the basement stopping on the other side of the table from me.

Rocco is my younger brother by five years, the youngest of the three of us. He reminds me a lot of myself when I was twenty-seven. I always rag on him for being short, although he isn't really short at five-foot-nine, but what kind of a big brother would I be if I didn't bust his chops? There is no question we're brothers though. Other than the height difference, we look like twins, right down to our thick eyebrows and big noses.

"Aren't you supposed to be at the car show?" he asks, confusion written across his face.

"I came back early because Lena's phone kept going to voicemail, and I haven't talked to her since Thursday night," I respond.

"Did you talk to her?"

"No. When I got home, she was gone, took her stuff, and left."

Rocco's eyes widen. "What? How is that possible?"

"If I knew, I wouldn't be sitting here drowning in my own misery," I retort.

"That explains why she got Shannon to cover her shift yesterday," he reasons. "When Shannon showed up, and I asked for Lena, Shannon told me that Lena had a doctor's appointment and needed coverage."

"That's it? Nothing else was said or happened? You

didn't talk to Lena?" I ask, digging for more information in hopes that he has something that will help me.

"Nah, bro. Lena is solid, always responsible. Honestly, I didn't think much of it yesterday," he tells me while scratching his head.

I thread my hands through my hair as I lie back in the chair, tilting my head up and letting out a long, deep sigh. Now it makes sense why she was crying the morning I last saw her. She wasn't fucking worried about my drive; she was saying goodbye. *Motherfucker!*

"All right," I say as I stand, nudging the chair with my leg. Circling the table, I stop a few feet from my brother and say, "I won't be back later today. You and Stella will need to deal without me until I figure this out, until I find Lena."

"Whatever you need, bro," he says. "I'll get tonight's shift covered since she won't be here."

"Thanks, Roc," I respond, turning on my heel and taking the steps up, two at a time, out of the restaurant.

Jogging down the sidewalk to my car, I flip my phone open and dial Luci's number. *Voicemail again, dammit! She never answers her phone. So frustrating!* I get in my car, slam the door, and start driving. I crank the volume and let Anathema's "One Last Goodbye" drown out the noise in my head.

Luci lives in the apartment she shared with Lena before we moved in together. I've been banging on the door wicked hard, and Luci still doesn't answer it. I need to ease up before the glass pane shatters. She must be passed out sleeping. I jog off the front porch, around to the side of the house, and find Luci's bedroom window at the back. I look like a stalker doing this, but I don't give a fuck. I need Luci to wake up so I can find out what she knows.

I knock three times and call out, "Luci! Open the door!"

A few moments later, the curtain pulls to the side, and Luci's face appears. "Massimo? What are you doing here?" she asks while rubbing away the sleep from her eyes.

"Open the door, Luci!" I say, walking away from the window toward the front.

Luci is opening the door and I push my way in, passing her by and walking into the house. "What the fuck, Massimo? Hello to you too."

Luci is petite, well, petite to me. She's five-foot-six and has a short pixie cut that's always colored some shade of red. But don't let her small stature fool you. Luci's personality is fierce, and she has a mouth on her.

She has no filter and doesn't sugarcoat. She'll cut you with her words without hesitation. She and Lena are the same age, twenty-five. Luci moved here from Italy with her family when she was eight, which is when she met Lena. They've been thick as thieves ever since.

"Where is she?" I demand as I'm pacing through the house, searching each room before moving to the next, with Luci following behind me.

"Where's who?" she asks.

I halt in the middle of the living room and get inches from her face. "Luci, don't fucking lie to me! Where's Lena?" I yell.

"You need to back up and chill out, dude. I have no idea what you're talking about. What do you mean, where's Lena? Why would I know where she is if you don't?"

"The last time I talked to her was Thursday night. She didn't answer her phone all day yesterday, so I left Mohegan early and came home because I was pretty worried about her. Turns out she ghosted. Packed up her stuff, left me some bullshit farewell note with her phone and ring, and disappeared into thin air," I tell her, exasperated.

"What?! That makes no sense, Massimo. Are you sure?"

"Am I sure? Yeah, I'm fucking sure. Why else

would I be here knocking on your door like some crazy person?" I yell, leaning into her.

Luci jumps at my words and takes a step back from me, extending her arms out to put space between us. "Massimo, calm down. You're scaring me."

"Sorry, Luci, but I am freaking the fuck out, and I don't know what's happening here," I confess, softening my voice as I let the reality of Lena's disappearance sink in. I stride across the room to the sofa and sit, letting my head fall forward in resignation.

"Did you call her mom?"

"First person I called. She told me Lena called her but didn't give her any details. I'm gonna go see her when I leave here."

"Massimo, I don't know what to tell you. I haven't talked to Lena since Thursday after work, and she sounded fine. We were supposed to hang out, but I canceled because I picked up a shift. She seemed normal, I swear. She didn't tell me anything about her plans to leave," she explains, worry spreading across her features.

"Now what?" I ask, tilting my head up to her. My eyes are burning from anger, hurt, betrayal, and the tears I'm fighting back.

Luci tries appeasing me and says, "I mean, she has to contact one of us sooner or later. When that happens, we'll get answers. In the meantime, I'll make some calls."

"What am I gonna do?" breaks free from my lips, and I can't fight back the tears anymore, as they start falling from my eyes. I hide my face from Luci, embarrassed by the emotions overtaking me.

"We'll figure it out." She's attempting to be optimistic, but her words are wrapped in pity as she watches me come undone. Luci places her hands on my shaking shoulders, trying to console me.

A few hours later, I'm home, and it's the last place I want to be. I had hoped that either Luci or Lena's mother would know something, but I'm no closer to having answers now than I was this morning when I got home to find her gone.

After a hot shower, I sit in the bay window seat that Lena loved. She would sit here and read her books for hours on end. Our apartment is on the top floor of a brownstone, and this window has a fantastic view. It was Lena's favorite spot.

TWO YEARS AGO

Lena's eyes light up the moment we enter the front door, and I tell the real estate agent, "We'll take it." We hadn't even seen the whole place yet, but seeing Lena happy, there was no question. She has a smile that stops me in my tracks, makes me feel things I've never felt before. I'd do whatever it takes—give her anything, just to elicit that look of happiness, to feel my heart swell the way it does when I'm with her.

I ask the agent if he'll give us a few minutes alone to explore the apartment because I want some privacy with my girl, want to fucking kiss her senseless. When the agent walks out into the hall, I grab Lena by her left hand, crushing her into me, and start kissing her soft lips. Her glasses get all dirty from our steamy make out session. She hates when that happens and tries to wiggle away from me, but I hold her tight while I continue kissing her lipstick-covered lips. If she'd let me, I'd fuck her right now while the agent waits in the hall, but my girl won't have it. She's all prim and proper when other people are around, but behind closed doors, she's an insatiable sex fiend that's all mine.

My phone rings, cutting my memory short. I shove my hand in my pocket, my hopes high that Lena is calling me, but when I see "Ma" lighting up the screen, my heart falls.

"Hi, Ma," I say, trying not to sound too disappointed.

"Massimo, Rocco called to tell me what happened. *Figlio, mi dispiace.* What can I do for you? You want me to come to the house?"

"No, Ma, I'm good. I just need some time alone."

"You want to talk about it?" she asks, her words blanketed in worry.

"Not now, Ma."

"*Figlio*, I'm worried for you."

"I know you are, but don't be. I'll be fine. I just need some time to clear my head."

"*Va bene figlio. Ti amo.* Call me if you need me."

"Thanks, Ma, love you too." I flip the phone closed and toss it on the couch.

When I look up, I notice that Lena left behind her beloved books, her bookshelf untouched, including the framed picture of us that sits on the top right. We went to a wedding last year, and she said this was her favorite photo from that night because we weren't looking at the camera, but instead, we were laughing and looking at each other. I stand and grab the frame. I thought we were happy. "WHY?" I scream at no one and hurl it against the wall, watching the glass shatter into a million pieces the same way my heart has.

CHAPTER NINE

1,301 Miles

MARIALENA

*T*HE KNOCK AT THE door jolts me awake. "Housekeeping," the voice says before knocking again.

The brightness of the sunlight peeking through the curtains causes me to squint until I can adjust to the morning light. My hand extends to pick up my glasses from the night table, and I put them on. When I glance at the clock next to the TV, it reads 9:07 a.m. After driving a little over ten hours yesterday, I had to stop for the night and ended up crashing at this hotel outside of Cleveland. What a long day it was.

It started with me packing the last remaining items

and loading up my car. Before leaving the apartment, I called my mother to tell her part of my plan. She's the only person I told about leaving. I contemplated not telling her anything, just like everyone else, but in the end, I didn't think that was the best idea. I opted to tell her I was leaving Massimo and Boston but not the reason or where I was going. She started with the usual guilt trip she's so good at giving. I'm used to her methods though, and know that I have to let her lay it on thick. Once she finishes, I can do the talking.

It took a lot of convincing to get her to understand that the best thing for both of us was for her not to know any details. Otherwise, Massimo would grill her until she gave in, and I didn't want to put her in that position. I also asked her to relay the message to my father. I'd have better luck talking to him once I was gone. With him, it's better to ask for forgiveness instead of permission.

Our conversation ended with my mother saying, "*Se dice el pecado pero no el pecador.*" This was my mother's not-so-subtle attempt at getting me to give her all the details because, in her mind, she can keep a secret and keep it well. Except this wasn't about her, it was about Massimo.

As soon as I hung up, I got in my car, drove to the bank, and then hit the Pike westbound. I wanted to get at least halfway to Des Moines, putting as much distance between Boston and me as possible. I knew Massimo would be frantic looking for me, and I couldn't risk it.

I kick the blanket off and swing my legs over the side to stand, tiptoeing across the rug. I hate carpets and don't understand why hotels have them. Cracking the door open, I leave the safety lever in place.

"Hi. I'll be checking out in about half an hour if that's okay," I say. The short, stocky woman nods, and I close the door and head into the bathroom.

A quick shower has me feeling refreshed and ready for another day on the road. But first, I need coffee and a quick bite. The front desk clerk checks me out, and before leaving, I ask him where the closest coffee shop is. He directs me to a Starbucks a mile down the road.

I buckle myself in and make a right onto the road with my large coffee in the cup holder and croissants in the bag lying on the passenger seat. While sitting at the traffic light, I put my Marc Anthony "*Todo a Su Tiempo*" album into the CD player and turn up the volume. I love this album, even if it does remind me of the first time I took Massimo to my family's Christmas Eve celebration.

God, I hope I made the right decision. I didn't have much time to plan, but with Massimo away this weekend, it was my best opportunity to flee without him finding out. He's probably freaking out already because he hasn't spoken to me. Ugh, I don't want to think about it. Otherwise, I'll start doubting my decision.

The highway blurs, exit after exit looking the same. I shift my eyes to the dashboard clock, and it reads 1:02 p.m. then check the gas gauge, which reads one-quarter tank. Now is an excellent time to take a break, stretch my legs, have some lunch, and fill up. I'm making good time, considering I got a late start.

It takes me another ten hours to get to Des Moines, Iowa, the place I'd chosen to be my new home. When I was in high school, I read the book *The Bridges of Madison County* and fell in love with the book's scenery. When the movie released, I fell in love even more. It seemed beautiful, idyllic.

The day I decided to leave Massimo, the book came to mind, and when I looked at a map, Des Moines was the biggest city closest to the Madison County depicted in the book—although it's a small city in comparison to Boston. Even though Madison County seemed beautiful, I'm still a city girl.

Driving through the quiet streets of Des Moines, I spot a hotel and pull into the parking lot. I check in for a few nights, and when I arrive at my room, I place the Do Not Disturb sign on the door handle, turning the lock and latching the safety lever.

I'm exhausted, so much so that I forego a shower and brushing my teeth; peel off my shirt, pants, and socks; and crawl into bed. By the time I pull the covers up and lay my head on the pillow, it's past midnight.

It's almost noon when I open my eyes. I have a headache, and I'm groggy, thirsty, and desperately need coffee. I tie my hair up and get into the shower, enjoying the hot water and extreme water pressure that streams from the showerhead, washing away the long drive from yesterday.

Once dressed, I grab some lipstick from the makeup pouch in my pockabook and stand before the mirror. Glaring at myself, I ask, "What have I done?"

Massimo must be looking for me. He must be agitated and calling everyone we know, driving them all crazy with his insistence. I can only hope it won't last long and that he'll accept that I'm gone and move on. That we can both move on.

I pull the top off the lipstick tube and swipe it first across my top lip, from the center down each side, and then across the bottom lip from left to right, smacking my lips together to spread the color, placing the cap back onto the tube. While checking my lipstick, I see a few stray hairs around my chin area. Ugh, how I hate them. I grab the tweezer from my makeup bag and tweeze the stubborn wire hairs until I can no longer see them.

I exit the hotel and take a left, strolling the two blocks to the coffeehouse last night's desk clerk told me I'd find. Roasters Coffee House isn't busy when I arrive. I appreciate the quiet. I can enjoy my coffee and bagel and begin planning what to do next. As I sip my coffee, my eye catches sight of a community board at the back of the sitting area.

When I finish breakfast, I rise and head back to the board to see what I find. It's filled with various flyers for events, live music, tutors, and a few for-rent apartments. I rip a live music flyer off, and my eyes continue roaming. I go back to the apartment rentals, tear off the phone numbers for them, and then return to my table to grab my jacket. On my way out, I stop and ask the young woman at the register if she knows where I can buy a mobile phone.

I walk the six blocks to the cell phone store, thankful for the sunshine because it's chilly outside. Once I have a new phone and number, I hurry back to the hotel because I want to make a few calls—to the apartments listed on the community board, my mom, and Luci. They must've heard from Massimo by now, and I want them to know I'm okay.

Before dialing my mom, I punch in *67 to block my number and press the green phone button to send the call. She answers on the third ring. "*Hola*."

"*Hola, Mami*," I say. "I'm—"

"*Marialena, estas bien? Dónde estás?*"

"*Mami*, I'm okay. I arrived in the city where I'll be living for a while and wanted to let you know." We chat for several minutes about my drive and that I'm looking for an apartment and will start looking for a job tomorrow. Finally, I ask, "Has Massimo gone to your house yet?"

"*Sí, me llamó* early this morning. Then he come to the house an hour ago. I tell him the truth, *yo sabía* you were leaving, but you no give me any information *porque* you knew he'd ask me for it," she tells me.

"Nena," her voice softens as she calls me by the name she's called me since I was a little girl, "he no look good. *No sé lo que está pasando*, but why you no talk with him? I never see him look this way. *Tiene* red eyes, dark circles under them, messy hair," she proclaims, her voice laced with motherly concern.

My heart hurts listening to my mother describe Massimo. It's exactly how I imagined he'd react, except it doesn't lessen the torrent of emotions her words cause.

"*Mami, por favor*. I know it's hard for everyone, for you. Please just trust that what I am doing is the right thing."

"*Bueno*, Nena. *No entiendo*, but I do what you want, even if I no agree," she concedes, sighing in resignation.

"*Mami*, I'll call you again. For now, I won't give you my phone number, *por si acaso* Massimo calls you again, or goes back to your house. If you don't know how to reach me, it'll be easier for you when you speak to him. This way, you don't have to lie."

"*Bueno*, Nena. *Te amo*," she says.

"I love you too, *Mami*." I press End.

The next call I have to make is to Luci. This one will not be as easy as my mother's because Luci will give me an earful. I dial her number, and when I get her voicemail, relief rushes through me. I hang up without leaving a message. I'll call her again later. My fingers hover over the keypad, itching to dial Massimo's number. Should I call him? What will I say? I start punching his number in but flip the phone closed before finishing. I can't. Hearing his voice will decimate me.

Instead, I fight the urge and grab my bag off the bed, looking for the several slips of paper I removed from the community board. I call each of them, someone answering each time, and I schedule a time to look at the apartments the next morning.

The event flyer from the community board advertised live music at a bar named The Last Drop starting at 9:30 p.m., just a few blocks from the hotel. At 7:00 p.m. I leave for the venue. I hope there are a few decent items on the menu—I'm hungry.

I notice there are a few bars along the way. This will be a good place for me to look for a bartending job. I'm hopeful that I'll find a job quickly. I have enough money to get me by for a few months, but would rather not have to use it all.

As I am walking, a gust of wind blows and chills me. I stuff my hands in my pockets and pick up the pace to The Last Drop. When I arrive, I catch a glimpse of a "Help Wanted" sign in the window. I make a mental note to ask someone about that later tonight.

The inside of The Last Drop is beautiful. It's all wood throughout, nestled in a renovated old building, yet the owner kept many of its original features—high ceilings and wood beams. The bar is long and made of dark wood.

I find a stool, two stools down from a guy wearing a White Sox hat, take off my jacket, and hang it on the back before sitting. A woman with braided blonde hair resting on her shoulders says "Hello," a slight twang when she does.

"Grey Goose and soda with two limes and a food menu as well, please," I say.

She pulls a menu out from under the bar and drops it in front of me before leaving to make my drink.

While waiting for the bartender to return, I look around. There are several TVs in various spots around the place, all playing one sporting event or another. The stage is medium-sized, and the restaurant has about thirty tables. Right now, the place is a little over half full, which means it probably gets busy in here. Most of the people in this place are wearing jeans and baseball hats or team jerseys. It's a laid-back atmosphere and family-friendly, as is evident from the few tables with kids using crayons to color their kid menus. Three Doors Down's "When I'm Gone" is playing over the speakers. It's loud, but patrons are still conversing. Local memorabilia adorn the walls—old street signs, license plates, and framed pictures and newspaper clippings. It's a very local place, and I like the vibe of it.

"Are you ready to order food?" the bartender asks, placing my drink onto a cocktail napkin.

"I'll have the wings and fries basket, with mild sauce, please."

"Sure thing, sweetie," she says, taking the menu from me and spinning away to input the order into her computer.

When the bartender returns, I introduce myself and ask her name. "Stevie," she tells me.

"Stevie, I saw the 'Help Wanted' sign in the window. Do you know what position they're hiring for?" I ask.

"We need another bartender," she says. "One of the guys gave his notice. His last day is next week, Friday. Why, you looking?" she asks.

"As a matter of fact, I am," I say. "I just arrived in Des Moines and am looking for a job. I bartended while in Boston. Bartending is my thing," I finish.

"Well, sweetie, Hank, our manager, should be here soon. When I see him, I'll have him come over so you two can talk," she says before shuffling down the bar to help someone.

When I finish my wings and fries, an older man sits next to me and says, "Hi, my name's Hank. Stevie here tells me you're looking for a bartending job." He has a receding hairline with salt and pepper hair and a cleft chin that accentuates his oblong jawline.

"Hello," I say. I grab the napkin and wipe my hands. "I'm sorry, my hands are a bit sticky right now, but it's nice to meet you. I'm Lena," I tell him, and with my knuckles, push my glasses up.

He and I chat for several minutes about where I'm from, my bartending experience, and how long I plan on being in town. He gets up to walk away, but before leaving, he asks me to fill out an application before I go, which is precisely what I do.

Back at the hotel room, I pull my phone from my pock-abook to call Luci again. Let's hope she answers her phone this time.

I dial *67 and her number, and she answers on the first ring. "Hello."

"Hi, Luci."

"Lena! Where are you? I've been friggin' worried about you! Massimo is freaking the fuck out! And why are you calling me from a blocked number? What's going on?" she spews.

"I'm okay. I'm calling from a blocked number because I don't want Massimo coming for me, which is exactly what he'll do if he finds out where I am," I tell her while I'm pacing back and forth in the room.

"I don't understand. Why did you leave?"

"I can't tell you that right now, but it's something I had to do. I promise I'm not in trouble or anything. I had to do this for Massimo."

"For Massimo? What does that even mean, Lena? This is really fucked up! You know that, right?"

"Yeah, I know. I'd probably be having a meltdown if the tables were turned. Someday you'll all understand. But for now, this is how it is."

"When are you coming back?"

"I don't know," I whisper.

"You don't know? So you left, and that's it?"

"For now, yes."

"Geez, Lena, you're scaring me."

"Please don't be. I'm fine, I promise. I'm in another city, thousands of miles away. Just know that I love you. I'll check in occasionally, okay?"

"It's not like I have a choice. You're making everyone's decisions for them. How fucking gracious of you!"

"I'm sorry, Luci, but this is the best way. The less you know, the less you have to lie to Massimo. I gotta go. I love you," I say and hit the End button before she can say anything else. I can practically hear her bitching me out.

I toss my phone across the bed and lie back onto the pillows. What a mess I've created. I hope it's all worth it in the end.

I stand from the bed and peel my shirt off, tossing it on the floor, unbuckle my jeans, letting them drop, and finish pushing them off with my feet, one leg at a time. I walk to the shower and turn on the water, letting it warm up as I unfasten my bra and hang it on the doorknob. I reach down, pull my socks off, and remove my undies. I place my frames onto the vanity then extend my hand to gauge the water temp. When it's hot enough, I slide the lever to run the shower. The last few days have been overwhelming, and that phone call with Luci was the culmination of it all.

I step into the shower and let the hot water burn my skin as I sink down and sit on my haunches. The water and my tears flow freely as one.

CHAPTER TEN

Black

MASSIMO

A FEW DAYS LATER

"YOU'VE BEEN IGNORING EVERYONE'S calls for days, and Ma is worried. She made me come here to check on you and make sure you're okay. We're all worried about you," my brother says. He crosses the room and turns the volume down, Pearl Jam's "Black" playing loud as fuck.

Lena left, and my world has tipped on its axis. I can't see straight. My thoughts are a jumbled mess. My chest is tight, constricting from the pain. Without lifting my head, I look at Rocco from where I'm lying on the couch. He's standing to the left of the stereo system, feet apart and arms crossed.

"I'm fine. You can fucking leave now!" I retort and close my eyes again.

"Yeah, because you look fine, wearing the same clothes you were wearing when I saw you a few days ago and smelling like whiskey," he huffs.

"I said I'm fine, leave me the fuck alone!" I roar.

"Stop being an asshole and get up. At least take a shower. I'll make you something to eat, and you can tell me about it."

I jump to my feet and dash across the room to get in his face. "Tell you about it? You want me to tell you about it, fine. The woman I'm supposed to marry in two months walked out the door without saying a fucking word. She snuck out while I was away and disappeared, leaving nothing but a bullshit note with her phone and ring. And then they didn't fucking live happily ever after! There, end of story, now leave me the fuck alone! I need to deal with this without you or anyone in my face. And leave your key on the counter on the way out!" I scream. I hit the back button on the CD player, cranking up the volume to drown in the lyrics that are currently my life.

"You're such an asshole sometimes. No wonder Lena left you," he says before leaving.

Several hours later, I feel terrible about how I treated my brother, but I can't get past my misery and anger enough to call him and apologize. He's right. I'm an asshole.

After showering, I call my mother because she gets worried, and that causes her blood pressure to rise. I need my mother in good health. I can't handle any more bad news right now.

"Hey, Ma," I say when she answers.

"Figlio, come stai?"

"I'm okay, Ma," I lie.

"You no sound okay, Massimo," she says in her thick Italian accent.

"I'm sad. I'm hurt. I'm angry. But I'll be fine, Ma."

"Massimo, why you no come here tomorrow, and I make you some *melanzane alla parmigiana*, eh? It's your favorite," she asks.

"Okay, Ma. I'll come over tomorrow, see you. *Ciao.*"

"Ciao."

I told Benny I'd meet him for drinks later tonight, but

first, I drive to Luci's house. She never answers her damn phone, and I want an update. Besides, the drive will do me good. The weather is finally warming up, so I take the scenic road down Storrow Drive with my windows open, Metallica's "The Memory Remains" pumping loud through the speakers.

Thirty minutes later, I park in Luci's driveway and sprint to the front. I rap my fist against the door several times.

"You're wicked impatient! You need to chill out!" I hear her say as she's unlocking it. Before it's fully open, I push my way inside.

"Sorry, I'm on edge, Luci. I've barely slept the past few days. I can't eat and I've been drinking too much whiskey. I'm a picture-perfect mess," I whine. I must sound like a fucking pussy, but I can't snap out of it. "Have you heard from her? Do you have any news?" I ask as I continue walking back to the kitchen, Luci shuffling behind me.

"Mass, first, you need to relax! Your attitude isn't helping make anything better!" Luci scolds.

"I'm not here for a fucking lecture! Anything new?"

"Well, then chill out!" she retorts. "Nothing new. I already told you that when I spoke to Lena on the phone, she wouldn't give me any details because she knew this—" gesturing her hand forward at me in an up-and-down motion "—is exactly how you would act."

"Fuck, Luci. I'm at a loss here. What am I gonna do?" I ask, more a plea of desperation than a question needing an answer. I pull a chair out from the kitchen table and sit. A flood of memories hits me.

THREE YEARS AGO

Lena invited me over for dinner because Luci is away for the week. She wanted to make Puerto Rican food; arroz con gandules, chuletas, and tostones. *I've never had Puerto Rican food, but if Lena is serving, I'll eat. I sit at the table while she sashays her sexy ass around the kitchen—opening the refrigerator to get ingredients, reaching into the cabinets for seasonings, bending to open a cupboard and get a pan. All of it makes my dick hard as a rock. I can't sit and watch her anymore. I stand, strut across the kitchen in three quick steps, wrapping my arms around her waist, her back to my front, and bury my nose into her neck.*

"Fuck, Lena, you're so sexy. I can't just sit there and watch you trot around the kitchen like that," I murmur into her right ear.

"Mmm, is that right?" she teases, lifting her hands, tangling them in my hair. "What are you gonna do about it?"

"Well, I'll start by—" I place my hands on her hips and spin her to face me "—kissing those sweet lips." I lift her glasses off, dropping them onto the counter. I put my hands around her face, our lips crashing. I force her lips apart with my tongue, and she moans. While I'm sucking on her lips, I drop my hands, dragging them up and down the sides of her thighs and to the front to unbutton her jeans.

"Please, Massimo," she sighs as I unzip her pants, forcing them down over her hips.

"Tell me what you want, Lena," I mutter, not wanting to distance myself from her, as my hands make my way into her panties.

"I want to feel you inside of me. All of you," she whimpers as her hands lower to my belt, which she begins unbuckling.

"Take what you want," I respond.

She finishes unzipping my jeans, pushing them down, and they fall to my ankles. I lift her up to rest on the side of the kitchen counter, and she guides me to her entrance, easing me into her wetness. She groans in pleasure.

"Everything I have is yours," I say as I'm gliding

135

in and out of her. Her arms wrap around my neck, and her body is lithe. She meets my strokes with her own thrusts until we milk each other dry.

"Massimo, are you listening to me?" Luci hollers, snapping me back to the here and now.

"What did you say?"

"You're such an asshole sometimes! It makes me wonder if you deserve what Lena did!" she spews at me. *Ouch, that hurts, but I deserve it because I'm pretty unbearable right now.*

"Fuck you, Luci!" I retort.

"I said, I know you don't want to think about it, but what are you gonna do about the wedding? It's still on. You have to start canceling stuff. People are traveling; it's the least you should do," she tells me, softening her tone. "I'll help you with what I can."

"Ugh, I don't want to think about that," I mutter, especially not after the memories that were just playing in my mind. "What if she comes back? I think I should wait," I say, trying to convince myself more than Luci.

"Well, I hate being the bearer of bad news but, let's face it, I don't think she's marrying you. I mean, she took her stuff and moved out of your place." Her words are like salt in a wound.

"I can always count on you to throw more wood in the fire, Luce, thanks," I snap back, getting up from the chair, marching toward the front door.

As she trails behind me, Luci says, "Look, I know you don't want to think about her not coming back, about the wedding, about any of it, but you have to deal with it. Rip the Band-Aid off already. Besides, I'm on your side right now because I'm pissed at Lena. This stunt she pulled is affecting all of us. It was fucking selfish of her to not say anything to any of us," Luci spouts off in anger.

I ignore her and walk straight out the door and to my car. The engine turns, and I need to silence the storm brewing within, so I channel surf and crank the volume when I hear Megadeth's "In My Darkest Hour."

"You look like shit," Benny says as I approach him sitting at the bar inside Prezza, the restaurant Nick bartends at in the North End. We often meet here to throw back a few drinks when Nick works the bar. The crowd is mostly locals, people who live in the neighborhood, or wait staff and bartenders from the other places in the area. Tonight, the bar is not that busy, and the dining room is half full. It's a nice place. Customers are well dressed, but not formal. There are no TVs anywhere, and the Gipsy Kings play through the speakers. I see one of my friends and his wife sitting at a table in the back dining room and wave.

"It's been a shitty week. What can I say?" I snort. Benny knows me well; he already has my whiskey sitting on the bar for me.

He and I have been friends our whole lives. We met in elementary school and have been inseparable since. He has five sisters—two older and three younger—so he spent a lot of time at my house, always trying to escape from being around all those women. He said they drove him crazy with all their bitching.

He nearly died last year in a car accident. Benny was driving to pick up Dom when some asshole T-boned him after running the light. He was in a coma for a week and in ICU for another two weeks at Mass General. After that, he had to do physical therapy and was out of work for months. It was a rough time for all of us. Benny used to always wear a buzz cut, but since the accident, he lets the top of his dark brown hair grow to cover the long scar across the side of his scalp. His arms are all scarred up too, small dark spots up and down both of them from the shards of glass that were embedded into his skin. What he hates the most, though, are the same small scars across his neck and face. Benny hasn't driven or been the same since. It fucked with his head—bad.

"No news?"

"Nothing," I say before shooting my whiskey back. "Give me another," I tell Nick as I place the empty glass down onto the bar.

"No leads, nothing? I mean, with all the people we know, nobody knows anything?" Benny inquires.

"Nope. I went to the bank and talked to Nina. She told me she saw Lena on Friday morning, the day she left. Said Lena made a big withdrawal, basically emptied her account, but didn't close it. Thinking about it, Lena probably did it that way so Nina wouldn't call me because she knows Nina and I are friends. Other than that, no one saw her," I explain, rapping my fingers on the bar top, waiting for my drink.

"Fuck, man. She planned this well," Benny quips.

"Thanks, Captain Obvious," I say, looking at him with side-eye while shaking my head.

Nick arrives with the bottle of Jack in tow, fills my glass, and leaves it on the bar. "It looks like you'll be sucking on Jack all night," he says with a low laugh.

I met Nick playing the courts. He was new to the neighborhood, which automatically made me wary of him. He had long hair, donned a ponytail, and was active around the rim. Over time, we became friends. He did a tour in the Gulf War, and when he came back, he moved in with his aunt here in the North End. Nick grew up down the Cape, but after the war, he wanted a change of pace. He fit right in with my crew.

"I'm guessing the bachelor weekend is off?" Benny asks.

"It's off as a bachelor weekend, but I definitely still want to go to Vegas. Need to go. After everything that's happened, I gotta get out of here, and what better place than Vegas to forget everything," I tell them.

In unison, they both say, "I'm down."

"Nothing like Vegas women to make you forget," Benny chimes in.

"You're friends with the manager at the Boston Harbor Hotel, aren't you?" I ask Benny.

"Yeah, why?"

"I need to cancel the wedding. We paid a pretty fucking penny for the down payment. Maybe he can do something to get some of the money back," I tell him.

"I'll call him, see what I can do for you. No promises," he responds.

"Story of my life. Nothing is promised," I say, and shoot back another whiskey.

CHAPTER ELEVEN

Apathy

MARIALENA

AUGUST 2004

THURSDAY NIGHTS AT THE LAST DROP are busy because it's the first night of the week with live music. Red Brick City, a local band that plays every Thursday night, has had the gig since before I started working here. They have a following that shows up for them every week. They're set to take the stage at 9:30 p.m. after the dinner rush ends, and most families have gone for the night.

"Hey, Lena, here comes your man," Stevie quips from the other end of the bar.

"He's not my man!"

"Keep telling yourself that," she says. "You've been sleeping with him for months, and he's like a dog, follows your every move. I'd say he's your man."

"Whatever!" Annoyed at her, I walk away, pulling slips from the printer to make some drinks for the service bar. I pour two beers and a gin and tonic and set them onto the service area with their tickets. When I look up, Nate is standing to my right, smiling.

Nate is the drummer for Red Brick City. We officially met a few weeks after I started working here when he sat at the bar during their break and asked for a Sam Adams. Stevie, always trying to be cute, said to him, "How funny, you love Sam Adams and the Red Sox. Did you know Lena is a Boston gal? Bet you'll love her too." That's how things started between us.

Initially, we talked when he was here to play their show. After a couple of months, he started coming in early to sit at the bar, eat, and chat with me. Nate's not the type of guy I'm typically attracted to, so I didn't think about hooking up with him initially. He's got dark blond hair, a shaggy look to it with the long pieces on top that stick up all over the place, which accentuates his piercing blue eyes. He's fair-skinned with a small, slightly crooked nose and thin lips.

Each week he came in, I got to know him a little

more. He grew on me. I thought it was cute that when we talked, he related most everything to a song. He would always sing a random lyric. He's a nice guy, sweet, and showers me with attention. In most circumstances, that would be a good thing, except when I met him, my heart was shattered, and I was not in a good place. It was easy to avoid talking about myself because I was usually working during our conversations.

The first few times he asked me to go out with him, I turned him down. I had told him I wasn't looking for a relationship. Eventually, I said "yes" because I thought it would help me fill a void. I thought hanging out with him would help me get over Massimo. I was wrong. Other than having great sex with him on the regular, it hasn't helped. On the contrary, it makes me feel like a terrible person because I'm basically using him for sex, and he doesn't deserve that. Not to mention, I still think of Massimo every day. Each time I have sex with Nate, it's Massimo I see. I'm such a jerk.

We've been spending time together a few days a week, although I don't ever spend the night at his place. It's been a little over six months since we've started dating, but I won't commit, can't commit. My heart isn't in it, which is awful of me because he's a great guy, deserves someone who will give themselves completely to the relationship. I know Nate wants that from me. Each time he brings it up, I avoid the conversation in some way.

"Hey, beautiful," Nate says, taking a seat on the stool next to the service bar.

"Hi." I place a bottle of Sam Adams onto the bar and lean into my right hip. "You know what you want to eat, or do you want a menu?"

Nate orders food, and we chat for a while between my serving customers until it's time for him to get ready for their set tonight.

"Want to hang out later?" he asks before leaving the bar, resting his hand over mine while he's waiting for my response.

"Sure." I pull my hand away and turn my back to him, feeling Nate's stare as I do.

"I want more," Nate says. We're lying in my bed, naked and uncovered, still breathing heavy from the sex we just had. I already know where this conversation is headed.

"More what?"

"Us. I want more." He sits up to remove the condom, ties the top in a knot, and places it on the floor.

"What do you mean?" I ask, sitting up to reach for

my glasses on the nightstand, grabbing my shirt from the floor.

"You know exactly what I mean. I've been trying to bring this up for weeks, and you always find a way to avoid having the conversation. So let's have the conversation now." He scoots closer to me, stretches his hand, and rubs the pad of his thumb across my beauty mark.

For the first time, his touch makes me cringe; the feel of his skin upon mine makes me feel dirty. I never should've let this much time pass. My gut feeling always told me this was wrong, and I ignored it. All it did was fuel his desires, lead him on, and give him false hope of having a relationship with me.

"You knew when we started hanging out that I didn't want a relationship. Nothing has changed. This is all I can give you." I stare at him but avert his gaze.

"This—" he gestures his hands between the two of us "—what is this?"

"We're friends with benefits, fuck buddies, whatever you want to call it." I yank my hand away.

Nate squints, and his mouth falls open. "We've been together for six months, and that's what you call us?"

I toy with the frames on my face and turn to look out the window. "Yes, that's what I would call us because we're not together."

"Lena, I'm trying to have a conversation with you. Can you at least look at me?"

I shift, and my eyes meet his again.

"If we're not together, then what are we?" His eyes are red and are pleading with me.

"I just told you. We're friends with benefits, nothing more."

"Why won't you commit to me, to us? We could be good together." He brushes the back of his hand across my cheek, and my stomach curdles.

I stand up, walking across the room, and stop next to the door. "I don't want a relationship, never have. I think you need to leave."

"What? Are you serious right now?" He jumps from the bed, darting across the room to stand before me, his proximity causing me to shudder away from him. "Lena, don't do this." His hand attempts to grab mine, but I jerk it back before he can grasp onto me.

"Nate, I'm sorry. You need to go. We can't do this anymore."

"Why won't you talk to me, open up? I'm trying here. Throw me a bone, something."

"Don't try, Nate. I'm not worth it. There is nothing for me to give you." I cross my arms.

"You won't let me ask questions. You won't talk to

me. You were closed off in the beginning, but I figured with time, you'd get over it, open up with me, and be willing to be in a relationship. Here we are six months later, and you're still the same closed-off girl. What happened to you?"

"I'm not talking about it with you. Now, can you please leave?"

"You know, Lena, what you're doing is really messed up. Has this been your intention the whole time—use me for sex?"

"Yes." I can see the hurt sprawling across his face at my words, and I am an asshole for saying that to him. But I have to end it with him because I can't give him what he wants. I'm empty inside, and I have nothing to offer.

"Wow." He picks up his jeans from the floor. Once dressed, he marches out of my bedroom and toward the exit. I follow.

Before opening the door to leave, he stops and says, "You know, I didn't expect the answer to that question to be 'yes.' That hurts a lot, and never in a million years did I think you capable of being such a cold, heartless bitch." He opens the door and leaves, slamming it behind him.

He's right. I'm a heartless bitch. The day I left Massimo, I lost my heart.

I'm driving to Winterset, Iowa, the town where all the covered bridges of *The Bridges of Madison County* are located—the bridges that drew me to escape to Des Moines in the first place. I've been here several times since moving to Des Moines last year, and the 30-mile drive is one that I enjoy. Long enough to clear my head but short enough to make it regularly. The radio plays in the background, and Chris Isaak's "Life Will Go On" streams through the speakers—it's like he's singing to me.

This drive reminds me of the ones Massimo and I used to take to Crane Beach in Ipswich, whether for the day or to stay for a few nights. We would eat at Woodman's of Essex or the Ipswich Clambake and stroll along the boardwalk, regardless of the weather. We are both lovers of the ocean, and Crane Beach was our favorite. Last September was the last time we were there together since we didn't have time to make it this past winter.

LAST YEAR

"Lena, let's go to Crane Beach. I rented a room at Shea's Inn for a couple of nights."

"I have to work tomorrow night. I can't go."

"I got your shift covered. Pack your bag."

It's mid-September, and the weather is still warm enough for the beach. During the summer, Massimo and I usually go to the beach once a week. Sometimes it was just the two of us, other times with a group of friends or family. He knows it relaxes me; the salty air and ocean waves are therapeutic. Massimo likes to say it's for me, but every time we're sitting in the sand, I sneak glances at him, seeing his face visibly relaxed. He's always busy and on the go, whether with the restaurants or with his family, and he rarely sleeps.

"Why the last-minute trip?"

"Why not? We've been busy the past few weeks with the end of summer tourist rush, and I want to spend a few days just the two of us. What better place than the North Shore for a quick getaway with my girl that's quiet, romantic, and has some of our favorite seafood restaurants?" He embraces me, dropping kisses along my temple.

Massimo likes surprises and last-minute trips. He's spontaneous that way, which I love about him.

"Okay, you know I love it there. I'll never say 'no'

to the beach." I go into my closet to search for my weekend bag to pack.

The old tattered sheet is spread across the sand, and we lie sprawled across it. The September sun is still warm, and I want to enjoy every last drop of it because the cold weather is creeping in. It's a Tuesday after-noon, and the sand around us is mostly empty. Gone are the summer days that filled the sand with umbrellas protecting babies from the sun, kids building lopsided sandcastles or digging holes to fill them with water, coolers filled with drinks and cold cuts for sandwiches.

Massimo always brings his radio to the beach. Today we're listening to some of his favorite Italian music. Claudio Baglioni's "Questo Piccolo Grande Amore" is playing. The first time I heard it, I asked him what the lyrics meant, and he told me it's about young summer love and the intense emotions that accompany it. He said his mother played this often because it re-minded her of when she and his father were young, and Massimo was a little boy. I wish I fully understood the lyrics because the melody is beautiful.

There's a couple near the shoreline sitting in beach chairs, letting the water splash at their feet while they

*watch a young child play. Two joggers run the coast-
line, one barefoot and the other in sneakers. I am leaning back on my elbows, looking out to the horizon,
Massimo's head resting on my belly. The ocean is calm
today, not roaring in its usual way that crashed the
waves at a furious pace.*

*"That'll be us when we have kids. I'm gonna buy
us a beach house so we can be beach bums."*

"Sounds perfect."

*Massimo gives me a quick kiss and springs to his
feet before saying, "I'm hungry, gonna run over to the
Snack Shack and get us some lobster rolls and fries.
You want anything else?"*

*"No, that's good. We still have some drinks in the
cooler."*

*Lobster rolls are my favorite summer food. It's
a tradition in New England. I like them served cold.
Massimo likes them served warm with drawn butter.
We always debate about whose tastes better.*

*After eating our lobster rolls, we lounge on the
beach until the sun starts dropping, and the chill in the
air forces us to leave. Days relaxing and enjoying each
other's company are few and far between. With the
schedules we keep, we rarely spend quality time like
this together, even if we live in the same apartment. I'm
glad we made one last beach trip before winter sets in.*

Winterset is a quaint and quiet town. I first stop to have breakfast at the Northside Café, a historic place in the center of town that has to-die-for eggs Benedict. After breakfast, I drive out to the Holliwell Covered Bridge. It's my favorite of the six bridges. The bridge itself is beautiful with its red and white painted wood, but it's my favorite because it sits over the Middle River, and listening to the water running downstream soothes me. I need a quiet place to think and clear my head.

When I still lived in Boston, that place was one of the nearby beaches. Winthrop or Revere always did the trick, even if they weren't my favorite. The crashing waves and salty air worked wonders to clear my head. The Middle River is a far cry from the ocean, but soothing nonetheless. I sit in the rocky area by the river to the left of the bridge and take in several deep breaths. My eyes sting from the falling tears, and my heart aches from the crushing weight of what I left behind and what my life has become.

I feel desperate, alone, and empty.

Breaking it off with Nate was the right thing, so why do I feel so bad about it? I know I had to do it, mostly for him, but for me too. Over the past six months, we've had a lot of sex. But, despite enjoying the sex with him, I was distant. My heart was off-limits. Rarely was I able to look him in the eye, and never did I express any feelings toward him. Sex with Nate may have physically satisfied me, but it emotionally drained me. What's worse is that I used him and was starting to hate the person I was becoming. Fucked up as it is, I felt like I was betraying Massimo, which is ridiculous, considering I left him. Regardless of how much time I spent with Nate, I can't stop thinking about Massimo.

One day at a time, regret eats away at me. I can't shake it, and it's been over a year. I thought by now it would've at least lessened, the distance making it easier to forget. Instead, despair gnaws at my skin, and everything I thought would be isn't. Every plan I made for myself unravels. Robert Burns said it best: the best-laid plans of mice and men often go awry.

Even working at The Last Drop reminds me of Massimo. It's the bar scene, mixing drinks, stocking the inventory, the day-to-day stuff that comes with the job. Although I bartended before meeting Massimo, I was new to bartending. It was Massimo who got me excited to join his family business. I miss everything and everyone in my old life. I'm spiraling into a funk and need to do something to stop myself.

"Hi, Luce." She answers my call on the second ring. "I'm glad you picked up. I really need a friend right now." I sit on my couch, crossing my legs, and cover myself with a blanket.

"What happened, Lena? Is everything okay?"

"Yeah. No. I don't know. I'm so blah lately. I don't know what to do with myself."

"Why don't you come home?"

"I'm not ready to do that yet."

"So, I guess you're also not ready to tell me why you left?"

"Ugh. No, but please don't lecture me, not today. I've had a terrible week and just need a friend."

"That's what friends do, Lena. They lecture you when you're stubborn and do stupid shit. It's literally my job description!"

"Will you come visit me?"

"What? You're going to tell me where you are?"

"Yes, but you have to promise me that you'll never tell Massimo or any of his crew."

"I don't see them or talk to them. How would I tell them? Besides, I'm your best friend. You can trust me."

"I know, but it was never about me not trusting you. It was about protecting you from Massimo's persistence. You know how he is."

"Do I ever! It was nearly every day after you left, but I haven't seen or heard from him in months. I'm guessing he moved on."

"I miss him! So fucking much! My heart aches for him."

All I can hear is Luci's steady breathing. I know she's trying to bite her tongue because she has no sympathy for me regarding my feelings for Massimo.

"Remember Nate, the guy I mentioned I was seeing?"

"Yeah."

"I broke it off with him. He kept asking for commitment, and I couldn't do it—couldn't give him more."

"I thought you liked him?"

"He's a nice guy, but that's it. I had always told him I didn't want a relationship, but he figured I would change my mind. I thought sex with no strings would be easy, but it isn't. It's just as complicated as a relationship—maybe more. The longer we continued, the worse I felt about myself. I started feeling shame because I was using him for sex. It's not who I am."

"At least you recognized it and know not to do that anymore."

"I guess. How fucked up is it that I felt like I was betraying Massimo?" I drop my head back, letting out a long sigh.

"You need to get over him."

"It was the biggest mistake of my life that I deeply regret, and I can't fucking take it back." Tears trickle from my burning eyes.

"I love you, Lena, but you made your bed. This is all your own doing. You chose to be selfish, so I don't feel sorry for you. I'm sorry I don't have kinder words, but you need to stop moping over it and move the fuck on."

"I know I have to, but I feel like I'm stuck on a hamster wheel." My heartbeat increases, and I exhale loudly to try to calm my nerves.

"Do something about it. In all the years I've known you, you've never been one to sit and dwell. What are you gonna do to change your state of mind?"

"I've been thinking about finding a new job, but really don't think that'll do it. I mean, bartending is bartending. Even that reminds me of Massimo."

"When we were growing up, you used to talk about being a lawyer, and you were gonna take the LSAT before you left. Have you given that any thought?"

"Honestly, I haven't given anything a thought. My brain has been mush lately. I need to snap the fuck out of this funk I'm in."

"Why don't you look into it again? You graduated from UMass with a 4.0 GPA. You're feisty, and you can argue anyone into the ground. Oh, and in case you didn't know, you're kinda stubborn. You'd make a great lawyer, and I'm sure you would get into law school! I've known you most of my life, and you've always accomplished everything you set your mind to. This is no different."

"True. I know I'm in my head now. I need to get out of my own way. I need to figure out how to move forward despite this persistent throbbing in my chest. I also haven't been doing any type of exercise. That's definitely not helping either."

"Look, I don't know why you left, and maybe I won't ever know, but it was obviously something you felt was important enough to walk away from the man you love."

"It was."

"Okay. There. That alone is enough. Remind yourself that all this headache you caused and put yourself through, that you put all of us through, was for a purpose and stop dwelling on would've, could've, should've."

"Talking to you always makes me feel better, even when you lecture me."

"I know, I'm awesome," she asserts. I can practically see her beaming through the phone.

"You truly are. I don't know what my life would be

without you, Luce, really. I smooch you."

"I smooch you more."

"So, will you come out and visit me? I'm in Des Moines."

"Iowa? I never would've guessed that's where you ran off to."

"Precisely why I picked it."

"Smart. I can probably go out in a few weeks. Let me check my work schedule, and I'll see if I can get a week off. I'll let you know in a few days."

"I'm wicked excited to see you. Seriously cannot wait to hug you. Let me know as soon as you find out so I can take the days off from work."

"Same girl, and I will. Talk soon. Bye."

"Bye."

"Let's have dinner at the new Mexican place that opened. I could use a few margaritas. Besides, I need details about why you broke it off with Nate," says Stevie.

Stevie and I both have Monday nights off and have a standing dinner date every week. She insisted on it after she forced her way into my life. I'm glad she did, though. Stevie's been a great friend. She reminds me of Luci in many ways. I know they'll love each other when they meet in a few weeks when Luci visits.

Stevie has long, blonde hair, thick and straight. She uses a curling iron to curl the ends in big, loose curls. Her heart-shaped face is always made up with foundation and blush. Her almond-shaped eyes never go without eyeliner or mascara, and her sharp lips are slathered in lipstick. It's the rare occasion I see her not wearing makeup.

I told Stevie about Massimo and most of my history of how I ended up in Des Moines, except she doesn't know my secret. I'm not ready to share that with her or anyone.

We order our margaritas and dinner, and I tell Stevie the details about what happened with Nate the other night since we haven't had much time to chat since then.

I sigh and take a sip of my margarita.

"You have been off lately. I've been meaning to ask you what's going on."

"I've been in a funk and feel stuck."

"Well, if I've learned anything about you since you moved here last year, you'll do something. You can't just sit still."

I drink some of my margarita, lick salt off the rim, and spread it around my mouth.

"Is that why you ended it with Nate?"

"I don't know." I shrug and play with the straw floating in my margarita. "I think I mostly ended it with him because he deserves someone who will reciprocate his feelings. That'll never be me. Besides, I was starting to feel terrible about myself."

"I thought you liked him?"

"He's a nice guy, but I don't want a relationship. Not right now, anyway."

"I know you loved Massimo, but you need to move on."

"That's the same thing Luci said to me the other day. It's way easier said than done."

"Yeah, but you can't keep on like this forever."

"I know. I think I'm gonna take the LSAT and apply to law school."

Stevie's eyes widen. "Law school? Wow, that's intense."

"Yeah, I'm sure it is. I was gonna take the LSAT before leaving Boston, but then my life fell apart, and I moved. But I can use the challenge right now and think I'm ready to do it."

"That sounds awesome. You should do it. Where would you apply?"

"I want to stay local. While I may need a change in my life, I don't feel like moving again. Drake University Law School is here in Des Moines, and they have a part-time program. I'm gonna drive down to the campus this week to pick up an admissions packet."

"How long is the program?"

"Not sure, but I think four years."

"That's exciting." Stevie extends her hand to squeeze mine.

"It is, and I feel really good about this. For the first time in a long time, I'm actually looking forward to something and getting excited."

"Well, whatever you need, I'm here to support you." We clink our margaritas and drink up.

CHAPTER TWELVE

First Born

MARIALENA

LUCI'S NAME FLASHES ACROSS my phone's screen. "Hi, Luce."

It's Saturday afternoon, and I take a break from studying to make myself a sandwich. I check the clock, 1:15 p.m. I have to be at work at 4:30 p.m. I can get a couple more hours of studying in before I have to leave.

My last final exam is next Tuesday, and then I'll have a week off before summer classes start. I still bartend at The Last Drop but now I only pick up shifts on weekends or to cover for someone when Hank needs the help. The extra cash is always welcome.

Last summer, I started working at an immigration firm as a law clerk for the attorney who works the criminal immigration cases. When summer ended, the attorney offered me a part-time position to stay on with the firm. Since I was a part-time student, I accepted. The pay cut from bartending hurt, but the experience was necessary for me to be ready to practice law after taking the bar exam. To help me out, I took out additional loans to help me with my living expenses. As long as I continued taking the number of classes I was, I would finish law school this December, one semester early. I took extra summer classes each summer to pull it off. I was ready to be done with school.

Law school was as intense as I expected it to be, which turned out to be a good thing. An occupied mind doesn't have time to think about anything other than the task at hand. The constant schoolwork kept the thoughts of Massimo at a minimum. Between classes, studying, and work, I had little time for anything else. Stevie and I moved our Monday date nights to Sunday brunch. It was my one constant that I looked forward to every week.

"Hi. What are you doing? Have a few minutes?" Luci asks.

"What's up?"

"I saw Dom last night. He came into my bar with a girl he was on a date with."

"Oh, how is he?"

"He's good. Looks great, as usual. I asked him about Massimo."

"Why would you do that?"

"What do you mean? Why wouldn't I do that? I haven't seen or heard from him in years, and I want to know what he's up to."

"And?"

"Are you sitting down?"

"Just tell me already!"

"He has a son, six months old—born last December."

Luci's words are a slap in the face. It's what I least expected to hear from her. My appetite is suddenly gone. I slide a chair out from under the kitchen table and sit.

"Lena, did you hear me?"

"Yes."

"Well, are you gonna say anything?

"What do you want me to say? I mean, I knew this day would come, but it doesn't lessen the sting."

"Are you okay?"

"Yeah, I'll be fine. You didn't tell Dom anything

about me, did you?"

"No, of course not."

"Good, keep it that way."

"I called your mom the other day. I want to start planning our trip for your graduation later this year."

"She told me. I'll have the exact graduation date in a few weeks and will text you. This way, you can purchase the flights."

"Marcus is waiting for the dates too, so the sooner, the better." I'm glad Marcus is coming to my graduation as well. We went from working together several nights a week to talking on the phone a few times a month. I miss him a lot!

Luci and I stay on the phone a few minutes longer before I hang up. I should get back to the books, but I can't focus on Business Entities right now. All I can think of is what Luci told me. Massimo has a son.

EIGHT YEARS AGO

"Maria is having a Fourth of July barbeque. We can drive there on the third and spend a few nights down the Cape," Massimo tells me as we're changing the sheets.

Maria is Massimo's cousin, and they have a house in Yarmouth just two blocks from the beach. It's the first summer we're together as a couple, and although I had met Maria several times at Massimo's family events, it would be the first time I would spend a few days with his family.

"Okay, but we gotta leave early on the third to avoid all of the traffic. Otherwise, we'll be stuck in it for hours."

"Zio Massimo, will you take us in the water?" Emilia asks.

Emilia is his cousin's daughter, but she and her brother Nico call him Zio. Emilia is seven, and Nico is five, and Massimo loves when they're around. He hangs out with them, plays games, and runs around the yard. He does all the fun things the kids want to engage in. We're at the beach for the Fourth of July holiday, and it's packed. Our umbrella and our chairs are spread out not too far from the shoreline.

Massimo stands from where he's sitting. "You bet, Bella. Let's go."

The kids jump up and down. "Yay!" Each of them grabs one of his hands, and they head toward the shoreline. No doubt the water will be cold. No matter how hot it is outside, the water is frigid.

"The kids love him. When I told them you guys were coming for a few days, they started screaming in excitement," Maria says. "Nico got his soccer ball and basketball ready because he knows Massimo will play with him for hours."

"He's really good with them," I tell her. His face always lights up, and after he spends time with them, he tells me that he can't wait to be a father.

"He's excited for you guys to have kids. He said he hopes his firstborn is a boy and that you'll start trying on the wedding night."

"Wedding night? We're not even engaged." I shake my head.

"You know him. Always confident when talking about his future, as if it's a given."

Chuckling, I say, "So much truth!"

Graduation is being held inside the school's auditorium since the December graduating class is small—there are only forty-seven of us. My parents, Luci, and Marcus flew in late yesterday. Luci and Marcus will fly home Tuesday morning, but my parents are staying here for Christmas since it'll be the first one we spend together since I left Boston. Luci rented an SUV so that we could drive around all together while everyone is here.

After the ceremony ends, we pile into the SUV and drive to Jesse's Embers, one of my favorite steakhouses, which is a five-minute drive across town. Stevie and her boyfriend are meeting us there.

Once at our table, we order drinks and food. After the waitress drops our drinks off, my father makes a toast.

"Nena, I'm so proud of you. I always knew you'd accomplish great things. You'll be a great lawyer."

"*Gracias, Papi.* Thank you all for being here. I'm so happy you guys came to support me. It really means a lot." I look around to everyone sitting at the round table. My father is sitting to my right, then *Mami*, followed by Luci and Marcus. Stevie is to my left and her boyfriend Andrew is next to Marcus.

"So, what are your plans now?" Luci asks.

"I'm taking off until Christmas since my parents are staying until the day after. Once they leave, I'll start studying for the bar exam, which is the last Tuesday and Wednesday in February. I won't be working during my study time, so I took out a bar study loan to help me with living expenses for the next two months.

I want to take one exam and be done with it."

"You quit your job?" asks Marcus, his eyes widening.

"No, just taking time off to study. My boss encouraged it, actually. He already offered me a job after the bar exam. I'll probably take a few days to relax right after it and start working the following week."

"Nena, *que bueno*, you have a job already," *Mami* chimes in.

"Yes, and full-time too. I mean, I'll officially work as a law clerk because I won't be a licensed attorney until I pass the bar, but being in the law firm environment will help."

"What do you do as a law clerk?" Andrew asks.

"I mostly research and write for the lawyers in the firm and help draft court documents, although occasionally I help out the paralegals or secretaries if they need it. Learning what they do is extremely helpful and important because it's not stuff that I learned in law school. Also, my goal is to work for myself once I have enough experience."

"I can definitely see you working for yourself," Stevie adds.

Luci clears her throat and asks, "Do you have any plans to move back home?"

I take a deep breath and adjust my glasses. "Eventually, but not yet. I need more experience, and I don't want to have to take another bar exam. I want to pass the Iowa bar on my first try, work here for a couple of years, then move back." I'm also not ready to face reality back in Boston yet, but Luci doesn't need to know that. "I'll eventually seek admission to the Massachusetts bar, but I need to wait until I'm licensed for five years. That's one of the reasons I also chose to work in Immigration Law. I just need to be licensed in one state, and I can practice in any state since it's federal. If all goes as planned, when I move home, I'll open my firm there instead of working for someone."

"*Ay si*, Nena, I miss you. I'm glad you'll be moving back. I miss you," *Mami* chimes in and extends her hand in front of my father, grabbing hold of mine.

CHAPTER THIRTEEN

The Market

MARIALENA

*D*ELUCA'S MARKET HAS ALWAYS been one of my favorite markets because it has a great selection of unique imported and gourmet foods. After the day I had, all I want is some cheese and wine, and it's the perfect spot to get everything I want to indulge in after a long day at the office. The market has been a staple in the Beacon Hill neighborhood of Boston for years. They offer imported products from Italy, a selection of Italian cheeses, salumi, and wines.

With a block of Asiago cheese, *soppressata*, and

gourmet crackers in my basket, I head over to the wine section to find the perfect bottle. I'm in search of a Barolo or Sangiovese, both smooth, red wines, and the perfect end to my long day.

As I browse the red wines, I hear, "Lena, what are you doing here?" I stiffen at the sound of his voice, which shocks me—unexpected yet so familiar. Disbelief is prominent in his words.

My eyes land on Massimo, and suddenly my chest feels tight. His black hair is still unruly, but it's now peppered with grays along the sides. He's aged like a fine wine in the nine years since I last saw him, and all I want is to drink him in.

I lift my eyes to his. Although words fail me, I search his dark brown hues. They're wild, filled with anger and hurt, which doesn't surprise me. The last time we looked into each other's eyes, I was kissing him goodbye, except he didn't know it would be the last time he saw me.

Seeing him again after so long confirms everything I've felt over the past nine years—I love him. I'm a fool for abandoning him. I crushed my soul for him and can only hope he'll understand why. It was always about him. For him. Because of him.

Right now, the wildfire burns in his eyes, and he's unreadable. Will he understand my truth, or will revealing my darkest secret be a nail in my coffin?

This encounter was inevitable, but today was not when I expected it to happen. For all the pep talks I gave myself, I am still not ready to face him. I don't know what's wrong with me, considering I knew this day would come.

"Lena, what the fuck? How long have you been back?" His words snap me out of my trance.

Massimo's tone is short. There are no indicators of understanding or forgiveness when he speaks. Instead, anger and bitterness ooze from his words. "A few weeks," I say in a low voice, finding it hard to speak, despite having plenty of explaining to do.

My voice is tight in my throat, and I feel lightheaded. I reach for the shelf to steady myself. Everything is spinning, and I can't control the force of my emotions churning within.

"Were you planning on coming to see me?" he asks in a softer tone, his eyes still boring into mine, pleading for me to say something, anything.

With the back of my right hand, I adjust my glasses. "I, um…" Words elude me, and I'm unable to complete a sentence. Seeing him after so much time has impacted me in a way I didn't expect. No matter how many times I imagined this day and what I would say, nothing could prepare me for this moment.

For looking the man I love in the eye.

For the heaviness in my heart.

For the words that would have to tumble from my lips.

"Lena, just answer the question," he retorts, irritation in his voice as he takes a step closer to me.

"Yes—" nodding to mimic my words "—I was planning on it once I got settled into work and my apartment."

He's a few inches from me, scrutinizing me with his eyes. I have the urge to reach out and touch him, run my fingers along his soft, warm skin, even if I have no right to do any of those things.

I begin extending my right hand toward him, his meeting me halfway. I watch his hand envelop mine, his fingers caressing my skin. I close my eyes, remembering his touch, and my skin prickles at the memories. When I open them, his eyes are wet and soft. Is that love I see? Is it possible that after all the damage I caused, he could still love me?

"Massimo, I—"

"Daddy, here are the crackers. These are the ones Mommy buys." Two small boys jog up to him, each handing him a box. I yank my hand back, staring down at the two boys, who are both looking at me with curiosity. They're unquestionably his with the same beautiful chocolate eyes, ink-black hair, and toothy smiles.

I shift my eyes back to Massimo's, where I see turbulent sadness and anger. My hand goes up to my mouth to cover the sob itching to escape. I shake my head and scurry away from him toward the front of the store. As I'm leaving, I hear him call my name. I momentarily stop before thinking better of it and ignore him.

I drop the basket full of groceries at the front and hurry out the door before Massimo can catch up with me. I jog down the street and around the corner to get as far away from him as I can.

Since I dropped everything and ran, I hail a cab to take me across town to see Luci, who's bartending at The Pour House tonight. If I needed a drink before seeing Massimo, now I need it even more.

Once inside the cab, I can no longer hold my tears back. I'm taking deep, measured breaths to try to calm my erratic heart.

I had convinced myself that I was ready to see him.

Ready to speak my truth.

Ready to ask for his forgiveness.

If what just happened back at DeLuca's is any indicator, I'm not ready for anything. A sob escapes me, and the cabbie looks at me through his rearview mirror. "Everything okay, miss?" he asks.

I nod. A blatant lie considering my steady flow of tears. Was that a glimmer of love in Massimo's eyes, or am I imagining it because it's what I want to see? And if it is, what does that mean for us? Is there even an us? I have to stop getting ahead of myself. First things first, I need to get a grip. His mere presence today shook me in a way I've never imagined it would.

The Pour House is a laid-back dive bar—dark inside, with random decorations strewn around the whole place and across the bar's top. There's a brick-wall mural along the entire left side, old bowling pins, a skeleton, trophies, plastic drink trays stuck to the air vents, and a pinball machine. Although it's a dive bar, it's been around for years, and the bar food is phenomenal, especially their burgers. Locals sporting their team pride with Red Sox or Patriots hats fill the booths along the brick wall or in the backroom.

When Luci sees me, she walks over, smiling, but as she gets close, she sees the tension and anxiety written all over my face and asks, "What happened?"

"Pour me a Grey Goose and soda, heavy on the Goose, with two limes and order me a mushroom burger, medium with onion rings, and I'll tell you about it,"

I tell her as I'm removing my jacket to place it on the back of my stool.

Luci and I have been best friends since the third grade, and I almost lost her when we were in junior high. In eighth grade, Luci was rescued from the house fire at her family home. She and her sister were sleeping in their bedroom with the door closed. Her father had fallen asleep on the couch while smoking a cigarette. Luci told me she was woken up by the firefighters outside the window, yelling to move back because they would be breaking through the bedroom window to rescue them. They later learned that their bedroom was spared from the fire damage because the door was closed. Thankfully her mom was at work that night, and her dad was okay. After that, her parents got divorced, and it was a rough time for her and her family.

Despite our lifelong friendship, I also betrayed her when I left Massimo all those years ago. She's mostly forgiven me for the hurt and betrayal, and I'm grateful for her love. I now know my decision hurt a lot of people. Hindsight is 20/20 and all.

"Spill it, Lena," she quips as she pours the Grey Goose over the ice-filled glass and tops it off with soda water before dropping two limes in and sliding it toward me. "The rush won't begin for about an hour. We have time to chat before it's a full house," she tells me, boring her eyes into mine with a force that says, "Don't fuck with me."

I hear Aerosmith's "What It Takes" playing from the jukebox behind me. How appropriate—singing about letting go and moving on. I grab the glass and give the straw a twirl before taking a sip. It's strong, burning as I swallow—precisely what I need.

"I went to DeLuca's after work to pick up a few things. Massimo was there, and he confronted me. He caught me off guard, and words failed me. I wasn't ready to see him yet. I basically ran away like a scared little girl. Oh, and he's still sexy as ever." I sigh before taking another sip of the liquid swirling in my glass.

"Whoa, slow down, Lena. What do you mean he confronted you?"

"He asked me what I was doing here and if I planned on seeing him."

"And?"

"And nothing. I barely muttered a full sentence. When I was working up the courage to say something, his two sons showed up, and it freaked me out," I spew, exasperated thinking about the encounter.

"That's rich, Lopez. What the hell is wrong with you?"

"I don't know, Luci. Massimo is the only one who makes me act like a fool. He's always had that effect on me," I remind her. "I guess he still does," I say, shrugging as I sip my drink again.

"Honestly, Lena, you've been back a few weeks, and I still don't know why you left. I can't imagine what he's feeling. Can you blame him?" she retorts, shaking her head. She leans into me and lowers her voice. "You were two months away from your wedding when you up and disappeared and left him a heaping pile of shit to clean up! One I helped clean up! You fucked him up pretty bad," she proclaims.

I glare at her because I need her to be my friend now and not scold me, even though I deserve everything she's throwing at me, and then some.

"Luci, I—"

"Don't *Luci* me, Marialena. Look, I love you. You're my best friend, but a spade is a spade, and you fucked up. Now own it and go make it right."

"I want to, but I don't know how."

"Oh, I don't know, maybe talk to him instead of running away."

A long sigh escapes me. "Touché." I slurp the remaining liquid in my glass.

I decide to walk home from The Pour House. It's a

mild night, and I need fresh air. Before turning left, I pull my iPod Touch out of my purse, pop my earbuds in, and hit play on Adele's "Someone Like You."

How I've missed my city. Being back is like seeing an old friend; she welcomes you with open arms. Boston is big city life with a small-town feel. She's old-fashioned yet contemporary, traditional yet chic. A perfect blend of old and new thrives here.

Boylston Street is relatively quiet tonight, and as I stroll home, I can't help but look up at the Prudential Tower lighting up the sky. The Back Bay is one of the areas I love most with all of its coffee shops, boutiques, and restaurants. When I was in college, I would be in this neighborhood often because the Boston Public Library is in Copley Square. Luci and I would spend hours studying in the Bates Hall reading room. It seems like a lifetime ago.

Luci's words hit me hard: "You fucked him up pretty bad." Although I know I hurt the only man I've ever loved, I didn't think he was that messed up over it. I mean, he's married, has kids. Ugh, just the thought of him belonging to someone else makes me nauseous.

The encounter at DeLuca's replays in my mind. I couldn't even string a sentence together. It's the Massimo Effect. He's like a magician who's had me under his spell since the first day he sat down at my bar, cocky and arrogant, but oh-so sexy. I still remember the day I met him as if it were yesterday.

THIRTEEN YEARS AGO

Cutting limes and fruit for the garnish jars that sit on the bar is what I hate most about bartending. When I hear the front door's open chime, I stop the knife mid-cut and raise my eyes. Massimo enters the Florentine and struts his way through the restaurant. He's wearing sunglasses, smiling as he greets the hostess, then saunters the length of the bar following its curve until he slides onto the last stool next to the servers' station. My eyes follow him the entire time. When he walks, he commands attention. His tall frame is lean, arms firm, the black ink on his upper-left arm peeks out from his solid black T-shirt snug around his biceps.

When he sits, I gait over to him and his friend, placing two cocktail napkins onto the bar. "Hi guys, what can I get for you?" I ask, smiling at them both, but Massimo is speaking with his friend when I arrive.

At the sound of my voice, he looks up, staring me straight in the eye, and says, "Hi." The silence hangs between us. Our gazes remain locked on each other for what seems like an eternity.

His friend breaks our trance by saying, "We'll take two Jacks, neat, please."

"What's your name, sweetheart?" Massimo asks.

I adjust my glasses to center them across the bridge of my nose. "Lena," I reply, in an attempt to flirt but fall flat when my voice cracks with nerves. He chuckles at that.

"Hi, Lena, I'm Massimo, and this is Dom," he says, gesturing to his right. "It's nice to meet you," he continues, extending his hand. I look down at his hand for a few moments before it clicks that I have to extend mine back.

"Nice to meet you too," I respond and place my hand in his, giving him a delicate handshake. Our hands remain joined there, across the bar, for longer than any handshake should last.

"Hey, Cassanova, let her get our drinks, will ya?" Dom says to Massimo.

I pull my hand back. "Excuse me," I say, "I'll be right back with your drinks," and spin away to break the spell before I start drooling all over the place.

For the rest of the night, I feel like a dog in heat circling that area of the bar as much as I can. Every time I approach that corner, I can smell him. His unique scent is alluring, and it makes my skin tingle. The sound of his voice gives me goose bumps, causing my legs to squeeze together from the wanton desire he's creating in me.

He and Dom sit at the bar for about two hours. Massimo steals glances at me throughout the night, smirking when our eyes meet. After they settle the tab, I say goodbye. Massimo rises and steps to his left to stand before the servers' entrance to the bar area, extending his hand. I move closer, taking his hand, and look up at him towering over me. I'm five-foot-eleven, and he's a few inches taller than me. It's rare to find a man taller than me, especially one as good-looking as him.

He kisses me, cheek to cheek, first my right side, then my left. Before letting go of my hand, he looks into my eyes and says, "Lena, thank you. I'll be back to see you soon. You can count on it." He drops a kiss on the backside of my hand before letting go. He turns, walks the length of the bar and out the front door while I stand frozen in place under his spell.

That night I went home, and while I showered, I masturbated to the thought of Massimo and the dirty things I wanted him to do to me.

The mere memory of that night has my panties wet. It was the beginning of a beautiful relationship. I crushed our relationship when I walked away from him, from our life, from our flawed future. Guilt and regret have dominated my thoughts every single day for nine years, and they're still raw emotions within me as if it was not nine years past. The heartache and tears today are at the forefront, just as intense as on day one, if not more.

Regret is a feeling that I hate. It seeps into my skin, permeates throughout my body, breeds self-loathing, and weighs me down. I usually don't regret the decisions I make but instead suck them up, accept them, and learn from them.

But this decision—to leave Massimo nine years ago—is loaded with regret and weighs on me like a ton of bricks, despite my knowing it was the right decision for him. It's dragged me down, made me bitter, and has been eating away at me from the inside, one day at a time. No matter how hard I've tried, I cannot get over it or accept it.

I need to make this right somehow, find the key to my redemption.

CHAPTER FOURTEEN

Square One

MASSIMO

"DADDY, WHO WAS THAT LADY?" Lucio asks me.

"A friend, buddy," I tell him.

Lucio and Leandro are my two boys. They both have dark hair, thick eyebrows, and crooked smiles—undoubtedly my kids. Although Lucio is four years old, he's an old soul. He likes to listen to classical music, play the piano, play basketball, and I'm teaching him to play chess. Leandro is three and imitates his brother every chance he gets, except he also likes the guitar, and I'm excited for him to start learning better when he's a little older. Both of my guys are musicians at heart.

"Come on. Let's finish getting the groceries we came for and go see Nonna. She's waiting for us," I tell them.

Seeing Lena at DeLuca's has my head spinning. I cannot believe she's back! Her beauty still takes my breath away. Her ringlets were cascading around her square jaw, and her full lips were colored in with vibrant lipstick. Sadness and regret smoldered from her green eyes hidden behind her blue frames. When I grabbed her hand in mine, her skin was on fire just as it was the day I met her, and memories rushed through me. She's back, and just like that, my world has tipped on its axis again.

I need to see her. Talk to her. Understand her. She said she needed to settle into her apartment and work, so it should be easy to find her. Despite it being nine years since Lena disappeared from my life, I never stopped thinking about her, even if I eventually gave up searching for her.

There's a piece of me that's missing, a part of my heart that will always belong to Lena. Now that she's here, she owes me an explanation, and I intend to get it.

Images of her crowd my thoughts during our walk from DeLuca's back to the apartment. We've been spending most of our days with my parents for the past two months because my mother's cancer has spread, and she stopped treatment. I want the boys to spend as much time with her as possible, create as many memories as we can.

"Hi, Pa," I say as we're entering the house.

After moving here from Italy, my parents bought a building in the North End because it's where many Italian families lived after migrating to the United States. They settled in this neighborhood and made a home for their family here. It's the only home my parents have known.

My father has aged tremendously over the past year since my mother was diagnosed with cancer, and the doctor recommended that her treatment be aggressive. The lines around his eyes have increased three-fold, and the circles around them are dark. His hair used to be a mix of black and white. Now, his mane is snow-white, yet it's still thick. My father has always been robust, tall with a belly from years of eating homemade pasta and meats, and drinking a lot of red wine. Since my mother became sick, his stomach has disappeared, and he's thinned out. My mother may be the one afflicted with cancer, but my father is wasting away at the same rate she is.

"Nonno!" Both Lucio and Leandro run up to my father to hug him.

"Where's Ma?" I ask.

"In bed. She's not well today. I called the doctor, asked her to come to the house."

"And?"

"She'll be here later tonight. She said after she finishes her rounds."

"Okay, well, I'm gonna hit the courts with the guys, and I'll be back later for when the doctor gets here."

"Okay, son."

Dom, Nick, and Paulie are already shooting basketball when I get there.

"Always running late," Paulie says.

Paulie and I have been friends our entire lives. Our parents migrated from Italy together in the late 60s, where they lived in Frascati, about twenty miles southeast of Rome. They've been friends since they were teens. Paulie is a year older than me, the older brother I never had. We went to school together at St. John's and spent most of the holidays together. Even though we're not blood-related, people constantly tell us we look alike.

"You know he always has to look pretty," Dom chimes in.

"Assholes," I say.

We play ball two-on-two for a little over an hour before Nick and Paulie need to leave. Dom and I walk back toward my parents' place. His apartment is two blocks from them. He and I became friends when we both worked at my uncle's restaurant together. I was bartending at the time when he started.

He had graduated from Suffolk University and didn't know what he wanted to do, so he waited on tables. We'd hang out several nights a week after work, whether we sat at a bar and drank or hit up one of the clubs. We became tight, and he fit right in with my crew. He now owns Gemelli's Liquor Distillery, one of the biggest wholesale liquor distributors in the city.

As we march down Prince Street, I give him an update on my mother's health. Before we part ways, I tell him, "Lena is back." Even saying that aloud is surreal. They're words I never thought I'd say.

"What?" he asks as he stops, facing me. "When?"

"I went to DeLuca's today to pick up some stuff to bring to the house, and there she was, looking for wine. I couldn't believe it, Dom. After nine years, she's back."

"What did she say?"

"Nothing, really. She could barely speak. I was trying to ask her questions, but she wasn't giving me much. She's been back a few weeks, has an apartment, and is working. That's all I know."

"How was it, seeing her again after all this time?"

"Fuck, man." My chest feels tight just thinking about her, and a flood of emotions hit me. Her eyes, piercing green with flecks of golden yellow surrounding her pupils, glowed with sadness and love. "She's as beautiful as ever. Still has that long curly hair, ringlets surrounding her face; her glasses are bigger than the ones she wore back in the day."

I was all torn up because I'm still pissed about how she left, disappeared from my life, and vanished into thin air, but when I saw her, I just wanted to kiss her senseless.

"My head is spinning again. It's like I'm back to square one. But I was with the boys, and there wasn't much I could say or do."

"Does she know about Camila?"

"No, I don't think so, but I have no idea."

"Are you gonna see her?"

"I'm gonna try. She was about to say something, but the boys interrupted us. When she saw them, she froze and ran away from me."

"Well, it must be hard for her to see you with kids. I mean, you two always talked about starting a family together."

"That's bullshit though! This is all her doing."

"That may be true, but it doesn't make seeing you with kids that aren't hers any easier."

I tip my head up to the darkening sky, letting out a deep sigh.

"What's next?" Dom asks.

"I have to find her. I'm gonna make a few phone calls, check to see if she comes up in a Google search."

"All right, man, let me know what I can do for you. Whatever you need." He gives me a fist bump, and we part ways.

When I get back to my parents' house, my father tells me Dr. Bova is in the bedroom with my mother.

"Has she told you anything yet?"

"Not yet, son. She asked to see your mother first, then she would speak with me."

"Where are Lucio and Leandro?"

"Your sister took them down to Modern's to get some pastries. I need to focus on what the doctor has to say."

We sit on the couch and chat for a few minutes. My father and I didn't have a great relationship when I was growing up. As a young boy, I would be frightened when I caused trouble, which was often because he would punish me at every opportunity. Since I'm the oldest, he made sure I set the example for my brother and sister. He was tough, would hit me a lot when I got in trouble, or disobeyed him or my mother. Sometimes with his fists, other times with his leather belt. He was no-nonsense and never hesitated to remind me of it. The older I got, the worse our fights became because I started rebelling against his attempts to control me. Eventually, he kicked me out of the house when I was sixteen, which is how I ended up living with my uncle and working at his restaurant. Now I look back and realize he probably didn't know any better because that's how he was raised. It was a different generation.

For years I resented him, but when Lucio was born, he started acting differently. I was wary at first, worried his behavior hadn't changed. But he was softer with Lucio, then Leandro, than he ever was with me. I wanted a better relationship with him for my boys. When my mother was diagnosed with cancer, it catapulted our relationship. He even apologized to me for being so rough with me as a kid. Although we still butt heads, I am glad I could get to know the man my father truly is.

Dr. Bova enters the living room, and both my father and I stand up. "Mr. DeLorenzo," she says to my father. "Rosa is not well; she's nearing the end and doesn't have much time."

My father's face goes pale, and he stumbles. I reach out and grasp his arm to help steady him.

"How long does she have?" my father asks, his voice shaking.

"It's hard to say," she says, extending her hand to hold my father's in hers. "Sometimes it's swift, a matter of hours or days. Other times it can be a matter of weeks. Because of the uncertainty, I recommend you let your family and loved ones know they should come to say their goodbyes. You should contact the priest; have him administer last rites."

My father moans at the doctor's words, and I help him sit because he's too shaky to continue standing.

"I'm so sorry, Mr. DeLorenzo," Dr. Bova says, patting my father's arm in sympathy.

"Thank you, Marina," I say to her. Marina and I grew up together here in the neighborhood. We went to St. John's together, and after high school, Marina went off to Boston University for her undergrad before going to medical school at Tufts. As long as I've known her, she's always talked about being a doctor, and here she is, treating my mother.

"I'm sorry, Massimo," she says to me. "I've known your mother since we were kids, and she's a wonderful woman. She'll be greatly missed by many," she says. "Is it okay if I let my mother know that your mom isn't well? I know she'd like to come say goodbye."

"You don't even have to ask that."

"Since I'm her doctor, I just want to make sure. Massimo, again, I'm sorry. I wish there were more I could do for her." She embraces me, her arms tight around me, offering comfort.

"Thank you, Marina. Truly. You've been a great doctor, a good friend. We appreciate it more than you'll ever know," I tell her.

"Thanks, Massimo. Good night." She quietly leaves through the front door.

My father is bawling, eyes red and swollen. "What am I gonna do without her? She's all I know. Forty-eight years we've been married."

"I don't know, Pa. But she's still here. Why don't you go sit with her? She likes it when you tell her stories."

"She can't see me like this. Why don't you go in with her, and I'll be there in a few."

My mother lies in her bed, blankets tucked just below her chin. She's frail, thin, her cheeks are sunken in, and her glasses look too big for her face. She has no hair left on her head, which is now covered in a red skully cap to keep her head warm. Classical music plays softly in the background.

I love music because of my mother. No matter what she was doing or where we were, there was always music playing, whether classical, opera, or her favorite Italian musicians.

"Hi, Ma."

"Massimo come, *siediti*." She pats her hand on the bed to her right.

I close the door behind me, settling on the bed, facing my mother.

"*Figlio*, Marina, she tell me I no have too much time."

"I know. She told us too."

"You need to be strong for your father. He no doing good, that's why he sent you in here. He no want me to see him. You see how skinny he is? He's no eat enough."

"I know, Ma. I don't want you to worry about him. We'll all take care of him." A tear leaks from my eye.

"And who take care of you, eh Massimo?" She lifts her hand, resting it on my cheek. "I won't be here no more, Mamma *se ne va*." Those words from her mouth cause me to let out a sob, tears dripping from my eyes as I lie down on my left side to face her, wrapping my arms around her.

"I saw Lena today."

"Lena? Where you see her?"

"I was at DeLuca's before coming here, and I ran into her there." My heartbeat quickens at the mention of Lena's name.

"She talk with you?"

"No, not really. She was surprised to see me and ran out before I had the chance to say anything."

"Massimo, you wait years to see her. No keep quiet now. You understand?" Her bony fingers pat my cheek. "You follow your heart. Camila, she's a good mamma to my Lucio and Leandro but you no love her. I see in your eyes for long time now. *La vita è corta.* No waste any more time."

My mother always knows what to say. She knows me better than anyone does, and I'll miss her, our talks, and her giving me advice. I'll even miss her scolding me because she often reminds me that I am still her little boy despite being a grown man. I am the man I am today because of her, the love she instilled in me, and the love she has given me.

"I love you, Ma. I'm not ready for you to leave yet. Lucio and Leandro are going to miss out on so many amazing memories with you." The words are muffled amidst my weeping.

"*Figlio mio*. I already live my life, and I'm old. You still have long life to live with my boys. *Ricordati*, follow your heart. *Ti amo*," she tells me, her hand rubbing my arm, consoling me.

At that moment, my father comes into the bedroom. I lift my head and see my mother attempting to raise hers. "Nino," she says, her smile lines blending with the wrinkles across her hollow cheeks.

I get up from the bed, kiss my mother, and give them privacy. I'm starving and go into the kitchen to grab something to eat. I find pizza from Umberto's and warm it up. I'm at the kitchen table eating when the boys come storming through the door.

"Daddy, look what *Zia* Stella got us. Cannolis and cookies from the pastry shop," Lucio squeals.

"And I got a lobstah tail," Leandro chimes in.

"Wow, they look delicious. Why don't you get your things together, and you can have your pastries before we go home," I tell them. They scurry out of the kitchen to go get their stuff.

"What did Dr. Bova say?" Stella inquires. Stella is two years younger than me. We're close, have been since we were young. I have always been fiercely protective of her and consider her my best friend. She's my go-to person when I'm in a dilemma or making a big decision. It was Stella who put me back together after Lena left. To get me out of my funk after Lena ghosted, Stella made me start running with her. She's an avid runner and has run the Boston Marathon several times.

I bring Stella up to speed. When I tell her that Ma could leave us any day now, her tears break free, and I hug her.

"I'll call Rocco and tell him. We need to be here for Pa. Need to make sure he isn't alone when it happens. I'm worried about him," I say.

When the boys finish eating their pastries, I start gathering their things to go home. Today has been a fucked-up day, and I need some peace and quiet. We say goodbye to my parents and sister and walk out to the car. I buckle them in and get into the driver's seat.

"Daddy, is Nonna gonna be okay?" Lucio asks.

"I don't know, buddy, but I hope so," is all I can muster telling my kids tonight.

Before I start driving, I turn the radio dial to WZLX. It's 9:02 p.m., and I am just in time to listen to "Getting the Led Out," the nightly installment of playing three back-to-back Led Zeppelin songs. Led Zeppelin is always good for the soul.

It's 9:45 p.m. when I pull into the driveway. I see Camila open the front door. She waits on the porch as I unbuckle the boys and help them out of the car. When they see her, they're excited. "Mommy, Mommy, *Zia* Stella bought us pastries," Leandro yells as they both run to her waiting arms.

CHAPTER FIFTEEN

Mr. Gentile

MARIALENA

ONE WEEK LATER

"ENA, YOUR 3:00 P.M. APPOINTMENT, Mr. Gentile, is here, and he's completed his intake sheet. Let me know when you're ready, and I'll take him back," my assistant Natalia tells me over the speakerphone.

"Okay, thank you. Give me a minute to finish up these edits," I tell her.

After law school and passing the Iowa bar exam, I worked for a local firm there doing Immigration Law, working in their criminal division, helping clients that were facing deportation. Because my mother is an immigrant, I was drawn to Immigration Law. This practice area also allows me to work in states other than Iowa with only my Iowa bar license because it's a federal practice. This permitted me to move back to Boston when I was ready without the necessity of taking the Massachusetts bar exam.

Before returning, I reached out to a female attorney who was a regular at the bar at Massimo's restaurant. I remember she had her office a few blocks away. When I spoke to her and reminded her where we had met, she instantly remembered me. I had told her of my intention to move back to Boston and that I would be looking to rent an office and start my firm. It turns out, she had an available office in her suite, which is how I ended up here on the 27th floor of 60 State Street.

When I finish making edits to the document I'm working on, I place it in the work folder to give to Natalia when she comes back with the client. I pick up the phone and dial her extension. "Natalia, you can bring the client back now, thank you," I say.

Moments later, I hear Natalia's knock on the door and look up. Natalia is petite and has shoulder-length, light brown hair. When I decided to move back to Boston, a friend of mine recommended her to work as my assistant. She's been a godsend.

My face goes slack when I see him stride into my office behind her. Massimo has a smug look of satisfaction on his face, yet anger is still prominent in his eyes.

"Mr. Gentile, this is Ms. Lopez, the attorney. Please, have a seat," Natalia tells him, gesturing for him to take a seat in one of the chairs across from me. She hands me the client intake sheet.

"Natalia, here—" I extend my hand and give her the work folder with the documents I was working on "—it's ready to be filed." She takes the folder and walks out, closing the door behind her.

I glare at Massimo. "Mr. Gentile, huh?" I ask, squinting my eyes at him as I speak. "I should've known you'd show up here like this." I crumple up the client intake sheet and toss it into the trash barrel to my right.

"I always get what I want, but you know that already, don't you, Attorney Lopez?" he says, leaning back into the chair, a smirk gracing his beautiful face. The stubble growing along his jawline is sprinkled with grays, his eyes rimmed with dark circles and crow's feet in the corners.

I stare at him for several moments before saying, "Why are you here, Massimo? This is my office. You can't be doing this." I rest my left elbow on the armrest of my chair and adjust the frames on my face.

He leans forward, resting his elbows on his legs. His eyes never break away from mine, and he smirks before asking, "Why are you so nervous?"

"I'm not." I am trying to keep myself calm, but it's not easy with him being in such close proximity. I can smell his unique scent, and just like it did the first time I met him, it makes my skin tingle.

"Have you forgotten that I know everything about you, and fidgeting with your glasses is your tell?" he says more than asks and licks his lips.

I snap my hands away from my frames and bring them down to my legs. I want to smack the smugness off his face.

"Why are you here?"

"Are you really asking me that question?"

"Yes, I am. I have a business to run and work to do." I scramble to answer, in a weak attempt to cover up the quivering in my voice.

"Look, I know you don't care about us. You made that quite clear when you left all hush-hush to do God knows what. But I deserve an explanation. I've been waiting nine years for it, and until I get it, I am not gonna leave you alone." His words are blanketed in anger and hurt, even all these years later.

His declaration hurts. None of what he believes is

true. But he's right; he deserves an explanation, just not right now. I can't give it to him here in my office with my assistant right outside the door and an office full of people I barely know. This is way too emotional of a conversation to have here. I cannot have a meltdown in my office.

"Despite what you think, Massimo, that's not true," I say, the words a hushed statement falling from my lips. Tears burn at my eyes, begging to be let free.

"Well then, Lena, why don't you enlighten me?" he quips as he scoots his chair closer to lean on the desk. "What is the truth behind your sudden and unexpected disappearance from my life?"

"Massimo." I shimmy forward in my chair and rest my arms on the desk, bringing my face inches away from his. I'm playing with fire, and with Massimo, I'll get burned. I've never been able to resist his energy and the pull he has over me. "I know you deserve to know the truth, and I am gonna give it to you, all of it. But that cannot happen right now, for many reasons, but mostly because I have a meeting after you leave."

"Many reasons," he repeats, contemplating my words. Massimo tilts his head slightly to the right, purses his lips, and runs his index and forefingers back and forth over his bottom lip. His eyes never leave mine as he searches for a response in them, studying me. He pushes his hands down onto my desk and stands, nudging the chair back with his leg.

He steps to his right, dragging his left hand along the desk while slowly circling it until he's standing to my left. With his right hand, he swivels my chair and lifts my chin, guiding my head up. I tremble under his touch. His hand stops when my eyes lock on his.

He bends down, bringing his lips to my left ear, and whispers, "Lena." My eyes close, memories of all the times he whispered words of love or sexual desire in my ear flashback through my mind. He pauses, his breath tickling my ear. "You want more time—" he gently skims his lips along my earlobe "—I'll give you time, even if you don't deserve it."

His breath is hot as he speaks, and my eyes flutter closed again in response. I squeeze my legs together to quell the tingling sensation. His lips graze the skin below my ear, and he drags them along my jawline until he's hovering over my mouth.

He rests his forehead against mine—eye to eye, nose to nose, breath to breath. We're still for several seconds, and it's slow, fucking torture.

My heart is bursting.

Racing.

Palpitating.

My breath is short and fast.

Massimo stokes the fire within me by bringing his lips to mine and resting them there, his breath searing me.

"Lena," he mutters.

"Massimo," I whisper back.

As quickly as his lips brushed mine, they're gone, and suddenly I feel cold.

And just like that, Massimo has pushed all my buttons. I am drunk on desire and need. I cannot think straight after feeling him close to me. My heart races and my mind is a flurry of thoughts, thoughts clouded by the yearning need for him.

"Lena," he says again, pulling away from me, a glint in his eyes and an arrogant grin sprawled across his face. "You have until tomorrow after work. We can meet wherever you like, but I'm done waiting," he commands as he lifts up and away from me.

"Oh…okay," I stutter, still coming down from my Massimo-induced high.

"Six o'clock at The Vault over on Water Street," he says as he starts walking away.

Massimo stops and glances back at me. "Don't be late," he says and struts out of my office.

After work, I drive to Newton to visit my parents. I haven't seen them in a week, and my father called me this morning to invite me to dinner. The drive westbound on the Pike is stacked with traffic. It never used to be this bad.

My iPod is on shuffle, and the music is keeping me company. Although it does very little to silence the thoughts of Massimo. When "Sad" by Maroon 5 starts playing, I turn up the volume. As usual, the song makes me question whether I chose the right path or not, and whether I will ever find another man like Massimo. Tears slide down my cheeks, the lyrics echoing my emotions.

Seeing him today was unexpected, and again, he got me all worked up. I need to get my act together to have a normal conversation with him without getting all flustered. I did notice he wasn't wearing a wedding ring, though. Was he wearing one the other day at the market? I don't remember and will have to pay attention when I see him tomorrow. Does him not wearing one mean he isn't married? Everything I remember about him tells me he's the type of guy who'd wear a band. I don't want to get my hopes up, but hope is all I have left right now.

When I arrive at my parents' house in Newton Corner, I sit in their driveway for a few minutes to gain my composure. I don't want them to know I was crying on my way here. They always have a slew of questions. I don't need to give them any more ammunition.

My parents moved to Newton in the early 1970s after moving to Boston from Puerto Rico. They had wanted to move to a neighborhood with good schools where they could raise their kids. Until he retired a few years ago, my father worked in a weapons manufacturing plant in the next town. My mother was a housekeeper for several families in Newton and neighboring towns.

I'm the youngest of six, and there are two or three years' age difference from one to the next. Newton Corner, my father told me, was the only part of Newton they could afford to buy a house since Newton was considered a more affluent city. But this part of the city was working class, yet would permit us to attend public schools here, which were amongst the best in the nation. Our Latino family was only one of a handful of Latino families in the city, which was predominantly Jewish and Italian when I was growing up.

I still remember starting pre-K, and on the first day of school, I didn't speak English. When my mother picked me up that day, the teacher told her, "Mrs. Lopez, you must speak English to your daughter because she doesn't understand anything we're doing. She speaks no English." My parents ignored the teacher's instruction and insisted that we only speak Spanish at home. Despite that, I learned English within a few weeks.

But growing up Latina in Newton wasn't always easy. With olive skin and a name like mine, I was often asked by kids and adults alike, "What are you?" or "Where are you from?" It made me self-conscious. I always looked different than most of the girls I went to school with because of my height and big, frizzy hair. When I hit my growth spurt in junior high school, though, I really stuck out. I was taller than all the girls and boys, had curvy hips, thighs, a big, round ass, bouncy curls, and full lips. I hated being a teenager because I always felt so different and didn't know how to love myself.

The ascent up the backstairs leaves me in the kitchen where my parents are making dinner—the aromas reminiscent of my childhood. It smells delicious, and the scent of Adobo seasoning fills the air. My father is standing over the stove, flipping something in the frying pan, and I kiss him.

"Hi, *Papi. Huele rico*, what are you making?" I ask.

My father is seventy, yet carries his age well. He's taller than me at six-foot-one, has thick curly hair, the gray hair evenly mixed with the black, and the wrinkles creasing his eyes show years of experience.

"*Hola*, Nena. Right now, *chicharrones*," he says. "I know you love them. The rest of the food is almost ready. We were waiting for you."

"Mmm, pork rinds. Thanks, *Papi*," I say, before turning to where my mom is standing at the counter. "*Hola, Mami.*" I lean down and kiss her cheek. My mother, also seventy, is petite with dark blonde hair and striking green eyes.

"*Hola*, Nena," she says. She's washing lettuce and spinach, probably to make a salad.

"Can I help?"

"*Si,*" *Mami* says. "Cut some bread. It's on the dining room table." She gestures to her left.

I pick up the bread from the table and see a picture of Massimo and me that my mom has in a metal frame on the china cabinet. I wonder why she kept this photo up. We're all dressed up, him in a black suit and me in a purple dress. We had been dating for about one year, and I asked him to be my plus one at my friend Gina's wedding, a couple of hours away from the city. We rented a hotel room for the night since we would be drinking at the wedding.

ELEVEN YEARS AGO

"Will you zip the back of my dress for me?" I ask.

Massimo sidles up to me—his front to my back—and nuzzles his nose below my ear.

"I'd rather take this dress off of you right now," he says, placing kisses along my neck between each word.

"You know I would love that too, but we're gonna be late. You'll have to save it for later."

Massimo's hands separate from me and he pulls the zipper up. "I'm gonna have a fucking hard-on all night watching you in that dress." His voice is deep and husky.

After he zips me up, I turn and see his shirt buttoned except for the top one, his purple tie loosely hanging around his neck. He's so handsome—lean and statuesque at six-foot-three with a chiseled jawline and a Greek nose. I could stare at him for hours on end.

"Are you ready to go?" I ask.

"Just need to fix my tie."

I watch him close the top button and adjust the tie, his left hand holding it while his right hand tightens the knot. His hands are large and olive-colored, with veins prominent along the top. How I love feeling them on my skin. They're masculine, yet he's so delicate when he explores my body with them, when he holds

211

my hands in his while walking.

Later at the church, we watch the wedding party enter. I'm sitting closest to the aisle, and Massimo is to my right. We rise to our feet to watch my friend enter on her father's arm, her wedding dress straight cut and simple with a long train. Massimo leans into me, whispering, "You're gonna look beautiful when I marry you." He softly kisses me on the cheek.

I blush at his statement, questions swirling in my head. Instead, I smile at him and continue watching Gina march toward her groom.

"Nena, where's the bread?" My mother's words bring me back to the here and now.

I love the memory this picture evoked. If Massimo had known then that I would crush his soul, he never would've asked me to marry him.

"Coming," I respond. I grab the bread off the table and return to the kitchen.

We enjoy dinner at the large round kitchen table, the same as we always did when I was growing up. We would all gather around the table, the space tight with the six of us kids squeezing in with my parents. They cooked together on most nights because they both worked all day, so it was their time to catch up with each other. They would steal kisses when they thought we weren't looking. Back then, it would gross me out to see my parents kissing or being affectionate with each other. Looking back on it, they set a great example of what love is.

"*Mami, la foto* of Massimo and me, why do you still have it there?"

"*Porque me gusta,*" she responds, matter-of-factly.

"I like it too, but we're not together anymore."

"Have you seen Massimo?" my father asks.

"Not yet," I lie. They don't need to know he was at my office earlier today. All it would do is require me to explain things I can't tell them yet.

"You know," he says, "I never told you how I felt about what you did, leaving Massimo in secret. You never wanted to hear it, always made some excuse about it because you weren't living here or were in law school, and I didn't pressure you. But now, you're going to hear it—no more excuses. We disapproved of it. You never told us why you did it or what happened. The truth is, the reason doesn't matter. It was wrong. He came here asking for our help, but you shut us out too because you know what I would've said had you told me your plans. You know I would've helped him find you. Massimo is a good man, and he didn't deserve what you did to him. And it's not the way we raised you. I hope you understand the damage you caused, the hurt you inflicted, and you seek forgiveness," he lectures.

My father is staring at me, disappointment in his eyes. He waits for me to respond to his admonishment.

"*Perdóname, Papi*. I'm sorry for hurting you—" I turn to my mother "—and you." She extends her hand across the table and softly pats my arm.

"It's not us you should apologize to," my father says before drinking from his beer bottle.

Despite being thirty-five, I'm left feeling like a petulant child because of my father's words.

CHAPTER SIXTEEN

Heart's Desire

MARIALENA

THE NEXT DAY

"WHAT'S UP, NATALIA?" I ask when she buzzes my office.

"Mr. Gentile is on line one for you. Would you like to speak to him, or should I take a message?"

"I'll speak to him," I say, smiling. I look at my watch, and it reads 4:28 p.m. I'll be seeing him in less than two hours, and I have butterflies in my stomach.

"Hi, Mr. Gentile. How can I help you?" I ask in a low, breathy voice.

"Lena, my mother passed away."

"Oh, Massimo, I'm so sorry."

"I'm. I. Fuck! Lena, my mother died," he croaks out.

I don't know what to say to him. I want to hug him, hold him, console him. But alas, I have no right to do any of those things anymore. Massimo was extremely close to her, especially since he didn't have a great relationship with his father. Because of that, I grew close to her during the time we were together. She was so caring and had a huge heart, took me in as one of her own as soon as Massimo introduced me to the family. She was the matriarch, always trying to keep everyone united. It saddens me to think she's gone and what it means for them.

"What can I do?" I ask.

"I'm at the Taverna in the North End. Can you come here?"

"Um," I begin, hesitant to say "yes."

"Don't worry about it, Lena."

"No, it's okay. I'm sorry, I'm just shocked by the news. Of course, I'll stop by. Be there soon."

"Okay," he says before the line goes silent.

I place the phone receiver back onto the cradle, and my hand lingers there. I'm stunned at hearing that my almost mother-in-law passed. I loved her and will never get the opportunity to apologize to her for the harm I inflicted upon her and her family. Life is unpredictable and can change in the blink of an eye. Death is always a stark reminder to not take anyone or anything for granted.

My heart hurts for Massimo. I haven't lost either of my parents yet, but the loss of a parent is devastating. Massimo always tried to keep up a tough appearance throughout our relationship, to not let emotions affect him, at least publicly. But as our relationship progressed, he allowed his feelings to show. He started opening up with me, sharing the turmoil that plagued him, the anger he carried, letting me see inside his hard exterior.

Massimo is the oldest of the three siblings and was always the leader of the family. Both of his parents and his siblings always look to him for everything. They all rely on him. He was always doing for others, giving to others, making sure everyone else had what they needed—putting himself last. Presumably, his father and siblings will do the same now. If that's the case, knowing him, he won't permit himself to grieve his mother's passing but will internalize it. Instead, he'll try and be the strong one for his father, his siblings, and his kids.

It's awful of me to think, but what terrible timing.

He's been so preoccupied with my return and hell-bent on finding out why I left. But he needs to deal with his mother's death before I unload all of my baggage onto him as well.

I roll my chair back and open the desk's bottom-right drawer to pull out my pockabook and place it onto the desk. I trade my dress shoes for my boots so I can walk over to the North End. After I lace them up, I grab my bag and strut out of my office, stopping at Natalia's desk.

"Why don't you wrap up and head home," I tell her. "I'm leaving for the day, and it's quiet."

"Okay, do you have the file for the Gomez hearing tomorrow?" she asks.

"I'll come to the office early before going to court. I'll get it then. Anything else?"

"That's all. Thanks, Lena. Have a good night."

"You too, Natalia," I say as I stride toward the office exit.

Before taking the elevator down, I stop to use the bathroom. When I finish washing my hands, I run them through my hair to tame some of the crazy curls. I find my makeup pouch and touch up my lipstick, glancing at my chin to ensure none of those stubborn wire hairs that grow in are visible. After our encounter in my office last week, I'm nervous to see Massimo. Despite knowing he belongs to another woman, I want to look my best, even if I know it's wrong.

A few minutes later, I exit the elevator, walking toward the exit on State Street, making a left once outside. I take the quickest route through Faneuil Hall. He owns three restaurants with his brother and sister: the one I worked at back in the day, which is on Franklin Street a few blocks from my office, one in the South End, and the one I'm going to now in the North End.

I still remember when they opened up Trattoria Lorenzo Restaurant & Bar, and he asked me to go work with him after we'd been dating for a few months. I was hesitant at first but ultimately decided to do it. Massimo had talked about expanding and opening up a few more restaurants with themed bars and that he wanted me to be the bar manager for all of them. So much for those plans—something else that I ruined.

I'm about to turn onto Salem Street when my phone rings. I ignore it because right now, my mind is on Massimo. As I approach the restaurant, I look left before crossing the street. Lorenzo's Taverna is located diagonally across the street from me.

Inside the Taverna, a few people are sitting at the bar to my left. There's an older man, his suit is dark gray, and the pant legs are tattered at the bottom. His orange tie hangs loosely around his neck, his shoulders are sagging, and he's sipping a martini. The couple in the corner by the window is young. They both wear suits, his black, hers a red skirt suit with black opaque tights. They look like newlyweds and can't keep their hands off of each other. Their drinks sit untouched next to the calamari that's getting cold.

A young woman approaches me. "Hi, how can I help you?"

"I'm here to see Massimo. He's expecting me. My name is Lena."

"Yes, he's in the office. Go through the back over there—" she points to the back door in the far-right corner "—and take the stairs down. Once downstairs, go through the kitchen, and you'll see the wooden door to your left."

I follow her directions, and when I find myself at the office door, I knock.

"Yeah," I hear Massimo say.

I nudge it open and poke my head through. "Hi, can I come in?"

He peeks up at me from where he's sitting on the couch, hands cradling his head, which hangs low. The radio plays softly in the background.

"God, are you a sight for sore eyes," he whispers. His gaze lingers on me for a few seconds before looking back down.

I enter, closing the door behind me, and lean up against it.

"How you holding up?" I ask him.

"I'm not."

"Is that why you're here holed up and not at your parents' house with your family?"

"Still know me after all these years, huh?"

"You're not an easy man to forget."

"It hurts so fucking much. I didn't get to say good-bye to her last night. We knew it was near the end but never expected it would be this quick. That my father would call me this morning and tell me she passed in her sleep. I didn't get to tell her so many things I wanted to say. My boys didn't get to say goodbye."

He barely mutters those last words, hurt overtaking him. As he shakes, I watch him move his left hand from his hair to wipe tears that must be dripping from his eyes. The absence of his wedding ring is glaring, but now isn't the time for me to be inquisitive. He's still looking at the floor, refusing to lift his head, most likely trying to hide his emotions from me, not wanting to expose his vulnerability.

I don't have any words to comfort him. Instead, I thrust myself off the door and pad across the office until I'm standing before him. I drop my bag on the couch and push my hands into his wild mane, down the back of his head, to the nape of his neck, spreading them to his shoulders to gently massage him.

His body stiffens, but I don't stop, although I should. I have no right to be doing this when he belongs to someone else, but I'm selfish when it comes to Massimo. His hands find my hips grasping them tightly, the feel of them evoking memories of him making love to me. He rests his head on my belly, and I move my hand back through his hair, tangling my fingers through the thick strands.

Massimo is shaking. I can hear his labored breaths and the sniffles that undoubtedly accompany the tears I cannot see. My heart breaks for him, and I want to ease his pain, so I continue tousling his hair with my fingers. It's all I can do.

We remain in that position for what seems like forever. The silence between us is filled with unspoken emotions, accompanied by Dave Matthews Band's "Crash Into Me" playing on the radio.

I am at a loss for words. I don't know how to console the man before me because he's no longer mine. Aside from our last two encounters, I haven't seen Massimo in nine years. The last place I expected to find myself is comforting him as I am now. There is still much unsaid between us, much I have to apologize for, yet now is not the time to get into all that. He needs to grieve his mother before he can do anything else.

"Lena," he murmurs while tightening his grip on my hips, the burning between my legs intensifying under his touch.

"I'm here."

Massimo lifts his head, peeking up at me, letting his gaze linger before shifting his eyes back down to my tummy. He moves his hands to the front and begins pulling my blouse out from where it's tucked into my skirt until my skin is exposed. He places his lips on my belly—the touch of them like flames licking at my skin.

My head tells me I should ask him to stop. My heart begs for him to keep going.

"I missed you so much, you have no idea," he mumbles, kissing the area above the skirt's waistband between each word.

My eyes burn when I hear his confession. I lean my head back to fight the tears from releasing. I should stop him, but my self-restraint has always been weak whenever I'm near him, his presence stripping me bare. Despite not seeing him in nine years, he's dominated my thoughts nearly every single day. I am selfish and want him to touch me. Having him so close to me fulfills all of my heart's desires. I let out a long breath, shifting my head back down to watch him.

Massimo begins unbuttoning my shirt, starting with the bottom button. He moves to the next, his large fingers struggling with the small buttons, kissing the skin he exposes with each one that comes undone. When he reaches my bra, he opens my blouse, placing his hands over each breast and squeezing.

I'm feverish and groan from the welcome pressure. His lips skim along the skin above the waistline of my skirt, his tongue licking its way up, stopping just under my breasts, leaving a trail of scorching heat along its path.

His kisses torch the wildfire within me, each stroke of his hands incendiary. My skin tingles and comes alive under his touch, at the feel of the stubble growing on his face scraping my skin. My hands play with his hair, back, forth, around—pushing and pulling it every which way in slow, circular motions.

Massimo's hands move over my hips and down the sides of each leg, landing on the bottom of my skirt, hiking it up until it's bunched around my hips. He kisses the skin along the top of my thighs, grasping the panties between his teeth. He drags his hands from my hips down to my apex, until his left hand finds its way between my thighs and rests on my panties, pulling them to the side. His right index and middle fingers rest on my heated folds just exposed. He begins rubbing them up toward my sensitive nub and back in a slow dragging motion.

I hiss at his touch, and my legs begin shaking. Fuck how I've missed him, his hands, his caresses. My breathing is labored. My eyes are hooded from the pleasure he's awoken within me.

I should stop him, but I don't want to.

I shouldn't let this happen, but I need it to.

I should end this, but greed overpowers me.

Massimo's index finger slips between my lips, pushing its way in, his thumb circling, and I moan in response. Lust clouds my thoughts, all reasoning I try to convince myself of, gone. Inside of me, his finger circles, and his middle finger joins, delving deeper within me, causing my legs to buckle from pleasure. I have to grasp onto him to keep from collapsing.

As he's rubbing and pushing, he lowers his head and flicks his tongue over my mound, resting its tip there before he begins drawing circles with it.

I mewl in pleasure and tug at his hair. He responds by licking my folds, dragging his tongue up to my nub and back down. All the while, his fingers stroke my insides, causing me to crash over the edge. He continues circling his thumb while his fingers rub me from within, carrying me through my climax.

When my breathing slows, Massimo pulls his fingers from me, and I instantly feel the cool air between my legs, hollow because I miss his touch.

I look down at him, and he's shifting his head back and away from me, raising his gaze to mine. His chocolate-colored eyes are hooded, dark, and burning with desire. I can still see the love there that I saw all those years ago.

He lifts his right hand to his lips and starts sucking on his fingers, slowly dragging them out and pushing them back in, savoring the taste of me.

Fueling my cravings to taste him. Feel him. Love him.

I bring my right hand from his hair down to his face resting my thumb on his lips, running it from left to right and back again. He flicks his tongue out, taking my thumb in his mouth, and begins sucking it. Our eyes bore into each other, and we cherish each other's touch.

"Massimo, I—"

"Shhh, not now, Lena, please." His eyes plead for me to stop talking.

His hands move to my waist and grab my skirt, adjusting it back into place before he buttons my blouse. When he finishes, he nudges me, and I take a step back, allowing him to get up. He stands, his eyes never leaving mine as he raises himself from the couch, his grasp still firm on my rounded hips. Massimo's eyes emanate a myriad of emotions—fear, anger, hurt, sadness, hope, love.

"Massimo, I think we should talk about what just happened."

"Please, Lena," he says, shaking his head as his thumb runs across my bottom lip, left to right, and back to the center, resting there, pressing my lips together. "Not today. Let me have this moment, you, what just happened. I have a lot to deal with right now, and I need something good to hold on to."

I resign to him, his plea one I cannot refuse. "Okay."

His mischievous grin appears before brushing his lips to mine. "Thank you for coming." He smirks and winks.

"Massimo," I pause but decide against saying anything further because he's asked me to wait. "Never mind."

At that moment, the door opens, and we both turn our heads. "Massimo, why don't you answer—" his sister Stella says as she's entering the office. She stops short when her eyes land on me.

"What the fuck are you doing here?" Stella demands, glaring at me. If looks could kill, I'd be dead.

Stella looks as beautiful as I remember. She and Massimo share the same lips, nose, and thick black hair, but she has striking round blue eyes like their mother, and her olive skin is always darkly tanned.

She and I spent a lot of time together before I left, and she was excited that I was marrying Massimo. She told me I was the sister she always wanted. I'm sure she feels betrayed by what I did and is angry with me for leaving not just Massimo, but her too.

Before I can answer, Massimo says, "She's here with me because I asked her to be." He tightens his arm around me, claiming me.

"Really, after everything she pulled? You just let her waltz back into our lives?"

"My life," he asserts. "And who I choose to be in my life is my decision. Stay the fuck out of it."

"Whatever. If you would've answered your phone, I wouldn't have come here and seen this bullshit." She gestures her hand in an up-and-down manner. "We need you at the house. Anthony from the funeral home is on his way." She storms out of the office, slamming the door behind her.

"I should go," I say.

"Yeah, I need to leave too. Where's your phone?"

"My pockabook."

He lets go of me, picks up my purse from the couch, and sticks his hand inside, searching for my phone. Once he has it in his hands, he slides the unlock feature and starts dialing. Moments later, his phone rings. After ending the call, he hands it to me with my bag.

I look at my phone's screen, Massimo's number in the most recent call slot. "You still have the same phone number," I whisper, lifting my eyes to his.

"I never changed it in hopes that one day you would call me." His revelation stings, another reminder of what a terrible person I am.

"I'm sorry," I mutter.

"I gotta go," he says. "I'll text you when I have details about the service. I want you there."

"Is that a good idea, after the way Stella reacted?"

"Let me deal with that."

"Okay." After what just happened, I want to kiss him goodbye, feel the warmth of his lips, but I have no right to ask for anything. I take a step toward the door when Massimo pulls me back into a hug. I reciprocate, wrapping my arms around his torso, feeling the firm muscles in his back, nuzzling my nose to his neck, inhaling his unique scent. His hands are circling on my lower back, and he drops kisses along my hairline. His arms envelop me in safety like I've arrived home after a long journey.

Before tears begin, I separate from him and step toward the door. "I'll wait for your text," I say, walking out of the office. The emotions are overtaking me, anxiety rising because I feel out of control of this situation. I need time away from him to let the fog lift. It's the only way I can think clearly.

When I'm outside of the restaurant, I welcome the fresh air. Late September is my favorite time of year in Boston, mostly warm days and cool nights. I decide to call Luci and see if she's off tonight to come over, but her phone goes to voicemail. I grab my iPod and pop my earbuds in, and hit play, letting Roxette's "Listen to Your Heart" calm my erratic heart.

Although it's dark and I can't see the water, the ocean is angry, the waves crashing with fury, mirroring the turmoil I feel within. Seems a storm is moving in. After getting home, I decided to drive to Revere Beach to sit along the wall, absorb the salty air, regroup my thoughts, and grab some fried clams from Kelly's for dinner. Comfort food always goes a long way.

The ocean air has a way of calming and centering me. And after seeing Massimo, my emotions are all over the place. The last thing I expected was for him to touch me the way he did, for us to be intimate. I know it's wrong, that I had no right to allow it, but I've missed him, and everything that happened in his office felt right. We need to talk, so I can tell him why I left, and we can discuss what just happened. If things were complicated before, our encounter just made it worse.

Even though I shattered his heart, Massimo still has feelings for me. I felt it in the way he touched me, saw it in the way he looked at me.

Selfishly, I'm happy about that. But my selfish behavior has already caused enough destruction, and I cannot do any more damage, especially not to him. He has a new life with his boys and their mother, and I won't ruin that for him. Except, once again, I noticed he didn't have a wedding band on. Everything I know about Massimo tells me he would wear one. He's too loyal not to, and I don't think he would've been intimate with me if he was in a relationship or married. I'm so confused.

As soon as he's buried his mother and he's ready to talk, I'm going to tell him my whole story, so we can both have closure and move forward.

CHAPTER SEVENTEEN

Should've Been Honest

MASSIMO

NTHONY FROM THE FUNERAL home spent a few hours with us, and we made the necessary arrangements for my mother's service. The wake is the day after tomorrow, with the burial the following morning.

It's past midnight when I walk through my front door, kick my shoes off, and go straight to my shower. I need to wash away the day. I turn the water on and let it warm up while I undress.

Amidst all the grief of my mother dying and making funeral arrangements, Lena was my bright spot—like she always was. Despite the years, my heart still swells when I think of her, touch her, taste her.

Feminine.

Sensual.

Delicious.

She was so responsive to me today. I didn't know if she would let me touch her, but I missed her so damn much I needed a taste. She's friggin addictive. When she didn't stop me, I knew she longed for me as much as I did her. I know she still loves me.

I step into the shower and welcome the hot water pounding my skin. My dick is rock hard thinking about Lena. I adjust the showerhead, sit on the bench to the side, resting my head against the wall, and begin stroking myself. Images of Lena are vivid in my mind.

How wet she was. How she mewled when I rubbed her folds, moaned when I flicked my tongue at her clit. Pulled my hair when I fucked her with my fingers, and she coated me in her milk. The taste of her on my tongue, my lips, and my fingers wasn't enough.

I'm greedy and want more. I want to grab onto those curvy hips and push into her. Feel her stretch around me as I enter her. Rub her walls when I'm inside of her. Suck on her nipples while plunging into her so that I can fill her with my seed. "Lena," I grunt as I'm coming, stroking myself until my breath evens out.

My legs are weak, and I have to remain seated for

a minute to regain my strength. Lena is at the forefront of my thoughts. My girl came back, and I need her in my life. I need to figure out how to make that happen.

Once I'm able to get up, I shower, brush my teeth, and hit the sheets. Let's hope I can get a good night's rest. Tomorrow is another long day, where I have to plan for the event after my mother's burial.

I spend most of the day at the restaurant in the North End since this is where everyone will come back to after we bury my mother—menu planning with the chef, phone calls with vendors, staff meeting to prep the team. Before leaving for my parents' house, I send Lena a text message.

Massimo: Wake is tomorrow 5-9 pm at Nardone's. See you there.

I arrive at the funeral home with my father. He was adamant that we arrive early to have alone time with Ma. I hate funerals; then again, who doesn't? Although this is for my mother, I dread that I have to be here for the next several hours and greet the ton of people who will show up. I'll have to be social when all I want to do is sip whiskey and mourn.

My father and I walk into the parlor where my mother's casket is. Flower arrangements fill the entire front of the room on each side of the coffin and behind it. Despite the magnitude of floral arrangements, it smells like death in here.

As we approach the front, my father's step falters, and he moans before his tears start flowing. Watching my father break down in such a manner humbles me. He was always so strong, a tough guy who never let me forget who's boss. To see him hurt this way, suffer and cry in a way I'd never thought possible, is jarring. With how tough he'd been when I was a child, seeing him now, weeping, sagging shoulders in defeat, is fucking with my head.

My parents were together their whole lives. She's all he knows, and I'm not sure how he's going to hold up without her. He's a changed man now that he's lost the love of his life.

I wrap my arm around my father, and side by side, we take the last few steps until we stand before the casket. I help him lower himself to rest on the kneeling rail, laying my hand on his shoulder. The tears fall from my eyes, despite my attempt to wipe them away and stop them from coming.

The woman inside that box looks nothing like my mother. In her final days, she was thin, pale, and bald. Cancer is a motherfucker and stripped her of so much. She was seventy, still too young to go. Her death has given me perspective—reminded me that our time here on Earth is short-lived.

I've checked the clock on the far wall more times than I can count—it's not even 6:00 p.m. yet! I crack my neck, shift my balance from my left foot to my right, and stretch my arms behind me. The funeral parlor is full. Full of faces I see every day and faces I haven't seen in years.

Aunts, uncles, cousins, second cousins, spouses, their kids. Friends, my closest friends, acquaintances from the neighborhood, and other business owners from the area. This tradition, or whatever the fuck it is, is too much.

We're standing in a receiving line, first the casket, then my father, me, followed by my sister and brother. My boys were standing with me for a little while but got tired and are now sitting with their mother off to the side. I've thanked so many people for being here that I'm now just going through the motions, people blurring one into the next.

I feel her before I can see her. Lena's energy is something my body reacts to. It's been like that since the day I met her. I know she's here; I just need to spot her. The room is packed with people. Everyone dressed in black, faces somber, people whispering to each other to keep the noise level down. But the whispers create a storm of noise in my head.

My eyes scan the room, left to right, and back. The line to greet us extends along the left side of the room and wraps around the wall. That's where I see her. She's standing next to Luci; they're talking, and she hasn't looked up yet. Her dark curls are loose and wild, with ringlets framing her face and falling halfway down her back. She's wearing her signature frames. Today they're black to match her black wrap dress with a deep V-neck, the swell of her breasts peeking out—making my dick twitch. She's wearing dark wine-colored lipstick, accentuating her bee-stung lips. She's beautiful. Her eyes shift and connect with mine, and her lips curl up on one side.

My sister breaks into my thoughts and whispers, "What the fuck is she doing here?"

I lower my mouth to her ear and say, "Don't. Not here. Lena is here for me. End of story!"

"Whatever!" She rolls her eyes.

I stand back up and shift my eyes back to Lena, who noticed the exchange between Stella and me. Lena mouths, "I'm sorry," and she looks away, starts talking to Luci again.

When Lena is standing before me, I wrap her in my arms, tightening them around her lower back. She tucks her arms around my torso, resting her hands below my shoulders.

I close my eyes, the storm within intensifying. My mother's death, Lena's absence and sudden reappearance, and the uncertainty of the unknown of what's happening between us cause my chest to tighten.

"Hi," I whisper into her ear. "You're the one person I've been waiting to see all night. Thank you for being here." I tighten my embrace, her coconut scent invading my senses, and a shudder runs through my body. I've missed her and holding her again like this is a stark reminder of how much.

"You're welcome," she whispers. "I'm truly sorry for your loss. I loved her too and feel terrible that I'll never have the opportunity to apologize to her for what I did to you." Her arms tighten around me.

Lena's words sear me, and I don't want to release her. "Thank you. Please don't go," I murmur into her ear. "Wait for all these people to leave. I want to talk for a bit." She nods in response. As she's stepping away from me, my eyes fall on Camila, who's glaring at me from the back of the room.

About two years after Lena left, Camila came into one of my restaurants for dinner. She checked into a reservation for two and waited at the bar. I noticed her sitting alone all night and approached her, which is when I learned her plus one never showed. She had been stood up for a first date. I was intrigued that this beautiful woman had been left waiting without so much as a call.

That night I learned Camila is from Argentina. She speaks English with a thick accent, has long, brown hair and hazel eyes. We stayed at the bar until past midnight, long after I closed the restaurant. The night ended with me asking her out. It was the first time I asked a woman out since Lena ghosted because it was time for me to move on. Although I had stopped looking for her, I still hadn't dated. I'd only casually hooked up with women when the opportunity presented itself.

Camila and I began dating and, after several months, became exclusive, even if thoughts of Lena always snaked their way into my life.

I wanted to forget Lena, wanted to not love her anymore, wanted to hate her for abandoning me. But the heart wants what it wants, and you can't dictate who you love.

When Camila told me she was pregnant, I took it as a sign I had to move on. Initially, I was upset, more at myself than anything. How could I let this happen with a woman I wasn't in love with? But I was thirty-seven and desperately wanted kids. If Camila was pregnant, I would be the child's father. Despite not being in love with her, I had to do the right thing, and we moved in together.

I knew I would never love Camila like I had Lena, but love comes in different forms, and I thought our relationship was good enough to withstand my frailty. That being parents to our child would help love, in some form, flourish. I settled, thinking my mind was stronger than my heart. I tried to do the right thing for my kids, tried to keep my family together, but it was disastrous.

I now know I was doomed from the outset, destined to fail, and was a fool to think otherwise. I should've been honest with her and myself from the get-go.

Lena is sitting with Luci and Dom along the back wall when the last of the visitors exit. Before going to them, I stop where Camila is sitting with the boys, both fast asleep. I lift Lucio into my arms, Camila carries Leandro, and together we walk out to the car. I place Lucio in his booster seat and buckle him in. Camila is about to open the driver's side door and asks, "Is that her?"

"Camila, don't. Not now, please."

"For once, can you please respond to my question?"

"Yes."

"Why? Can you at least answer that?" she pleads.

"No. We've already had this conversation."

She rolls her eyes, opens the door, and climbs into the Escalade. I close the door behind her and wait till she drives off before returning to the funeral home.

Lena was long gone from my everyday life, but she was very much a part of my relationship with Camila.

FOUR MONTHS EARLIER

"Camila, I'm moving out," I say to her as I'm entering the kitchen.

"What? Why?"

"You know why."

"Actually, I don't. Why don't you tell me? I deserve the truth."

"We have our boys, and we'll always be their parents, but that's it. We're not a couple anymore, we haven't been intimate in months, and I spend my days working long hours to avoid coming home, so we don't fight." Camila's eyes widen because she didn't expect to hear those words, but the truth is inevitable. A truth I've avoided for too long.

"You know, you've always been distant, kept a part of yourself hidden away from me, and I never understood why," she tells me.

"It doesn't matter."

"It does matter!" she says, her voice getting louder with each word. *"To me, it matters! We've been together for years, we have kids, and I do everything for our family, for us! But despite this seemingly perfect life we've built—"* she screams, throwing her arms in the air *"—it's not real! We're missing the foundation. You won't commit to our family, won't marry me! It doesn't matter how many times I ask you to!"*

Camila has tears streaming down her face, and seeing the hurt I caused her hammers home that I'm a bastard and was selfish in my actions. I know I should comfort and embrace her, but the defeat I feel over *what I've allowed my life to become is too powerful to let me, even if I am the cause of her pain.*

My heart isn't satisfied, hasn't been since that fateful night Lena disappeared from my life. I can no longer pretend that everything between Camila and me is fine. The words fall from my mouth before I can stop them. "I'm not in love with you, Camila; I never will be."

"Why can't you love me? Why won't you love me?!" she yells, thrashing my chest with her fist-clenched hands.

"I can't tell you that because I don't know," I say, moving away from her to stop the onslaught of her fury.

"That's bullshit, and you know it! You do know, but you just don't want to say it to spare my feelings! Newsflash, Massimo, you've already shattered me, so spare me and just tell me the truth!"

"Please, Camila, don't do this!"

"If you're gonna ruin my life, at least be a man about it and say it to my face!"

"Why? It's not gonna change anything!"

"Because that bitch walked away from you and destroyed your heart! I was the one who was there for you! I'm the one who gave you the children you so desperately wanted! Yet you're incapable of loving me, of loving anyone but her! She robbed me of your love

and robbed your children of having a complete family. She's a ghost that lives in our house and sleeps in our bed! I just don't understand how you can still fucking love her!"

"I can't explain it. Not to you and not to myself. I just do," I respond, shoulders sagging in defeat.

"You know what, Massimo? Fuck you! I deserve so much better than this, than you!" she retorts, storming out of the kitchen.

"You're right, Camila, you do. I'm sorry for everything. But mostly, I'm sorry I hurt you. I'll be gone by tomorrow."

Back inside, Lena is still with Dom and Luci. I take a seat next to Dom, resting my elbows on my knees. "Thank you for being here."

"Of course, you're my brother, and I'm here for you. Always! Can I do anything for you before leaving?"

"I'm good. Thank you."

"All right. If you need anything, just let me know. We're taking off," Dom says, as he and Luci stand. I look at him, then at Luci before glancing over to Lena, who purses her lips and shrugs. Lena stands and hugs

Luci before sitting in the chair next to me, her hand resting on my lower back, caressing me.

"Long day, huh?" she says, more a statement than a question needing an answer.

"Doesn't even begin to explain it."

"There were a lot of people here. I waited in line for more than an hour before I was even in the door. Your mother was loved, and tonight was a testament to that."

"Yeah." I stand, extending my hand to Lena. "Let's get out of here; I don't want to be here anymore."

My car is parked to the far right of the funeral home, and when we reach it, I open the passenger side door for Lena and ask, "You want to go the South Street Diner, grab some coffee, maybe a bite?"

She lifts her left wrist, pulling back her jacket sleeve, and looks at her watch. "It's 10:30 p.m. I can't have coffee now because I have a hearing at 8:30 a.m. tomorrow morning and need to stop by the office first. I'm sorry."

"Okay. I'll drive you home." I close the door and walk around to get into the driver's seat. Her rejection stings like a motherfucker.

"Where do you live?" I ask.

"Beacon Hill, 79 Pinckney."

"Oh, you fancy now, huh?" We both chuckle.

"Just a small one-bedroom apartment on the third floor; I couldn't resist the view," she says, shrugging.

Before pulling out of the parking lot, I search my phone for music to play, something Lena will like, and decide on Daughtry's "It's Not Over." When the music starts, Lena glances over at me and gives me a crooked smile. I extend my hand to place it on her leg, squeezing just above her knee.

The ride to her house is silent except for the music playing. Even though I'm with Lena and I wanted to talk with her, I'm not in the talking mood. Between my mother's death, Camila, Lena's return, our being intimate a few days ago, and now her rejection, I'm drained. It seems she isn't much for conversation either. Or maybe she still reads me like a book and knows I'm in my feelings right now.

The drive over to Beacon Hill is quick, and when I turn onto her street, I park the X6 along the fence at Louisburg Square. We exit the car, crossing the street to Lena's place, and sit on her front stoop.

"Thanks for driving me."

"No need to thank me. You know I wanted to spend some time with you."

"I won't be at the service tomorrow because I have court. I'm sorry I can't make it."

"I know. It's all good. Thank you for being there

tonight. It means more than you know."

Lena stays silent. She lifts her legs one-step, bringing her knees closer to her chest, wrapping her arms around them. There's a chill in the air tonight, and she's cold. I wrap my arm around her, pulling her into me, kissing the top of her head.

"Are you ready to talk about it?" I ask her.

"Not tonight," she says. "I'm sorry. I know we're long overdue to have the conversation, but it's late, both of us are exhausted from long days, and we both have to be up early. The conversation we need to have is one that needs more time than we can give it right now."

I contemplate her words, see the sincerity in her eyes. "Okay. I don't like it, but you're right."

"Thanks. I'm gonna head inside. I need to go to bed." She stands up, and I follow.

"Hey, after we bury my mother, I'm driving to Newport with the boys. I need a few days to decompress, away from everything, everyone. I'll let you know when I'm back, and we'll meet, finally have our much-needed conversation—yeah?" I brush my knuckles across her cheeks, which are red from the chilly fall air.

"Okay, that works." She nods.

My hand cups her face underneath her chin, and I

brush my lips to hers. They're warm and soft as they always are. I'm greedy and want to taste more of her, so I kiss her again, this time with more force, swiping my tongue between her lips to open her mouth, and she lets me in, her breath hot.

"Massimo," she says, ending our kiss. "I'm—I don't think this is a good idea."

"What? Why?"

"Good night." She pulls the keys from her pocket and opens the door, disappearing behind it. After the way she responded to me the other day, her rejection is another slap in the face! Yet I keep coming back for more.

I return to my car and lean against it, watching the building to see when she gets upstairs and turns the lights on. I can't understand what's going through her mind. It seems like she's hot and cold, but I can't figure out why. It's like she wants me to touch her but then rejects me, and it makes no fucking sense. Her indecisiveness torments me, more so than I already am, if that's even possible.

I had resigned myself to live a life without Lena, to be the best father for my boys, and put relationships on hold. After all the hurt I caused Camila, I just need to focus on them. But fate intervened, and Lena returned. Stella thinks I'm an idiot for even speaking to Lena.

My head tends to agree. She wrecked me. But my heart shouts in joy that she's back, hoping it's for me.

Am I imagining that she came back for us? And if she did, can I forgive her for abandoning me? Everything inside of me screams that Lena still loves me. I can see it in her eyes, feel it in her touch, and in the way her body still reacts to me.

My mother's death reminds me that life is short, and we need to live for ourselves. Do things that make us happy. Except Lena's rejection is something fierce. So what the fuck is going on? I can't risk being betrayed—my heart can't handle that again.

Once I see Lena's light on, I climb into my car and hit shuffle on my phone. The torrents of emotions coursing through me are overwhelming, and I need the loud music to soothe and calm me.

CHAPTER EIGHTEEN

The Vault

MARIALENA

LAST NIGHT, MASSIMO'S TEXT message asked to meet today at The Vault, the same bar we had planned on meeting at last week before his mother passed away.

As I leave my office, I send him a text.

Lena: On my way—see you soon.

Massimo: At the bar—far end.

My stomach is a bundle of nerves as I'm walking to

The Vault. I've been rehearsing how to tell him, when I should tell him, and no matter how many times I try, it always sounds wrong. Of course it does. I should've never left the way I did. I shouldn't have left at all.

It takes a few minutes to arrive from my office to the entrance of the bar. Before entering, I take a deep breath and whisper to myself, "You can do this."

Inside, the tables to my left are nearly full, and the bar area to my right is standing room only. All the seats are taken, and people are crowding the space. Most of the people don suits, ties removed, top buttons loosened, suit jackets off. Everyone is here to drink away the stress of their workday. The voices are loud, and I have to force my way through the crowd to reach the far end of the bar. Nearing the back of the restaurant, I spot Massimo sitting in the second to last stool; he saved the one in the corner for me.

He's wearing his signature black T-shirt, snug around his biceps, his ink now covering almost the entirety of his left arm, stopping just short of his wrist.

When I reach him, he stands to make room for me to get by and into the corner.

"Hi," he says, leaning down to softly press his lips to my cheek.

"Hey, have you been here long?"

He shakes his head. "I know Tom, the bartender,

and haven't seen him in a while. Figured I'd get here early to catch up with him and ensure us a seat."

As I hang my jacket and pockabook over the back of the stool, I hear Massimo say, "Grey Goose and soda, with two limes for Lena, and another Jack for me, thanks." He slides his stool closer to mine and sits on the side of it; his face is just inches away—his scent intoxicating, his nearness dizzying.

"How are you?" I ask, looking into the depths of his dark brown gaze.

"Better, now." He grins, showing those smile lines on each side of his face. His hand lifts to grab one of the locks of curls framing my face, twisting it around his fingers.

"How have you been since burying your mom?"

"Okay, I guess. I don't think it's hit me yet, ya know?

"Death is hard. Take it one day at a time. It's really all we can do."

"You can say that again."

"Look at that sleeve tatt. It's impressive. Let me see it." My fingers trace the ink, and Massimo lifts his arm so I can get a better view of it. When I met him, he had just a laurel wreath with a large rose in the middle of it. He had told me the laurel wreath was related to his family's name back in Italy and that the rose in the middle was for his mother, whose name is Rosa. Said he placed it in the middle of the wreath because she's the center of the family, the rock that holds them all together. Now, he's added to the lower part of his arm. A Roman gladiator with his two boys' names inscribed on the shield and along the underside of his forearm the Roman Colosseum. I lift my eyes to his and say, "It's incredible. Why a gladiator?"

"You know Rome is my favorite city, and I'm a lover of history." His eyes flit down away from mine to his ink. "Besides, I've lived through a lot; gladiators are a symbol of strength. After my boys were born, I had their names added along the shield, at the forefront of everything."

I cringe at his words about being through a lot, knowing I played a massive role in causing him so much pain. "I have no doubt," I say, raising my eyes to meet his gaze, where pride glows he speaks of his boys.

"How was work?" he asks.

"It was work, nothing exciting." I shrug.

"Law school, huh? You finally did it. I always knew you were destined for great things."

I grin at his words. "When I was in Des Moines, I was in bad shape, emotionally and mentally. I was self-sabotaging myself and felt like I was drowning in my

253

own despair. I failed myself, my family, my friends—"
I pause to exhale because my emotions are churning
"—you." I break my eyes away from his, the intensity
of his gaze right now is too much for me, and I push
my glasses back up to sit on the bridge of my nose.

With my eyes hidden from his, I continue, "Nothing was satisfying me anymore. Don't get me wrong, I
loved bartending, but I was in a rut, and honestly, being
behind the bar reminded me of you and of our plans
to have various restaurants. I needed a change and
something challenging, something to keep my mind
focused. I had a conversation with Luci about how I
was feeling, and in typical Luci style, she whipped me
back into shape. Gave me the pep talk I needed to snap
out of the funk I was in. That's how I ended up in law
school."

"Do you like it, being a lawyer?"

"Most days, yes. I work for myself, so that's important to me because I can choose the cases I take and
the schedule I work."

The bartender had left our drinks on the bar, and
I sip from mine. The burning feeling of the vodka
soothes the ache constricting my heart. I begin peeling
back the layers for Massimo to see, exposing my vulnerabilities, and need my drink to give me the courage
to continue. I push the ice around with the small plastic

straw floating in my glass.

"Self-sabotaging, huh? Tell me about that." Massimo pushes the hair back from over my eye, and with his index finger at my chin, turns my face to him. His eyes search mine, telling me he's listening.

I've buried my feelings and emotions over abandoning Massimo and my subsequent regret for years that it takes me a moment to gather the courage to speak up, to give him what he deserves.

"I was miserable and bitter and tried to drown those feelings by having meaningless sex. The sex made me feel worse about myself. It was a vicious cycle."

Massimo recoils at my words. He swallows, his Adam's apple bobbing. The betrayal reflects in the pool of his eyes, and questions churn in their depths, but he doesn't ask them and instead lets me continue.

"Anyway, I became good friends with the girl who worked the bar with me, Stevie. When I trusted her enough, I shared most of my story with her. She was my only friend in Des Moines for a while. When I found myself in a rut, she and Luci were the ones holding me up, encouraging me to do better."

"Those are good friends to have."

"Yeah, Stevie is one of the good ones. When Luci visited me the first time, they hit it off and bonded over their love for calling me out on my bullshit." I smile at the thought of my friends.

Massimo's eyes turn up at my words. "I like doing that too."

He leans in just inches from my face and whispers, "Lena, you have no idea how much I missed you. No fucking clue." His left hand moves up. I again notice the absence of a wedding ring.

I want to ask him about it. Need to know whether he's married, especially since we were intimate last week. Thoughts of him and the mother of his boys have haunted me all week—wondering if I am intruding on a relationship, taking what isn't mine, stealing from another woman. Last week at the wake, I saw her with their boys, and she's gorgeous. When I recognized who she was, my heart twisted, and jealousy erupted inside of me.

I know if I ask him now, he'll think I'm deflecting and doing everything I can to avoid having the one conversation he's been waiting nine years to have. I swallow my need to ask until I tell him why I left. He brushes the back of his fingers across my cheek, my eyes fluttering at his touch.

"I looked for you for a year. Every day I hoped you would come back to me, but you never did." Agony is in his voice as he recounts the pain I caused him.

"I'm sorry. And I know those words may not mean

much, do very little to ease the heartache I caused you, but I want you to know, I made the decision because I thought it was best for you."

"I don't think I'll ever understand how you ghosting me was the best decision for me." His head shakes in unison with his words.

Massimo's thumb rubs back and forth across my beauty mark as he speaks to me, his attempt at relaxing me. Back in the day, he would always use touch to soften me, to draw me into him, and tear down my walls. He knew how to manipulate me with his hands, my puppeteer.

"Do you remember when you proposed to me?" I ask.

"How can I forget? Easter hasn't been the same since."

TEN YEARS AGO

Easter dinner is at Massimo's parents' house, and we invited my parents to join us. It'll be the first time both families will be together to celebrate a holiday. To say I'm nervous is an understatement. Massimo's mom asked me to make my Mami's flan. I had made it for her the first time I went to their house to meet them, and it was a hit.

My parents arrived not too long after us. My mom made arroz con habichuelas *to accompany the lamb that Massimo's mother was making, as it was their tradition to eat lamb on Easter. We have traditional Puerto Rican food,* pernil, arroz, yuca, *and potato salad at my house during the holidays. This year would be different for them, which made me a little nervous because they're kinda old school and stuck in their ways.*

We gather around the dinner table—my parents, his parents, and his siblings. His father asks Massimo to say a prayer before dinner.

Massimo rises from the table, moving his chair back, and stands in the empty space before kneeling.

"Lena." He takes my hand. For a moment, I'm confused until I see he has a small box in his hand. My eyes widen, mouth agape, heart racing.

"That first day I sat at your bar, I knew you were my girl. You're the woman who has opened my heart in a way I never imagined was possible. You're on my mind from the moment I wake up until the moment I fall asleep and in my dreams each night. When we were at Gina's wedding, I knew I would marry you, that you would be mine. I want you to be Mrs. Massimo DeLorenzo and my life partner. I want you to be the mother

of my children because we'll create the most beautiful little humans together. Will you be my Mrs.?" He opens up the box, inside a beautiful Asscher-cut diamond on a thin white gold diamond-encrusted band.

Tears stream down my face, and I have to remove my glasses. I swipe my fingers underneath each eye to wipe away the wetness and try to compose myself because I'm blubbering from emotions.

I nod. "The answer is always yes!"

He slides the ring on my finger and kisses me, deeply and passionately, there in front of our parents. I blush and pull away, nervous at everyone looking at us. When I look up at our family, joy fills the room. My mother is crying, a grin spread across her face and leaning into my father, who's smiling at me—his eyes wet at the creases.

Stella rises from her seat. "Get up. I want to hug my new sister," she says. When I do, she embraces me tightly. "I'm finally getting the sister I always wanted. I'm happy! For you, for Massimo, for us. I knew I loved you the minute he brought you home."

"Love you too, Stella." I pull back from her, and we're both crying happy tears.

"I cannot wait to help you plan this wedding! Ahh, I'm wicked excited!" Stella is ecstatic. She and Massimo are tight, and because of their close relationship, *my relationship with her has grown into one of friend-ship.*

My parents both stand from their seats and come over to us. "Nena, que alegría. *I'm so happy for you," my mother says, hugging me.*

"Gracias, Mami."

"You know, Massimo nos pidió permiso *before ask-ing you. He wanted to make sure* que *we approved," my father adds, looking between Massimo and me.*

"He did?" *I ask, glimpsing at Massimo. My heart is exploding with happiness knowing that he sought out my parents' blessing to marry him.*

That night when we return home, Massimo starts talking about wedding plans and babies. "I cannot wait until you're pregnant with our child. Other than you being my wife, it's what I want most in the world, to make babies with the woman who makes me feel alive."

"What does the day I proposed to you have to do with this?" he asks, pulling a piece of paper from his wallet and sliding it across the bar.

I extend my hand and pick it up. It's the handwrit-ten note I left for him when I skipped town. It's torn at the edges and creased from the years he's kept it in his wallet.

"You kept this?" I wasn't expecting to see this slip of paper. I reread the note I wrote to him nine years ago and wince when I see my callous words.

Massimo,

Writing this is the hardest thing I've ever done. I love you, and because of my love for you, I'm walking away. You deserve so much more than I can give you. By the time you read this, I will have left Boston. Don't bother looking for me. I left so you can live out your dream. Thank you for loving me.

~ Lena

"I read it so much that I have it memorized." His eyes are red. A tear trickles from his right eye.

I reach out and wipe away the tear with my thumb.

"Massimo, I know there are no words to console you for what I did, for the way I betrayed you. I'm sorry will never be enough."

"Lena, just tell me already. Why did you run and leave this note?" His eyes plead with me, searching for answers that only I can give him.

I fidget with my glasses, straighten them out. "I'm barren."

"What?"

"I can't have kids."

"I know what the word means. I'm asking what, as in, what, that's the reason you left?"

"Yes, but I did it for you," I murmur, my eyes dropping from his.

"You ghosted me because you can't have kids? Are you fucking kidding me?" His voice is louder than it was just a moment ago, causing the man next to him to look over at us.

"Massimo, please lower your voice."

He leans into me, his face hovering over mine. "Unbelievable! Pretty selfish to make such a life-altering decision all on your own, don't you think? Who the fuck are you to decide for me? And you couldn't look me in the eye to tell me that? Get the fuck out of here!" He sticks his hand in his pocket, pulls out his wallet, and drops a hundred-dollar bill on the bar.

"Massimo, please stop. Look at me, let me explain." I reach out for him, but he yanks his arm back from my hand.

He kicks his stool back, causing it to make a loud screeching sound before it crashes into the wall behind us. Massimo quickly turns to leave, grabbing his jacket from the stool. He forces his way through the crowded area. The faces of the patrons he's shoving are angry at his aggressiveness. His behavior causes everyone around us to gawk at me, pity dripping from their stares, whispers about what just happened wafting through the air.

I jump to my feet, scrambling for my jacket and bag, and attempt to push my way through the crowd, tears streaming down my face. When I reach the street, I see him jogging away from the bar, but he's at the end of the block, near Liberty Square, disappearing into the crowd of people. I reach for the wall to my left to balance myself. Defeat is hitting me; pain is constricting my heart.

Massimo reacted exactly as Stefano did by getting angry and storming out of the restaurant, humiliating me. It's not what I expected and is truly disheartening. I knew he'd be upset, but to react with such anger without allowing me to explain, fuck!

Once I regain my composure, I begin walking until

I see an available cab and hail it. When it stops, I climb in. "Pinckney Street, Beacon Hill, please."

Although the ride is a short distance, the traffic is heavy, and we're barely crawling down Cambridge Street. Massimo had said he wanted an explanation, and the minute I gave it to him, he didn't want to hear it. He embarrassed me just like Stefano did all those years ago. Maybe it's his way of getting even with me, a cruel payback for me to feel the slightest bit of humiliation he's felt all these years. But that doesn't seem like something he would do, at least not something he would've done when I knew him. Maybe my leaving changed him.

Is this it? Now that he knows why I left, I won't ever see him or hear from him again? Although that's the most likely scenario, I hope it isn't so—especially after what happened between us the other day.

I have to try to give him the full story. He deserves to hear it. This way, I can close this chapter once and for all. If he still wants nothing to do with me after that, I'll be crushed but will have to accept it. If that's what he decides, it'll be the consequence of my decision, and I'll have no right to demand otherwise.

Thunder rumbles as the skies turn a dark and ominous gray, mirroring the storm brewing inside of me.

I have the cab drop me at the Beacon Hill Market, a block over from my apartment. I need to pick up something to drown my emotions in. I wander the store and decide on a sleeve of Oreo cookies.

Inside my apartment, I toss my pockabook on the bench next to the door, and untie and kick off my boots. I peruse my CD collection in search of my Chayanne "*Cautivo*" CD. Chayanne is one of my favorite Latino artists, whose songs often sing of love and heartbreak. I haven't heard it in a while, but right now, sorrow suffocates me, and I need to drown my emotions in music and Oreos.

CHAPTER NINETEEN

Cover Story

MARIALENA

"HI, LENA. IT'S GOOD to see you. Tell me, why are you here today since you just had your annual pap smear four months ago?"

"Hi, Dr. Ahmed, it's good to see you too, even if I'd rather not be here." She gives me a half-smile and leans into the counter behind her.

"I've had my period for eight days, and I am still bleeding heavily. As you know, my cycle is extremely irregular, and when I do get it, it's never more than two or three days. I have my usual back pain and leg pain, but this time around, the cramps in my belly area are way worse. The pain has been horrible. Bad enough that I've been taking six ibuprofen a couple of times a day, so I thought it was time I come see you."

Dr. Ahmed writes some notes down on the chart she's holding in her hands. "You shouldn't be taking that much ibuprofen. I'm glad you're here. Can you explain what you're feeling?"

"A shooting pain here." I use my hand to signal just below my belly button. "It's like someone is gutting me with a knife and twisting it inside of me." She writes down a few more notes.

"That's concerning. Have you been feeling anything else?"

"Other than my usual leg and back pain, no."

She puts the chart down onto the counter behind her. "Lie back. I'd like to feel your abdomen if that's okay." I lie back onto the exam table and lift my T-shirt, unbuttoning my jeans and pulling the flaps back.

Dr. Ahmed places her hands on the area below and around my belly button. Her fingers are cold. "I'm going to apply pressure. If you feel any pain, let me know." She presses into my belly with mild pressure.

I flinch. "Owww, yes. I feel that a lot!"

"Is this the first time you're feeling this pain?"

"Yes."

"Okay, you can sit up and close your jeans." She steps away from the exam table and makes additional notes in my chart. "We're going to need to run tests, see what's causing this because this doesn't sound like the typical PCOS symptoms women have. We'll start by drawing blood to recheck your hormone levels and an MRI. Let's get you in for one right away." She pulls a small booklet from her pocket; it's bound in black leather. She writes me a script and hands it to me. "This is the script for the MRI. One of the ladies at the front desk can schedule it for you before you leave. I'll leave your blood work requisition form at the front for you."

"Thank you, doctor."

"You're welcome. Have a good afternoon." She exits the room.

I meander to my car, worry pooling in my belly, and my gut feeling is that something is wrong. When Dr. Ahmed diagnosed me with Polycystic Ovarian Syndrome (PCOS) a few years ago, she told me that I could feel pain sometimes if any of the cysts in my ovaries ruptured. But today, she didn't think the pain I was feeling was associated with that. She had a concerned look on her face and didn't have many answers, which worries me. Luckily I was able to get an MRI appointment for this Friday morning. I'll need to get my lunch shift covered and come up with a cover story for Massimo. I don't want to tell him about any of this until I know what's going on.

Before my MRI appointment, I stop by the lab to have blood drawn. Eight tubes of blood later, I'm walking from the lab to the Imaging and Radiology department at St. Elizabeth's Hospital. I've had several MRIs in the past. I'm not worried about the actual procedure. The only thing that concerns me right now is that I have to work tonight and need to be at the restaurant by 4:00 p.m. but first need to stop by the apartment to get dressed. As long as I don't have to wait too long, I should be good.

As expected, getting the MRI was a breeze, and I'm driving back to my apartment with plenty of time to get to work. The radiologist technician said my doctor would receive the results in approximately five days. Five days of anxiety-filled waiting until I get the call from Dr. Ahmed.

I arrive at Trattoria a few minutes early and head down to see Massimo in his office. "Hi, babe," I say upon entering the office.

"Hi. How's your mom? How'd her appointment go today?" He drops the paper he was reviewing onto the desk and looks up at me.

"She's good, and it went well. Results will be back next week." I lie to him as I approach him sitting behind his desk. I feel terrible about using my mother as an excuse, but I know he won't ask questions this way.

"I'm glad. Now let me kiss you before the rest of the crew gets here." I settle on his lap, and he kisses me with his soft, warm lips.

I'm in the kitchen, putting groceries away, when my phone rings. I scurry to grab it out of my pockabook hanging on the coatrack by the front door. When I finally have it in my hands, I see Dr. Ahmed's name flashing on the screen.

"Hello."

"Hello, Marialena. This is Katie from Dr. Ahmed's office. I was calling to let you know that the MRI results are back, and everything appears normal."

"Oh, well, that's good news."

"Yes. However, Dr. Ahmed would like to schedule you for a laparoscopy. It's an outpatient surgery, and she performs them here in the hospital."

"What kind of procedure is it?"

"She'll make a small incision in your abdomen and

take a look inside with a tiny camera."

"When does she want me to do it?"

"I have an opening next week, Monday. At 10:00 a.m., if that works for you?"

"How long does it take, and can I go to work after?"

"The procedure should only take 30–45 minutes. While it is an outpatient surgery, you need to relax after the procedure is complete and should take at least two or three days to recover from it. You'll also need someone to drive you because you'll be given general anesthesia." I ask Katie a few more questions about the procedure, which she answers and finishes giving me instructions to prepare for the surgery.

I hang up, sit at the kitchen counter, and think about the news I just received. The doctor is concerned enough that she wants to insert a camera inside of me to see what's going on. Those nerves at the bottom of my belly twist and my gut reminds me that something is wrong. I exhale a long breath of both frustration and concern.

I grab my phone again and dial my mother to ask her to take me to the surgery next week and if I can stay with my parents for a few days. I tell her that since I live on the fourth floor and there is no elevator, I need to stay at her house. Fuck, I better start taking notes of all these stories I'm telling.

It's a rare night that both Massimo and I are home for dinner. He's making his mother's sauce, meatballs, and linguini, and I'm making a salad. I love when he cooks—he's very good at it, and he enjoys doing it.

We both love cooking, yet both prepare different dishes, him Italian and me Latino. Massimo is definitely the better cook between the two of us. The days we're home together, we like to spend time in the kitchen experimenting with different foods. While one prepares the meal, the other helps, or prepares drinks.

After tuning the radio to Magic 106.7, I remove a bottle of wine from the rack and begin cutting the capsule open. It's a smooth, even-bodied wine and is one of our favorites, which Massimo sells at the restaurant. We brought home several bottles to add to our collection.

"My mother got her MRI results back. They're normal. But the doctor is having her go in next week for a laparoscopy to check things out." I push the corkscrew into the cork and twist it, pull it out, and rest the bottle on the counter while I get two wine glasses from the cabinet to my left.

"What's that?" His back is to me, and he's stirring the sauce, adding seasoning to it.

I pour myself a taste of the wine, swirl it to lift the aromas to smell the bouquet better, sip to let the flavors absorb on my palette, and pour us each a glass.

"The doctor will take a look inside with a tiny camera. Have a better idea of what's going on. I'll take her since my dad works and stay with her for a couple of days while she recoups." I smell the wine again before sipping it. "I love this wine. I can't get enough of it." I hand Massimo his.

"Salute." We clink our glasses.

"I love you, Mrs. D." He brushes his lips to mine, swiping his tongue across my lips to pry them open.

"Staking your claim before it's time, are you?"

"Our wedding date just makes it official. You're already mine." He deepens his kiss, placing one of his hands on my back so I can feel the arousal beneath his jeans. He puts his wine glass on the counter and takes mine out of my hand, placing it next to his.

Massimo lifts me up and onto the island. He's hungry for me. His fingers press into my rounded hips. "I want to fuck you," he murmurs while kissing me.

"I still have my period," I say, placing my hands on his chest and nudging him back from me.

"I don't care. I need to be buried inside of you."

"You know I'm not into that." I jump down from the counter, dropping to my knees before him—my eyes level with his waist. I peek up at him while my hands work at unbuckling his belt. When I manage to open it, I pop the button open and pull the zipper down—his jeans swiftly falling to the floor. Massimo wears tighty-whities; they hug his lean, flat hips, accentuating his V and trail of dark hair running from his chest down and hiding behind his briefs.

I rise up on my knees and lick around his belly button. Massimo threads his hands in my hair, tangling his fingers in my curls. My tongue licks down the trail of hair, and when I reach the top of his briefs, I bite the elastic to pull it down. My hands tug at them until his beautiful erection is before me, glistening. The thick vein on its underside is prominent. My mouth is watering to take him in.

"Is this what you want?" I ask, grasping his length with one hand while licking and swirling my tongue, my eyes never leaving his.

Massimo grips my hair, his head dropping back. "Fuck yes."

My mouth opens, taking him in, and I hear him grunt. He's moist, his unique scent mixed with the saltiness of his arousal. I adjust myself to take him further in, covering his length until I feel him rub the back of my throat. I flick my tongue up to tickle him, begin slowly pulling my mouth back until reaching his crown, then slide back down.

"I love fucking your mouth while you're wearing lipstick."

I peek up at him. His eyes are dark and hooded, lust flaring. My mouth continues to glide up and down his shaft, sucking my cheeks in for him to feel the pressure of them, his hands guiding me.

I remove him from my mouth, my hands holding his length. "I want to drink all of you." Wrapping my lips around him, I scrape my teeth slowly down his shaft until he's fully seated in my mouth, and Massimo yells in pleasure. My lips cover my teeth, gently soothing his iron length as I glide it out. I hear Massimo groan, and he begins to rock his hips, taking control of the movements, which means his arousal is building, his release on the cusp of exploding.

He increases his speed, tangling his fingers further in my hair, tugging at it until he grunts. "Lena, I'm gonna come." I move my hands to his firm glutes and push him toward me until he lets go, emptying himself, his cream filling my mouth. When I feel Massimo's legs relax and his hands loosen in my hair, I pull back and look up at him, licking my lips from satisfaction.

"Fuck, woman, your mouth is like fucking magic.

You're gonna be the death of me," he proclaims as I'm rising up.

"Good." I wink at him. "Let me go wash up, and we can have dinner."

A week later, I'm at St. Elizabeth's Hospital for my laparoscopy. My mother waits in the waiting room while I go back with the nurse. Once in the procedure room, the nurse asks me questions to ensure I understand what is happening. Dr. Ahmed and an anesthesiologist come into the room and begin explaining the procedure. I'll be given general anesthesia and will be asleep for approximately thirty minutes. The doctor will make a small incision on my abdomen area and will insert a tube with a camera on the end to take a look around, and images will be captured.

When I wake up from the procedure, I'm groggy, and my mouth is dry and loose. The nurse helps me to the dressing room where my mother is waiting for me. My mother helps me into my sweatpants, T-shirt, and hoodie, and we exit the surgical center. By the time we get to my mom's house, I'm more awake, yet my body is tired. I lie on the couch and call Massimo.

"Hi," I say when he answers.

"How'd it go with your mom today?"

"Good. She's resting right now. I'm gonna probably take a nap too since we got up super early. You know I'm not a morning person." The lie slips from my lips with ease.

"I know how to get you going in the morning," he tells me in a low voice.

"Always thinking about sex."

"I didn't say anything about sex. You did," he says.

"Yeah, yeah. Anyway, just wanted to check in and let you know that everything went well. I know you're at work. I'll call you later."

"Okay. Bye, babe."

"Bye."

Four days later, Dr. Ahmed's office calls to schedule an appointment to discuss my results. It can't be good when the doctor wants to see you in person. Bad news is on the horizon.

CHAPTER TWENTY

Clarity

MASSIMO

OCTOBER 2012

MY FEET POUND THE pavement as I'm running the trail along the Charles River, Volbeat's "Heaven Nor Hell" streaming through my earbuds. Running usually gives me clarity and lets me sort through the storm in my head. My legs burn from the miles they've carried me, but my head is still a fucking mess.

It's been four days since Lena told me she can't have kids.

Four days with her words ringing in my ear.

Four days and I still can't get my act together.

Four days with a tightly wound knot in my chest.

I can't understand why Lena would ever think she had to leave because she can't have kids. Is there a logical explanation behind it? Even if there is, will I accept whatever excuse she gives me for shattering our lives?

I know I need to talk to her, but I'm still so upset about everything that I can't, not yet. I need to let my anger subside. Otherwise, I won't be able to have a normal conversation with her.

My reaction to her confession wasn't how I should've reacted to the news, but I was blinded by her words, angry that she would make such a decision about my life, our life, without speaking to me first.

I know I was wrong. She probably thinks it's my reaction to her inability to have kids, which it's not. It's about her ability to lie with such ease, her callousness at making such a life-altering decision on her own. Here I was expecting her to say she was with another guy or in love with someone else. I probably would have handled it better. Who am I kidding? I definitely wouldn't have.

I check my watch; I've been running for over an hour but need to head back, or else I'll be late to pick up the boys from their music lessons at the North End

Music & Performing Arts Center. I run toward the Dartmouth Street Footbridge to cross Storrow Drive and jog the last few blocks to my apartment.

After picking up the boys from music lessons, we walk down to Regina Pizzeria to grab a pie for dinner. The boys love pizza, and you can never go wrong with Regina's. Thankfully, when we get there, there's no line. There are times the line here stretches down the block in the dead of winter; that's how good the pizza at this place is.

As usual, it's a full house inside. Lots of locals sprinkled with tourists. It's a casual place, most everyone in jeans, donning their favorite sports team hats or hoodies, with a few after-work-crowd people still suited up.

We're taken to the back-corner booth next to the window, past tables of people and families chatting, eating, and laughing. The boys love sitting along this wall because they look at the pictures hanging one right next to the other and ask questions about the people in them, most of them celebrities, both local and well-known. They can also see all the police and fire department patches that adorn the wall from different places.

As I sit here staring at my little guys, I can't help but think about Lena, and the last time we came here a few weeks before she left me.

NINE YEARS AGO

Her sister, brother-in-law, and their four kids are visiting from Florida for a week during the kids' school vacation in mid-March. It's the night before they have to return home, and we meet them here with one of Lena's brothers, his wife, Lena's other sister who lives in Medford, and their parents. There are thirteen of us, and we take up most of the area back here. Whenever we're with Lena's nieces or nephews, she always sits with the kids no matter where we go for dinner. She wants to be among them, laugh with them, tell jokes, draw, or listen to their stories.

I like sitting across from her because when she's with the kids, her face glows. Her eyes turn up and crinkle from laughter. She's relaxed with them, and the kids are drawn to her, all wanting to sit next to her or on her lap. Being with the kids is like second nature for her. Every time I see it, all I can think about is what a great mom she's gonna be.

"Dinner was fun tonight. I love it when the whole family is together. My heart is full when we're all gathered around a table," Lena says while removing her jeans in the walk-in closet. "I wish we all lived in the same city. I miss those kids a lot, am missing so much of them growing up."

I join her inside the closet and take her into my arms. "I can't wait to grow our family, put a baby in your belly," I tell her while drawing circles on her stomach. "You're fucking beautiful," I say, as I pepper kisses along her face, down her neck, over her breasts, stopping at her belly and resting on my knees. "But when I get you pregnant, and you're wicked swollen with our baby, you'll be," I pause, "I don't have words to describe it—Lenalicious." I howl back in laughter. I have a huge grin sprawled across my face because thinking of Lena with a swollen belly, swollen with my baby, a baby we created from love, makes my heart burst with happiness, makes my dick hard.

"You say the craziest stuff." She chuckles, running her fingers through my hair. When I look up at her, Lena shifts her eyes away from mine while fiddling with her glasses.

"I am crazy! Crazy for you, for us, and for the family we're gonna have." I pop up to my feet and open the bottom dresser drawer. "I know this is way early, but

last week when I took my mother to Target, I saw this and couldn't resist buying it." I pull out a tiny white onesie and unfold it to show her. It says, "50% Mommy, 50% Daddy, 100% Perfect," in stacked lettering.

She starts crying. Not even like tears dripping from her eyes, but full-on gushing tears and runs out of the closet.

"What's the matter?" I ask, following her.

"Why would you buy that? We're not even pregnant."

"I know we're not, but I'm just excited and couldn't resist because look how cute it is." I hold up the onesie closer for her to see. "It's fine! We'll be pregnant soon." I wrap her in my arms and kiss the top of her head.

"It's not fine! What happens if we never get pregnant?" she screeches, wrestling out of my arms.

"Lena, what's wrong with you? We'll get pregnant when we get serious about trying. Stop freaking out over it. It's just a onesie. Seriously, it's not that big of a deal."

"Actually, it is a big deal, but whatever!" she yells while slamming the bathroom door behind her.

283

"One large cheese pizza," the waitress says, placing it on the table.

I serve the boys and grab a slice. "Wait a couple of minutes, guys. It's too hot right now, don't want you to burn your mouth. Blow on it a little, so it cools off."

"Daddy, you remember the time I burned my mouth?" Lucio asks.

"Yes, buddy. I do."

"I never burned mine, right, Daddy?" Leandro asks.

"No, you didn't, which is why you have to be careful now."

My thoughts go back to that night when I showed Lena the onesie I had bought. Now it makes sense why she started crying and freaked out the way she did. That night she already knew she couldn't have kids. Why wouldn't she have told me? None of it makes sense.

When we were in bed later that night, she had told me she didn't want to talk about it, was tired, and went to sleep. I didn't bring up the topic again because I didn't want to upset her any more than I already had. Figured when the time was right, we would talk about it. Had I known, I would've forced us to have the discussion. I had put the onesie back into the bottom drawer. I still have it, tucked away with all my workout gear.

After dinner, we go to the Taverna on Salem Street. Rocco is down the Cape, and Stella is at Casa Lorenzo in the South End. I need to close up here and check in with Patty, the manager at Trattoria downtown, to make sure she's good and doesn't need anything. As we're walking the three blocks, I text Camila to let her know she can pick up the boys.

Massimo: At Taverna—boys are ready when you are

Camila: OK—be there in 30

Once at Taverna, I slide the boys onto stools at the bar and ask Antonella, the bartender, to get them each a Shirley Temple to drink while we wait for their mother to pick them up.

It's a Monday night, and the restaurant is quiet. A few couples are sitting at two-tops along the right wall. An older couple in the back corner, the man is balding, wears glasses, and has his hand extended across the table. He's caressing his wife's left hand, or whom I presume to be his wife since they're both wearing wedding rings. At the two-top in the middle of the banquette are two young women, maybe in their late twenties, looking like they came for dinner after work,

SHELLY CRUZ

one dressed in a pants suit, the other in dress pants and a cardigan. The table next to the window is a young couple, both of them looking at their phones, not paying attention to each other. What's wrong with people? They're out to dinner. Put your fucking phone down and look at the person in front of you. You never know when they won't be there anymore.

We sit at the bar while we wait for Camila to pick up the boys. We're sitting near the servers' station, and the boys are talking to Kelly, one of the servers. They're telling her about their music class and that they like to play soccer. Kelly is one of the servers who's been working in our restaurants since I opened Trattoria downtown over ten years ago. The boys have known her their entire lives, and they love seeing her because she gives them a lot of attention. Before we know it, Camila shows up and leaves with the boys.

I text Dom.

Massimo: Where you at? I'm at Taverna—come have a few drinks

Dom: Can't—with Luci tonight

Massimo: Luci? Lena's Luci?

Dom: Yeah =)

Dom and Luci? When did that happen? I've been

caught up in all my drama. I had no idea. And Dom is so chill, he'll just let me sulk, bitch, and be miserable and not say anything about it. That's why he's my brother. He's always there for me, no questions asked. I decide to text Benny. I need some company tonight. Drinking Jack solo won't cut it.

Massimo: At Taverna—drinks?

Benny: Be there later, 9ish

It's 9:15 p.m., Kelly dropped the check on the last table in the dining room, and I've sent the other servers home. "Antonella, pour me a Jack, neat, please," I ask, as I'm sliding onto the stool near the front window. I remove my phone from my back pocket and see one missed call from Lena and two text messages.

Lena: It's been 4 days. We need to talk

Lena: Please stop ignoring me

She's been calling and texting since I stormed out of The Vault last week. I've ignored her because I'm not in the right headspace to deal with it yet. My fingers hover over the keypad, on the fence whether or not I should respond. I know I have to; I can't put it off much longer.

I wanted an explanation, and the moment she gave

it to me, I didn't want to hear it. There must be more to the story. Part of me is still wicked pissed. Pissed that she made such a colossal decision for me, ruined my life, and ripped my heart out. I had zero say in any of it. But, if I want to have a normal conversation with her, I need to chill out.

"What's up?" Benny says, extending his fist, which I meet with mine.

"Antonella, another Jack, please. Then you can go. I'll finish up."

Benny slides into the stool next to me, drops his fedora onto the bar, and says, "What's going on?"

"Did you know Dom and Luci are dating?"

"Yeah, he mentioned it a few weeks ago."

"I must be the only one who doesn't know."

Antonella places two tumblers in front of us, each half full of whiskey.

"You've had a lot going on the past few weeks. You know how Dom is. He'll never let you in on what's going on with him if he knows you're going through something."

"Speaking of, I saw Lena last week. She finally told me why she left."

"Oh yeah, how'd that go?" he asks before sipping his drink.

"Terrible, that's how. As usual, my temper got the

best of me, and I stormed out before I said things I would regret."

"Some things never change."

I side-eye him for calling me out, but it's what I need right now.

"Why'd she do it?" he inquires.

"She can't have kids."

"That's fucked up!"

"That was my exact reaction too. I don't understand why that would make her leave."

"I was referring to her not being able to have kids, in general, and not to that being the reason she left. But yeah, it doesn't make sense to leave over something like that," he clarifies.

"So I'm not crazy for thinking that. I've been racking my brain about it. I mean, she made this decision that would change both of our lives, except she forgot to consult with me. My head is all sorts of fucked up over it. Between her and my mother's death, I'm a mess."

"What are you gonna do about it?"

"She's been texting and calling, but I've ignored her. Giving myself time to chill out because if not, I'll ruin shit again."

"To not ruining shit." Benny raises his tumbler to mine, and our glasses clink before we both throw back our drinks.

CHAPTER TWENTY-ONE

La Verdad

MARIALENA

THE NEXT DAY

MASSIMO HAS IGNORED MY calls and texts for five days. I know it's his way of processing what I told him the other day. When we were together, he'd always take time away from the person he was upset with, including me. When we would argue, he wouldn't delve into the issues until he had time to sort it out in his mind and calm down but never went this long. Of course, the difference is now he owes me nothing and has no obligation to discuss anything with me.

Even though I know he's still upset and trying to work through his anger, I need to set the record straight with him. I want to respect his need to come to terms with everything before discussing it, but the entire situation's uncertainty gives me anxiety. I haven't had a good night's rest since that day last week, and I can't focus. I cannot continue this way. It's starting to affect my work.

I know he's usually at Trattoria during the week. I open a web browser on the desktop computer and type Trattoria Lorenzo Restaurant into the search engine. When the number displays, I reach across my desk to pick up the phone receiver, dialing the number.

After four rings, a woman answers, "Trattoria Lorenzo."

"Hi, can I speak with Massimo, please?"

"Sure, may I ask who's calling?"

Quickly, I hang up the phone. I push my chair back, slide off my heels, replacing them with my Dr. Martens, lacing them up but leaving them untied. I grab my jacket and pockabook and rush toward the front door.

"Natalia, I'll be back later. Please reschedule my 2:30 p.m. phone conference for later this week, if possible. I'm not sure if I'll be back before you leave." She's about to say something, but I dash toward the exit before she has a chance to.

Once outside my building, a burst of cold air jolts me. I zip my jacket up and stuff my hands into my pockets to keep them warm. Clouds blanket the sky, and the day is gray, matching my mood. I beeline it to the restaurant, which is six blocks away.

Trattoria is still full from the lunch crowd, even though it's past 2:00 p.m. I scan the dining room searching for him, but he's not here.

"Hi, table for one?" a young lady I've never seen before asks me.

"I'm here to see Massimo. Is he downstairs?"

Her posture stiffens. "Um, let me check." She picks up the receiver and punches a few numbers on the keypad. "Hi, Massimo, there's a woman here to see you." She moves the receiver from her mouth and asks, "Your name, please?"

"Lena," I say, exasperated. I know he's downstairs. Will he turn me away?

"Her name is Lena," she pauses. "Okay." She hangs up the phone.

"You can go downstairs. It's through—"

"I know where it is, thank you." Her eyes widen at my rudeness.

I dash through the dining room, and in no time, I'm at the door in the back corner where stairs are leading down to the cellar. When I reach the bottom of the stairs, the office door is only a few feet away from me. Images from when I visited him at the North End restaurant a couple of weeks ago flash through my mind, and I clench my legs at the thought of Massimo's touch. "Focus, Lena. I need to make things right with him and not let myself be seduced," I tell myself, taking in a deep breath.

I knock on the door before pushing it open. I don't wait for him to respond; I enter the office, closing the door behind me.

Massimo is sitting behind the desk, papers strewn across it in messy disarray. The dim yellow light causes me to squint, and Matchbox Twenty's "Back 2 Good" plays softly in the background. His eyes lift from what he was working on. His hair is wild, sticking up in all directions. No doubt he's been running his hands through it in frustration. He dons a five o'clock shadow, and the dark circles under his eyes scream exhaustion.

I lean against the wall behind me and unzip my jacket, letting it hang open. "You've been ignoring me."

"I have."

"Ignoring me won't resolve this," I say, gesturing my right hand between us.

"I'm ignoring you because it's what's best for you."

He crosses his arms over his chest.

"I fucked up. I know that. But right now isn't the time for you to teach me a lesson. What I need is for you to listen."

"And why should I give you anything that you need?" He leans back in his chair, intertwining his fingers and resting them on his head, elbows out to each side. His stare is penetrating, unrest and turmoil emanating from him.

"You wanted an explanation. I'm trying to give it to you, so let me. You deserve to know why I made the decision I did. When I'm done, I'll walk out that door, and you'll never have to see me again." Saying those words makes my stomach curdle.

"I'm listening."

"We always talked about kids. But after you proposed, it was nearly every day. You would often talk about what our family would look like, where we would live, things we would do. You even picked out names."

"Luca, if we had a boy, Giulia, if we had a girl," he says.

"Yeah, I remember. But that's my point. You were obsessed with talking about it. Your eyes would light up whenever you did. Your excitement over it was always at the forefront of every conversation." I take the few steps across the office and slide into the seat across from him, dropping my pockabook onto the chair to my right.

"A few weeks before I left, I got my period. It was super heavy. My cycle was always irregular because of my PCOS, but never heavy like that."

"Because of your what?"

"Polycystic Ovarian Syndrome. Instead of ovulating regularly, the eggs stay in the ovaries and form cysts. They're not harmful, and it doesn't hurt until they burst—then they hurt like a motherfucker. Anyway, it causes severe hormonal imbalances, irregular periods, sometimes causes acne, and causes these annoying wire hairs to grow." I point to my chin line with my right index finger. "When my doctor diagnosed me with it, she told me it would be difficult to get pregnant."

He takes a deep breath and places his hands on the desk, fingers spread wide. "I never knew any of that," Massimo mutters, shaking his head.

"I bled for over a week, and the pain and cramping were more intense than it had ever been in the past."

"I'm pretty sure I didn't know that either."

"I didn't tell you about any of it because I didn't want you to worry about me."

"How cavalier of you."

I take a deep breath, knowing that I have to be patient with him because he's angry with me, and I probably deserve all the sarcasm he dishes out, but it doesn't make it less frustrating. The tension in the room is so thick you could cut it with a knife.

"Anyhow, I went to the doctor because that much blood wasn't normal. She sent me for an MRI, and when that came back normal, she sent me for a laparoscopy."

"What's that?"

"It's where the doctor looks inside to see what's going on. It's done with a thin tube with a camera on the end of it. Remember when I stayed with my mother for a few days because I needed to take care of her after a procedure? Well, I was the one who had the procedure, and I stayed with her to recoup for a few days."

"Wow, so you got good with the lies!" He slams his hands on the desk, and I flinch.

"You know, I'm trying here. Can you cut me some slack and let me finish?"

His tone and demeanor are pissing me off, but I need to keep my cool.

"By all means." He gestures his hand out.

"The results showed I had stage 4 endometriosis. That's when the tissue that normally grows and lines the inside of the uterus grows outside of the uterus.

Stage 4 is the worst, which is why I was bleeding so much. It also explains why I always had intense pain every month during my periods."

"Why didn't you tell me any of this? Here I thought we shared everything." The sarcasm drained from his voice is now replaced with a softer, concerned tone. His eyes soften and squint. Hurt is written all over Massimo's face, his head shaking.

"I'm getting there. When the doctor diagnosed me with the endometriosis, she told me I had to have a hysterectomy and I would never carry a child. I felt numb," I say, shifting in my seat. Massimo's eyes widen and become damp, and his mouth goes slack.

Talking about all of this is more challenging than I'd imagined. I thought I had come to terms with everything, but maybe I didn't because it was buried so deep, hidden away from everyone—including me.

I exhale deeply before continuing, "It's one thing when a woman decides not to have kids. But when that choice is stripped away from you because your body fails you, it's devastating. I was robbed and had zero control over my body. I've never cried so much in my life." Tears trickle from my eyes. The memory is raw, even after all this time. I pull my glasses off and lay them on his desk, shifting my eyes to avoid his.

"Jesus, Lena," he mutters, running his hands

through his hair, sighing, pity snaking its way into his words. Pity that I don't want him to feel. It's not why I'm here.

"All I could think about was you, how you always wanted kids, a family, to be a father. I was gonna crush that. You would never have the family you wanted had I stayed. You would have resented me. I would have resented myself, knowing that I had taken that away from you. I couldn't do that to you, couldn't live with that resentment for the rest of our lives. It would've destroyed us."

"Lena," he says, sliding forward in his chair, getting closer to me. "Why would you ever think that?"

"Please, I'm not done."

He lifts his chin, a nod to signal I should continue.

"Remember the boyfriend I had when we met—Stefano?"

The corner of Massimo's lip lifts in a sneer, and he nods yes.

"We had been together for almost a year. We were out to dinner one night, having a conversation about our relationship and where it was headed. As usual, I was nervous to talk to him about something important but decided to tell him about my PCOS and what the doctor had told me—that getting pregnant would be difficult. Instead of discussing it or understanding, he was furious with me and said some really hurtful things. He screamed and insulted. Told me I'd probably done something in my life to deserve that kind of karma. Said he'd wasted his time because he wanted a family and what was the point of being in a relationship with someone who was broken."

As he listens to me, Massimo's nostrils flare, his teeth clench, his jaw hardens. "That guy was always a douchebag."

"Stefano stormed out of the restaurant, left me at the table after I had opened up to him. Tears streamed down my face, and I was embarrassed at the scene he'd made, by how he had humiliated me in front of the entire restaurant. I tried to fix things with him. Called him, went to his work, but he wanted nothing to do with me. He wouldn't even look at me. His reaction to my confession confirmed what I felt—broken. Looking back, I was an idiot! I saw the signs and ignored them all. And to make matters worse, I even tried fixing things with him. It wasn't until much later that I realized how awful he was to me and that I deserved better."

My friends always tried to warn me about Stefano. I never listened; I wanted to believe they were all wrong. Sometimes, you don't see what's right in front of you and only realize what's really happening by taking a step back and removing the horse blinders. After Stefano humiliated me and would no longer talk to me, I started thinking back at all the things that had occurred throughout our relationship. The more I thought about it, the clearer it all became. In retrospect, he never respected me, and in turn, I never respected myself.

"Lena—"

"Please let me finish." I rub my fingers together to ease the nervous clenches twisting inside of me. Massimo appeases me and remains quiet, but I can see his thoughts churning, his gaze scrutinizing me.

"Because of what happened with Stefano, I was jaded. It caused me to lock up my secret and not tell anyone, not even you," I whisper, reaching my hand across the desk in search of Massimo's. "I'm sorry I let him poison our relationship. I should've known better. I should've been stronger."

Massimo covers my hands with his, his eyes burning with betrayal and sadness.

I exhale and flip our hands, letting my fingers curl around his. "A few months before I left, we went to my friend David's house to celebrate him and his wife adopting a little boy, remember?"

"Yes."

"On our drive home, we argued."

TEN YEARS AGO

"That was a nice celebration to welcome home their new son. He's such a cutie," I say, as Massimo makes a right onto Main Street. David and Brenda live in Woburn, and they had a "Welcome Home" celebration because they adopted a four-year-old boy last month and were ready to celebrate now that he was settled in.

"Yeah, I guess so," Massimo mumbles.

"Uhh, okay. Why do you say it like that?"

"Why did they adopt that kid?"

I shift in my seat and stare at him. His tone is annoying me. "What kind of question is that? They adopted him because he needed a home and because she can't get pregnant."

"I don't know. Adoption is not something I can get into. Raising a kid that isn't mine? Nah, not for me."

"You would never adopt a child?"

"No. I've told you that before."

"Why?"

"Because I don't want someone else's kid! Now, I don't want to talk about this anymore because it's not us. End of conversation!" I jump when he raises his

voice.

His words cause tears to well in my eyes, and we drive the rest of the way home in silence. The traffic down 93 to the city is bumper to bumper, and it takes an hour and a half to get back to our place. I rest my head back, staring out the passenger window, watching the drops of rain bead and glide down the glass.

I can't believe Massimo is so upset. I can't believe he isn't open to adoption. I can't believe he'd be so cruel as to not love a child that isn't his.

I haven't told him about my health issues, and after that reaction, how can I? He'd probably be an asshole about it the same way Stefano was—fucking men.

"I walked away because I knew you would never accept me not being able to have kids, and there would be no alternative. Not after the conversation we had in the car when we drove home from David's house. I figured you would react the same way Stefano did when I told him." At my words, Massimo's eyes widen, and his mouth goes slack.

"Lena, I—"

"I'm not done." I raise my hand, suspending it between us, open-palmed.

"How could you continue in a relationship with me, knowing that I could never give you what you wanted most? You wouldn't have. I assumed you would've reacted as Stefano did, and—"

"I'm not Stefano!" His nostrils flare.

"I know. Except last week you did react like him."

"That's not fair. The circumstances aren't the same, but you're right, I did and shouldn't have. For that, I'm sorry."

"No, you shouldn't have, but I understand. We probably should've had that conversation in a more private place."

"Lena, what you—"

"Let me finish, please. I've been waiting years to get this off my chest."

Massimo nods in acknowledgment.

"I'm sorry for ever thinking you would've reacted like Stefano. It was wrong of me to assume. But I felt like a failure, empty, out of control, and less than a complete woman. Turns out Stefano was right. I'm broken. I will never carry a child. I don't even have a womb anymore." A desperate croak escapes me, the tears gush from my eyes, and my chest heaves. I wipe away the tears with the heels of my palms.

"Lena." He rises from the chair, walking around the desk to stand before me. He forces me to my feet, wrapping me in his embrace, soothing me with his hands, dropping kisses along my hairline. His arms are warm and robust.

This is where I belong. I inhale his scent, how I've missed it, missed him. Now that I've been reminded of everything I used to have, I don't know how I'll survive without him. I need to finish what I came to say and get the fuck out of here. My heart can't take much more.

"You deserve to have the kids you always dreamed of," I say. "I knew you would be hurt, but eventually, you would forget me, find someone new, and start a family. I would never be able to give you children. I thought, why should both of us suffer without kids? I loved you and chose to sacrifice my love for you so you could have them. It's the one thing I could control. Guess I made the right decision. Love is a sacrifice, right?" Tears continue streaming down my cheeks.

My body trembles. "I'm sorry, Massimo. I'm sorry I left the way I did, but I did it for you."

"Shhhh, it's okay," he repeatedly murmurs in an attempt to console my broken soul.

"Massimo, I—"

"Lena, I'm sorry. So sorry for everything."

Massimo's arms remain firm around me, his embrace comforting and soothing me. His touch relaxes me, as it always has.

My tears begin to lessen, and as I rest my head on his shoulder, my nose scratches his neck, his scent intoxicating. Massimo's arms are the one place that have comforted me, given me shelter, and protected me. Each and every time. Although at this moment I feel comforted, I know the feeling will be short-lived.

CHAPTER TWENTY-TWO

Shall Set You Free

MASSIMO

LENA DROPPED A BOMB on my heart with her confession. Yeah, she fucked up and vanished, but to think I could've had something to do with her decision makes me feel like an asshole. She suffered through all of what she just told me, and I knew nothing. My heart tightens in pain. Pain I feel for the hurt I caused, the hurt she went through, the loss she endured, and the loss of our relationship.

This woman, she owned every part of me, and I was oblivious to the agony she was living with. How is that possible? To add insult to injury, I basically did what Stefano did and stormed out on her when she was the most vulnerable. My actions proved that I reacted exactly as she feared I would, solidifying that I'm still an asshole. I can't deal with my shit right now. I still need answers from her.

Lena's breathing has evened out. She's no longer sobbing, and her breath is hot at my neck. "Hey, you okay?" I ask, lifting my hands to her face and gliding my thumbs across her cheeks, over her signature beauty mark.

"It's the first time I've said all of that out loud to anyone. I've kept it locked away inside of me since the day I left. It's such a relief to finally let it all out."

"Lena." I look up to the ceiling and let out a deep sigh before turning back to face her. "I can't begin to understand what you felt. What you feel about everything you lost. I had no clue about any of it. I should've been more attentive and more open. For that, I apologize." I kiss her forehead and let my lips linger there.

I grasp her face and stare into her eyes. "I'm sorry that we never had the conversation about kids, and I just assumed we would have them." Lena's eyes widen at my apology for my insensitive behavior, something she wasn't expecting to hear.

"My assumptions pushed you away. Made you think you couldn't have a conversation about it or about your health. We were gonna get married, and we should've discussed what we wanted, and what was happening with you, with us. I was wrong."

Tears slide down her cheeks. "Thank you," she mutters. She lifts her hands and rests them over mine, which are still embracing her face.

"There are not enough words to express how sorry I am for making you feel like you couldn't talk to me about what was happening to you. But I don't understand how you could ever think I would love you less. That never would've happened."

"You don't know that." She shakes her head.

"I do know that. But, if that's what you're sticking with, then neither do you. I fell in love with you, your heart—" I lay my hand over her heart, resting my palm there "—your kindness, your sense of humor, the way you're shy yet confident, your laugh, and these curls."

I grab a ringlet that's hanging over her left eye and twirl it between my fingers. "Having kids would have been a bonus. Yes, I wanted children with you, but we would've made it through together. We would've made a life without kids. You didn't even allow me to do that. You took that away from me, from us."

"I'm sorry." Her eyes dart away from mine.

"Lena, look at me."

She hesitates before turning her eyes back up toward mine, moisture brimming at their edges.

"Help me understand. I have questions. Will you answer them for me?"

She nods her head yes.

"No more lies."

She lifts her eyes back to mine and nods.

"The doctor, she told you that you needed a hysterectomy, and you'd never carry a child. Did you get a second opinion?"

"I planned on getting one in Des Moines."

"You planned on it? What does that mean?"

"I had been in Des Moines for about four months. Had found a job, an apartment, and was trying to normalize my life, establish a routine to forget you. My body was in pain, but I ignored it. I took ibuprofen and worked through it all. I pretended the pain was a result of all the drastic changes I had made."

NINE YEARS AGO

It was a busy Thursday, and after working a double, Hank, my manager, let me go home early. I wasn't feeling well and had shooting pains down my legs for most of the day from my period, which is heavy again this month. When I get home, I take a shower to wash the day away and take a few ibuprofen to dull the pain.

I've been meaning to contact a doctor, schedule an appointment to get a second opinion, and see if Dr. Ahmed in Boston was right. Still, I keep putting it off, making excuse upon excuse to myself to avoid facing reality. The truth is, I don't care. I am wicked miserable, have been since leaving Boston, leaving Massimo. I miss my old life, miss everything about it. But mostly, I miss my man. I regret leaving him, regret being here, but I know if I go back to Boston, Massimo will tell me it's okay that I can't have kids, and we can have a life without them. But I know better. He would resent it. I would know he was always unhappy without kids, and it would destroy our relationship. I left because I cannot bear the thought of him leaving me. After all, I had no control over what was happening to my body, and I can't have children. At least this way, I am in control of my misery and heartache.

It's the middle of the night when I wake up from the abdominal pain. The sheets beneath me are soaked. I reach to the nightstand and turn the lamp on. Blood saturates the sheets. What the fuck is happening? *I attempt to stand, but my legs buckle, forcing me to sit back on the edge of the bed as blood streams down my legs. I grab my phone and dial Stevie's number.*

"Lena? It's four in the morning. What's the mat-

ter?"

"Hi, Stevie. I woke up in a pool of blood and can barely stand. Can you come here and drive me to the emergency room?"

"What? Yes, of course. I'll be there in ten minutes. Keep your phone close."

I lie back down in a cradle position to alleviate the pain, tears streaming down my face. I'm so alone. I could die, and no one would ever know. What have I done?

Stevie used her key to enter my apartment. After entering my room, she helps me up from the bed and walks me to the bathroom to clean up. She hands me a wet towel to wipe my legs while she's searching for clean underwear, pants, and a top. As I'm cleaning myself, I notice I am still hemorrhaging golf-ball-sized clots. When Stevie returns to the bathroom and sees me, she says, "Lena, I can't take you bleeding that way. I'm calling 9-1-1."

The EMTs are in my bathroom minutes later, a male and a female. The female helps me stand and supports me as we cross the room to the stretcher waiting at the bedroom door. They lay me back, place an oxygen mask on my face, and strap me in. The pain in my stomach is like a twisting knife, and I'm crying from how much it hurts.

"Lena, I'll meet you at the hospital." Worry laces Stevie's voice.

Once at the hospital, the EMTs roll me to a room and transfer me to a bed. The air smells sterile, and it's freezing in here. I shiver until someone drapes one of those flimsy white hospital blankets over me. A nurse begins placing those small sticky dots on my chest and arms, takes my blood pressure and temperature, and sticks an IV into my arm. Two doctors enter when the nurse is finishing the IV placement, and they begin asking questions.

I tell them my medical history, what Dr. Ahmed told me, and that I have not seen a doctor since, nor did I do any treatment. I do my best to explain the pain I feel down my legs, across my back, in my abdominal area. The doctors tell me they will keep me for observation and attempt to stop the bleeding. But when I'm still bleeding several hours later, the doctors tell me they're taking me into surgery to perform an emergency hysterectomy but that until we're in surgery they won't know what type of hysterectomy they'll do."

Lena lets out a sob. She bows her head and rests her forehead on my shoulder.

"Jesus, Lena, you could have died."

"Honestly, I didn't care whether I did or not. That's how fucked up I was at that point. I had never felt so sad and lonely. It was like I was being punished for what I had done."

"You weren't being punished, you were sick, being stubborn, and ignored your body. Not quite the same thing."

She scowls at me.

I attempt to soothe her with the one thing that has always worked, touch. I tighten my arms around her torso, gliding my thumbs back and forth over the area where they rest. When her breaths are even again, I caress her arms, up and down in slow, steady motions before asking, "What happened after your surgery?"

"I was in the hospital for six days. The doctor explained that she removed my uterus but left my ovaries in. She said she didn't think they posed a problem, and since it was not something we had discussed, she didn't want to remove them without first consulting with me. She also had to do bladder reconstruction because the endometriosis was growing on a substantial part of my bladder."

"She left your ovaries in? Does that mean you still have eggs?"

"Yes."

"You could—"

"No, I can't. Don't say it."

"Hey, stop," I say. She glares at me. "Let me finish. What I was gonna say is that you could have called me after you had the surgery."

"No, I couldn't have. Because you would have come to find me, and things would still be the same. I would never give you the children you wanted."

"So stubborn!"

"If I would have stayed, or called, or whatever, you wouldn't have your two beautiful boys. Forgetting everything else in our past, those two guys make it all worth it for you, for both of us. Unquestionably you're an amazing father to them, which means I made the right choice for you."

"I want you to know you're not broken. Just because some asshole said that to you doesn't make it so. You not being able to have kids doesn't make you any less of a woman. You have a beautiful heart. I know it because I've been on the receiving end of your love."

Tears stream down her face, and she sniffles.

"Why did you take so long to come back?" I wipe tears from her cheeks with the pads of my thumbs.

"When I learned you had a son, it hurt—a lot! I had a final exam a few days after finding out and just barely passed. I was so distraught. I felt a lot of sadness and

315

resentment again, thinking it should've been me to give you a son. It should be me who's the mother of your children. Of course, that was crazy of me to think." She hides her eyes from me, attempting to conceal the guilt that accompanies her statements. I'd be a hypocrite for telling her she's wrong for thinking that way because that very thought has crossed my mind numerous times and has caused the same feelings of guilt.

"As soon as classes started again, I focused on school and pushed away thoughts of you again because I had to finish. I wasn't ready to come back and face reality, so I stayed to work for a bit and gain experience before returning. I hoped time would heal me."

"Did it heal you?"

"Not really."

"What does that mean?"

"It means that I regret the decision I made. That regret has eaten away at me from the inside out. Every single day! It's the only decision I've ever made that I haven't come to terms with. Regret that I'll live with for the rest of my life even if I know it was the right decision for you."

She drops her eyes to the floor, her hands clenching into fists. Although painful for her, her words give me a glimmer of hope—the unknown future of us.

"If you could do things over again, would you

make the same choice?"

"I don't know; it's hard to say. I'd like to think I would do things differently because I wouldn't feel so sad and wouldn't feel so much regret. But I don't think I would. Because then you wouldn't have your boys."

"*Grazie.*"

"What are you thanking me for? All I did was wreak havoc and cause you heartache."

"I disagree with the way you handled everything, but now I have Lucio and Leandro. They're everything to me. The love I feel from those two little guys is indescribable. The only other time my heart felt that happy was with you. You're not their mother, but you sacrificed your life, your happiness, the love you felt for me so I could feel the love of being a father. It's hard for me to accept how it all went down, that what you did was for me, but those two little boys make it difficult not to."

Lena attempts a weak smile. Another tear leaks from her right eye, and I stop it with my thumb, wiping it away and kiss the wet spot it leaves.

"I'm sorry I stormed out of The Vault the way I did, for reacting exactly as Stefano did. I should've listened to you, let you explain, and tell me your story. I was furious, and I couldn't control my temper. You told me that right after my mother's death. I wasn't in the right frame of mind to hear what you said. Between my mother's death and your reappearance, my head is spinning. It's not a valid excuse, but it's the truth. Thank you for coming here today and for forcing me to have this conversation. We needed this."

"Well, thinking about it, it was probably a good thing you walked out. Did you see the dirty look the guy at the bar gave you when you raised your voice? Imagine if he saw me sobbing like I just was, he probably would've wanted to knock you out or something." Lena attempts some humor, and I'm relieved to see her sense of humor still there underneath all the pain and heartache.

I lift my wrist to look at the time. I need to close out the lunch crew, but I am not ready for Lena to leave. We still have things to discuss. There are things I need to know, wrongs to make right. We need to make up for lost time.

"I'm sorry. I know you have things to do. I'll go."

"No. Well, yes, I need to close out the lunch crew upstairs, but we're not done here."

"We're not?" Her eyes widen.

"Not even close. Will you have dinner with me tomorrow night?" She purses her lips and stares at me, her eyes crinkling in the corners. I can see the thoughts racing through her mind. "Lena, it's not a difficult question to answer."

"I'm not sure if that's a good idea."

"Of course it is. Meet me tomorrow at Billy Tse's, 6:30 p.m."

A deep sigh escapes her. "All right, I'll be there."

I grasp Lena's face and brush my lips to hers.

CHAPTER TWENTY-THREE

On the Mend

MARIALENA

LEAVE MASSIMO'S RESTAURANT and walk toward Post Office Square to sit in the park. I need to absorb everything that just happened. As I stroll down Franklin Street, I feel lighter. Our conversation was emotional and cathartic. I've kept it buried for so long it weighed me down. It's what I needed to start healing from all the destruction I caused.

Massimo's reaction at the Vault last week was unexpected and felt like a slap in the face. The way I left was pretty fucked up, so I get it. It's not like I can blame him. If our roles were reversed, who knows how I would've reacted. Besides, his mother just passed away and he was already grieving.

I was worried about how he'd react to me for just showing up at his restaurant to demand we have a conversation, but it turns out it was the right move. I didn't think he'd understand, but it seems he came around and even apologized to me. His apology was unexpected, but welcome. I'm glad he recognized his role in my decision. For the longest time, I blamed only myself, but with time I realized his behavior didn't inspire confidence that he would accept me as I am—a woman who would never give him children.

Despite all the damage I caused, he was still the one comforting me, which shouldn't surprise me. Looking back, he was always like that, and I don't know why I didn't see it when we were together. Part of me thinks that I should've told him the truth, that we would've dealt with whatever came because then we would've probably continued our relationship. But the other part of me knows that my inability to have kids would've been something that caused a rift between us, even if Massimo thinks it wouldn't have. At this point, it doesn't matter what any of us think.

Decisions were made, lives were disrupted, relationships were damaged, and none of it can be undone.

In the end, I am my own worst enemy because I would've been the one to always ask myself whether he resented me. I would've nitpicked at everything, created drama that likely didn't exist. I would've looked for a hidden meaning in his words or actions, and it would've made me angry and bitter. I self-sabotaged because Stefano made me feel worthless, unloved, and broken. I never truly healed from it, and part of me believed Massimo was capable of the same. Of course, in hindsight, that's ridiculous to think since Massimo is so different than Stefano. I had no business comparing the incomparable. This is what happens when I get in my own head.

I'm not sure where we go from here, but I know we're on the mend after the conversation we just had. Hopefully, Massimo will forgive me for all the hurt I caused him. I still love him, part of me always will, and given our last few encounters, I think Massimo feels the same. Except there's the mother of his children.

My heart aches at the mere thought of her and that she now gets to raise a family with the man I love. Thoughts of her cause jealousy to rear its ugly head. We haven't talked about her, their relationship, and the absence of his wedding ring. Although he did tell me his heart has only ever felt happy with his kids and me. What does that mean? Is there hope for us? Tomorrow night I'll have to ask him because I do not want to break up a family. I've already crossed too many lines with him without knowing his relationship status. I cannot be a part of that.

I find an empty bench to sit in the sun that finally made an appearance, look up toward the sky, and let the rays warm my face. There is a chill in the air, but it's still early enough in October that the sun still warms when it's unobstructed. I close my eyes and take deep breaths. I need to decompress and clear my head before I go back to the office. Otherwise, I won't be able to get any work done, and right now, I need to focus. One of my clients has a removal hearing next week, and I've been reviewing the file and preparing the evidence to meet with him and prepare his testimony.

My phone vibrates in my purse, and when I find it in my pockabook, I see a text message from Massimo.

Massimo: Thank you for stopping by today. We needed it.

I stare at my phone. Yes, we needed it. I should've told him a long time ago. Who am I kidding? I probably should've never done it in the first place, but I can't dwell on the past. I can only move forward. I think about the text I want to send back, how much I would like to say, but decide to keep it simple.

Lena: You're welcome. =)

Tossing my phone back into my bag, I stand and walk back to the office. For the first time in a long time, I feel some peace within me.

I check the time. It's 7:48 p.m. I need to leave. I'm supposed to meet Luci and Marcus for dinner at 8:00 p.m., and I'm going to be late. I leave everything sprawled across my desk, so tomorrow I can pick up where I left off. A few more hours of preparation, and I'll be ready for my client meeting.

When I exit the building, the cold sucker-punches me, and the wind howls as it tunnels down Congress Street. Thankfully, the cab stand is at the curb in front of the building, and there are a few available cars in line. I sprint over to the first one, open the back door, and climb in.

"Hi. Giacomo's in the South End, please. On Columbus Ave." I open my pockabook and search for my phone to text Luci.

> **Lena:** Running late. Just got in a cab & should be there in 15.

Luci replies instantly.

> **Luci:** OK. See you soon. Me & M already

drinking wine :)

Of course, they are. Luci is the reason I started drinking wine. I was never a fan of it, but that's because I never knew what to order. We'd go out to dinner, and she'd pick a wine to pair with my food. Eventually, we graduated to drinking bottles with dinner.

When I started working at the Florentine, during our pre-dinner meeting, we would have an employee meal, which was always accompanied by a wine tasting. The owner wanted the staff to know about the wines we sold because it would make the upsell easier.

After I started working at Massimo's place, I suggested he do the same because it made a difference at the Florentine in sales numbers. He was reluctant at first but decided to try it. After that, he hired a wine sommelier to work the dinner shift four nights a week, and he quickly saw an increase in sales.

The sommelier was impressive. The restaurant carried over 1,000 varieties of wine. Each night our employee meal was paired with a white and red wine, and we had a tasting accompanied by a short instruction. Our wine glasses only had two to three sips of wine in them, but it was enough to swirl the wine, take in the bouquet scent, and taste it. We'd learn about the best wines to complement the specials and menu items. It made the experience of working at a restaurant enjoyable and entertaining.

The dining room at Giacomo's is full, as expected. It's one large room with approximately fifteen tables and high-top counter seating at the back facing the kitchen. They serve Italian food, specializing in seafood and pasta dishes.

Luci and Marcus are sitting along the left wall. There is a bottle of Santa Margherita Pinot Grigio on the table, and their glasses are each half full. As I approach the table, Marcus stands and hugs me.

"Lena, I've missed you so damn much." He squeezes me tight.

"Me too," I say. I know we talked on the regular, but it's not the same. "Feels good to be home again."

"I'm super happy you're back, too," says Marcus.

"Hey, Luce," I say. She slides down the banquette, and I lean down to give her a cheek kiss.

"Hi, Lena. We've nearly polished off the bottle waiting for your ass," she tells me, giggling.

"That's okay. I'm sure there's plenty more where that came from. Luci, your hair looks amazing. When did you get it done?"

Luci's hair is freshly cut, a typical short cut, extremely short in the back with longer pieces on top, and colored auburn.

"I went to see my uncle on Saturday. You know he

loves to experiment with my hair."

"I love it, as usual," I tell her.

"Everything okay at work, Lena?" Marcus asks.

"It's been quite the day. But first, wine." I pull a chair out and shimmy into the seat next to Marcus. The restaurant is small, and the space is tight. I take my jacket off and hang it on the back of the chair as Luci pours me some wine.

"What happened now?" She holds her glass up, waiting for me to raise mine.

"Salute." We clink our glasses, and I sip my wine. "Work kept me late. I have a removal hearing next week that I'm preparing for."

"What's that?" Marcus asks.

"It's basically a trial for someone who has a deportation order. At the removal hearing, my client has an opportunity to make his case as to why he shouldn't be deported."

"Sounds intense."

"It is. Let's not talk about work. I think about it all day already. I'm dying to catch up with you guys since we haven't had time to since I've been back. Marcus, how's work? Do you like working at Mistral?" Mistral is an upscale, trendy French-Mediterranean bistro a few blocks away from where we are now.

"It's okay. I miss working at the Florentine. I make

more money at Mistral, but it's a different vibe, ya know?"

"I was surprised when you told me you were leaving the Florentine. You worked there for years," Luci says.

"Fourteen years, to be exact," Marcus adds.

"You think you'll stay there? Nothing worse than working somewhere you don't like," I say.

"Actually, I called the manager at the Florentine and asked if there was any possibility of me returning. She was gonna let me know. Guess they're not a fan of the bartender that replaced me. I'll know more in a few days."

The server comes to our table and takes our order, and I fill Luci and Marcus in on what happened with Massimo—giving them all the details of our conversation, including why I left.

"You left because you can't have kids? Jesus, Lena! Why didn't you share that with me? I'm your best friend and would've never judged you." Luci's mouth twists in disbelief, her eyes are rimmed with water, and she's fighting back the tears. Another one of my victims.

"Luce, I'm sorry. I know those words don't do much to take away the pain my actions caused, but I want you to know it's not because I didn't trust you or because I was afraid you'd judge me. I just knew that Massimo would go see you and pressure you, and I didn't want to put you in that position." I extend both my hands across the table and grab her right hand in mine.

"Wow, Lena, I don't even know what to say right now. You lied to me for so many years about something so monumental. I get why you did it, but it's so fucked up."

"I never lied to you. I just never told you the whole truth," I say.

"Semantics. You lied by omission. It's the same fucking thing!"

"I'm sorry." I squeeze her hand. "I never meant to hurt you. I love you, and I hope that one day you'll forgive me for the pain I caused you."

"I'm not gonna lie and say I'm not hurt and that I forgive you because I need some time to let it all sink in. But I'm sure I'll come around eventually. And I love you too, even when you do things you shouldn't." She squeezes my hand.

"You girls are gonna make me cry, and I didn't come to shed tears tonight. I know you ladies will kiss and make up. Now let's drink," Marcus says and raises his glass. "To us, our friendship, and being back together." That's one of the things I love about Marcus.

He always lightens the mood when the conversation gets serious.

"I'll drink to that," I say, looking first at Marcus and then at Luci. My gaze remains on Luci, hoping that she can see that I truly love her. We've been friends our entire lives, she's my sister, even if not by blood, and I know that I wounded her. Hopefully, she'll find it in her heart to understand and forgive me.

"Me too," Luci says, and her lip curls up on one side.

"So, I am dying to hear about you and Dom," I say. "I saw you guys being all hush-hush at the wake for Massimo's mother but honestly didn't think much of it. I just thought you were keeping your voices down because of the circumstances. But when you left together, I was intrigued. Are you guys an item now or what?"

Luci bites her lip. "We've been out a few times, nothing official yet."

"Girl, spill. You know we're not gonna be satisfied with that," Marcus proclaims.

"Exactly! I want all the details," I add.

"A few weeks ago, I was in the North End picking up a ricotta pie and a few pastries at Modern's for a work thing, and I ran into him. We talked for a little while, and when I had to leave, he asked if he could call me. That day I didn't realize he meant he wanted to ask me out. I wasn't thinking about him that way. He called me the next day. At first, I was surprised to hear from him that soon, but then he invited me to dinner. We've been out a few times since."

"Are you into him?" I have so many questions for her.

"Surprisingly, yes. I've known him for years but never thought about a relationship with him. But he's sweet." Luci shrugs and takes a sip of her wine.

Marcus quips, "Have you slept with him? Is he good in bed?"

"Don't hold back, Marcus," I add.

"Oh, stop! You know you want to know just as much as I do," he responds, and I chuckle, shaking my head.

"Well, yeah, but figured I'd work my way to that question."

Luci's eyes widen. She shakes her head. "You guys have no shame! You want to get right to it."

"That's right, now spill it. How is he in bed?" Marcus insists and chuckles.

"Considering I went back for seconds and thirds." Luci shrugs, smirking.

"Where was your first date?" I ask.

"His friend owns a restaurant in Woburn, so we had dinner there."

"How was it?" I ask.

"Incredible. Every time I've met him, he's always been quiet, but he's quite conversational. He wants to take me out for my birthday in a few weeks, and of course, I said yes. It's been a while since I've dated someone seriously, and I like him. He's not pushy, we have good conversation, and since I've known him for years, I know he's not a serial killer."

"You forgot to mention he's fine!" adds Marcus.

"Yeah, that too," Luci confirms.

Luci glows when she talks about Dom. Her eyes are upturned, and she dons a smile while speaking about him and their time together. I'm happy for her. She's only had a couple of serious relationships over the years. I'd like to think that fate had something else in mind for her with Dom. I got to know him relatively well when I was with Massimo, and I liked him. He was always polite, has a good sense of humor, is a loyal friend, was always there for Massimo or any of his friends when they needed it most, and he's a good-looking guy. Besides, Massimo is friends with him, and he's weird about the friends he lets into his inner circle, which speaks volumes about Dom.

"Luce, I'm happy for you. Dom is a great guy, and I really hope it works out for you guys," I tell her.

CHAPTER TWENTY-FOUR

It Was Always You

MASSIMO

'M ANXIOUS TO MEET Lena tonight. After she showed up here unexpectedly yesterday, we made progress in starting to squash our negative history. I was annoyed that Patty was out, and I had to fill in for her because it cut our conversation short. I hope now that Lena told me why she left, she won't close up on me. After our conversation, getting work done was torture, and it took me twice as long to close everything out.

Work was the furthest thing from my mind. All I could think about was our exchange. She kept so much about her health from me, and I can't help but wonder what I could've done differently that would've made her open up to me. I played a huge role in her choosing to vanish from my life. For years I blamed only Lena for everything. But I was as much responsible for our heartache as she was. That's a tough pill to swallow.

Even with everything I learned, my stomach twists in knots when I think about what she did. But when I think about why, I almost understand, which is fucked up. What does that say about me? Does it mean she's right, that I would've resented her because we wouldn't have been able to have kids? I'd like to think not, but I'm known to be an asshole, and the truth is I don't know what I would've done. My head is so fucked up over the whole thing, although at this point, I guess it doesn't matter. What's done is done—could've, would've, should've, and all that.

I feel terrible that I reacted exactly how she predicted I would and left her at The Vault the way I did. I wish I could take it back, but thankfully she accepted my apology.

And what a fucking douchebag Stefano is. I knew the guy was bad news and that things between him and Lena ended badly, but I never knew the extent of it. He fucked with her head, and that spilled over into my relationship. I should've beaten his ass when I had the opportunity to. Let me stop thinking about that asshole before my mood turns sour.

The clock on the wall reads 4:19 p.m. The staff is probably having their meal and their pre-shift meeting—let me join them. Before heading upstairs, I shoot Lena a text.

Massimo: Still on for dinner at BT's?

The wine sommelier is doing his usual wine tasting with the staff while they have dinner, and I take the opportunity to speak to Patty.

"I'm heading out soon and won't be around tonight. Of course, if you absolutely need to, call or text, but try not to need me," I say, giving her a half-smile.

"I'll be fine, but you know that already. Do what you need to do, and don't worry about us."

"I know, Patty. I trust you, but you know I'm a workaholic and control freak."

"You? Really? Thanks for the 4-1-1. I didn't know." She rolls her eyes and starts laughing, then returns to the staff meeting.

Patty has been my manager since day one. She used to work at my uncle's place with me as a waitress, taught me most of what I know. I offered her the management position when I opened up because I knew I could trust her to run this place like her own, and she does.

I saunter to the end of the bar, pull a bottle of Jack from the back shelf, and pour myself a shot. I need to take the edge off. I feel my phone vibrate in my pocket and grab it.

Lena: Yes—see you soon =)

I'm sitting on the brick wall outside the restaurant when I see Lena crossing the street. She has a black scarf wrapped around her neck and is bundled up in her black leather jacket. Her hair cascades down her back. As usual, her lips are painted, today with a dark red stain. Fuck, her beauty still shines. When she's near, I stand.

"Hi. You look cold," I say, kissing her cheek. Her nose is red, and her cheeks are flushed.

"I forgot how crazy the weather is in Boston. One day it's warm, and the next, it's frigid." She's rubbing her hands together.

"Come on," I say, reaching for her hand and walking to the entrance.

Billy Tse's has been a part of the neighborhood since the 90s. The food is phenomenal and has been since the restaurant opened its doors. With a full bar and a late-night lounge, my buddies and I would come here a lot after work to grab a bite and have a few drinks when I worked with my uncle.

"You want to sit at the bar or a table?" I ask her.

"Um, let's get a table in the back in case it gets busy later." She gestures toward the back by lifting her chin while she unzips her jacket.

The hostess takes us to a table, and we're the only two people in the dining room. Six thirty is early for dinner in the city, and this place tends to get full on the later side, which is okay because it will give us the privacy we need.

Once seated, Lena says, "It's been years since I've been here. We have a lot of great memories from here." Her eyes crinkle and turn upward at the corners as she's looking around. "Nothing's changed. It looks literally the same as it did all those years ago, yellow walls and all." She chuckles.

I lived across the street at the Lincoln Wharf Apartments when Lena and I started dating, and we would regularly order takeout from here and walk down to pick it up. Sometimes we would sit at the bar for a few drinks and eat in, often running into someone we knew and would hang out for a little while.

"It's been a minute since I've been here too, I think maybe last year," I say.

"I hope the scallion pancakes are as good as they always were. I never found any in Des Moines that were worth getting. Most places didn't have them, and those that did just didn't cut it."

"You want to look at the menu, or should I order us our usual?"

"The usual. We never went wrong. Plus, I'm starving."

The waitress arrives, a slender Asian woman with her hair in a low ponytail.

"Hi, welcome to Billy Tse's. Are you ready to order, or do you need a few minutes?"

"Grey Goose and soda with two limes, a Tsingtao beer, and two glasses of water, please. As for food, an order of scallion pancakes, spring rolls, crab rangoon, and *Chun Liu* chicken with white rice. If you could, please bring the food together."

"Will do. Thank you." The waitress walks off, and I turn to Lena and extend my hands across the table, curling my fingers with hers, our eyes meeting.

"Nine years gone, and here you are sitting in front of me. It's so surreal. I didn't think I'd ever have this opportunity again," I say. Her eyes are soft, vibrant green behind red frames.

"Do you think you'll ever be able to forgive me for leaving you?"

"That day at The Vault, I didn't know if I could. I was so mad at you. I couldn't believe what I'd heard. But as the days passed, I thought to myself, 'There has to be more to the story,' and there was. After everything you told me yesterday, part of me gets angry that you made such a big decision without me, a decision about my life—our life—and you had no right to do that. You took that choice away from me, except I played a huge role in the decision you made, and I'm furious with myself for it because I was oblivious. Until yesterday, I always blamed you for our destruction, but now I know I was just as responsible for it. That realization is humbling. You're not the only one who needs to ask for forgiveness."

The corners of her mouth tug upwards, and she squeezes my hands.

"I also understand why you ghosted me. You sacrificed everything for me, and I'm so grateful because now I have my boys. Had you not left me, Lucio and Leandro wouldn't have been born. Does my understanding your actions mean I would've resented you? I don't know. My feelings about the whole situation are all over the place, and I can't reconcile them. My head is all sorts of fucked up, ya know?"

"And therein lies the conundrum. That's what I've been living with every day since Dr. Ahmed told me I needed a hysterectomy—regret despite knowing it was the right decision for you. I know exactly what you're feeling and how it twists you up inside." She drops her head, looking down at the table, her fingers tracing the lines of my palms.

At that moment, the waitress comes back with our drinks and places them on the table. Lena lets go of my hands and grabs her glass, squeezing one of the limes and stirring before taking a sip from the straw.

I pull from the beer bottle before saying, "Please look at me." She lifts her head without question and meets my gaze. I take her hands in mine again, intertwining our fingers.

"You broke me, broke my heart. Before I met you, I never imagined I would love the way I loved you. When I got back from the casino and you were gone, I was a mess. I hated you, myself, shut my family and friends out, and was a complete asshole to everyone. Without you, nothing made sense. You shattered my world in an instant and left a gaping hole in my heart, one I've never recovered from. I didn't know how to cope with losing you. A whole year hoping you'd come back. Benny's friend does some PI work, but he didn't have any luck finding you. And back then, we didn't have these smartphones like we do now, so it wasn't easy."

"I didn't want to be found, which is why I never told Luci or my parents my plans."

Her words cut me. It's like she's driving a dagger into my heart despite me knowing the reason behind it.

"You did a good job."

"It's probably no consolation to you, but I was miserable. I pined for you. I thought about you every day. It was always you." She licks her lips before pursing them.

"You're right. It's no consolation."

"There will never be enough words to express how sorry I am for the pain I caused you. Now that you know the truth, I accept whatever comes."

"What do you mean by that?"

"You don't have to forgive me. You don't have to accept anything from me. I have no right to demand anything from you. Whether you choose to forgive me or not is entirely up to you, and I'll have to live with your decision, even if I don't like it."

We sit in silence. Words hover in the air as we stare at one another, my hands still holding hers, with our fingers linked. My heart constricts, and my stomach twists. Our tortured history mixed with my feelings stirs the storm within me. I never stopped loving her. Because of her, I was never able to commit to Camila, despite years of trying. Now I have the opportunity to resolve all of that, to finally settle the chaos Lena left in her wake after leaving.

The waitress breaks our silence when she begins putting food on the table, and we let go of each other's hands. Talk about bad timing. I was hungry, but with our conversation being so heavy that I'm in my feelings, my hunger has subsided.

"Why'd you come back to Boston?" I ask.

She stares at me, lets her response teeter on her lips before saying, "For you. When I left, I knew it was the right thing to do for you, even if I knew it would destroy us, destroy me. I came back to set the record straight and give you the truth you deserve to hear. I knew that you needed it. I needed it. I wanted to apologize and ask for your forgiveness. Neither of us had closure, which we need to move forward."

"Now that you've done that, how do you want to move on?"

She shakes her head. "No, Massimo. Not this time. I'm done making decisions for others. You decide."

I contemplate her words, the sincerity in them, and say, "Call me a masochist, but despite you shredding my heart, I could never let go of you."

Her eyes widen at my confession. "Oh. So, what does that mean?"

"I want us to try again."

She fidgets with her glasses and adjusts them to sit on the bridge of her nose. "What about your relationship with the boys' mother?"

"Camila? What about her?"

"Uhh, she's the mother of your children, and you're in a relationship with her."

"She is their mother, and that'll never change, but we're not together anymore."

Lena's mouth goes slack. "You're not?"

I shake my head fervently. "Camila and I have been over for a long time, but I made it official and moved out earlier this year. She's an amazing mother to our boys, and she deserves someone who will love her completely, but that isn't me."

Lena's face is still, her eyes wide.

"I met her a couple of years after you left and believed I was ready to move on. I tried. I thought a new relationship would help get you out of my system, head, and heart. Then she got pregnant, and I took it as a sign that I was supposed to let you go—especially because I desperately wanted kids. By that time, you had been gone for almost four years. I wanted it to work out for us because of Lucio. We were doing well for a while, or so I thought, which is why I agreed to have another child with her. But no matter how hard I tried to convince myself that I should be committed to her, my heart wouldn't let go of you. It's like a part of me was missing."

"Oh."

"Is that so hard to believe?"

"It's just that I thought you were married."

I shake my head. "I couldn't commit. She kept asking me to get married, wanted to make our family official, and I couldn't do it. I wanted to, for her, but I felt like a phony, a failure. When I thought about marrying her for our kids it felt wrong and deceitful because my heart wasn't in it."

"Does she know why you couldn't commit?"

"At first, I didn't tell her. But she wanted to know, so eventually, I did, even if I was reluctant to do it."

"I'm sorry."

"Don't be. It was the best decision for her. I would've never been able to give myself over completely, and that would've been an unfair mistake. I had already made way too many mistakes and hurt her enough. She's still upset with me, but she'll eventually get over it, and she'll find a good man that loves her completely. In the meantime, we have our boys that we have to raise. We will be the best parents we can be in two households."

"So, where do we go from here?"

"I don't know, but you're back, and suddenly I feel

like a darkness has lifted. Even with all the stuff I've learned lately. The gaping hole in my heart is already starting to heal. I want to see you, spend time with you again." I stretch my hand across the table, caressing her beauty mark, and she leans into my touch. "Maybe everything I remember about us is just history that I'm nostalgic about," I tell her. "But maybe we'll be able to bury the past and start fresh. We were really fucking good together! I don't know, I'm thinking out loud here."

"Wow. I'm not gonna lie, that's surprising and not what I expected to hear."

"No? What did you expect?"

"Considering I thought you were married, it wasn't that you wanted to spend time with me. But if I tell you the idea of spending time with you and trying again doesn't excite me, I'd be lying." Her cheeks are pink, and her eyes are teary.

"Look, I can't make any promises and don't know how it'll turn out. We can at least see where things go. What do you say?" I rest my elbows on the table and open both of my hands out, palms facing forward, waiting for her response.

"I'd like that," she whispers. Her hands meet mine, and our fingers intertwine. I kiss the back of her hand before letting them go.

"Now let's eat. I'm starving."

We stand from our table and put our jackets on. Once I have mine on, I step closer to Lena and ask, "Will you come back to my place with me?"

Her eyes soften before she nods yes.

I park in my spot in the alleyway behind my building, and we get out and walk to the door.

"Why'd you move back to this neighborhood?" she asks.

"Camila and I lived in Brookline, but once I moved out, I decided to come back to the city to be closer to work. It was just easier, and this is close enough to her and the boys. Besides, I liked living in this neighborhood."

We climb up the stairs to the second floor. I stick the key in and unlock the door, nudging it open with my foot. "Make yourself comfortable. I'm gonna put some music on." I remove my phone from my pocket and connect it to the audio system, hitting shuffle. It's chilly inside, so I grab the clicker and turn my fireplace on. I draw the curtains to give us some privacy.

Lena is sitting on the couch, her legs crossed. I bend over and tug on her hair, lifting her face to mine, dragging my thumb over her mouth. "Fuck, how I've missed you." I kiss her, prying her lips open. She complies and runs her tongue along my teeth, causing my dick to strain in my jeans.

I've been waiting years for this woman—I want to both rip her clothes off to fuck her and gently undress her to make slow love to her.

Lena pushes her hands into my hair, starts tugging at its ends. I uncross her legs so I can straddle her, kiss her deeper, savor her sweetness. She's pulling my T-shirt, pushing her hands underneath it. Her fingers burn my skin as they're exploring. My heart thunders in my chest, and I drag my lips along her soft skin, landing at her ear. I softly sing Scorpions' "Still Loving You" as the melody plays, and Lena's grip tightens around my waist. Our breathing is labored, and her eyes are glowing with longing, lust, and love.

I stand up and grab the blanket that's over the back of the couch, spreading it open on the area rug in front of the fireplace. I toss a few throw pillows onto the blanket and sit. "Come," I say, patting the floor next to me.

Lena rises from the couch and pads over to me,

crouches, and sits to my left, crossing her legs. She pushes the hair behind her ears and adjusts her glasses.

"Are you nervous?" I ask, rubbing her leg.

"Oddly enough, I am."

"Why?"

"I don't know, really. For years, I dreamed of this day, of how it would be between us if we ever had the chance again, but never thought it would come true. Now, here we are, and my stomach is a bundle of nerves despite our steamy make out sessions."

"Here, let me help you with that." I remove the frames from her face, placing them on the windowsill behind me. I run my fingers along her jawline before our mouths collide. Her lips are hot and supple. She returns my kisses softly, passionately.

I ease her back, guiding her to lie on the pillows. I kneel beside her, her long curls sprawled out around her. She looks like a fucking siren lying before me, calling out to me, luring me in.

I want to rip Lena's blouse open but think better of it and start unbuttoning it instead. I start at the top button and make my way down until her olive skin is exposed. She's wearing a gray laced bra, and looking at her breasts spill over the bra's fabric makes my dick twitch.

I cup her breasts in my hands, feeling their fullness.

Her nipples perk up under my touch, and she closes her eyes, absorbing the moment, relishing in me worshiping her. I brush my knuckles down her midsection until I reach the button on her slacks and tug, causing Lena to open her eyes and nod—giving me permission to continue exploring.

She lifts her hips, allowing space to shimmy her pants down her legs. I pull her socks off one at a time and run my finger up one foot then the other, remembering it gives her goose bumps when I do.

I kiss her foot and begin working my way up her leg. She's watching me, love oozing from her emerald gaze. When I reach her panties, I bite at them, tugging them away from her apex. I slide them to the side and lick her folds, causing her to buck her hips and moan. She tastes sweet as my tongue glides over and through her lips. Her response encourages me to suck her sensitive nub and swirl my tongue around it. Lena's pulling and tugging my hair in rhythm with my tongue, and my cock is begging to be let free from my jeans. I give her mound one last flick before pulling away.

My eyes lift to meet hers so she can watch me lick her honey from my lips. I slide up, begin removing her panties, and that's when I see it.

She has a thick, dark-colored scar running from below her belly button to her groin area. I glance up at her, and her eyes are moist. No doubt mourning all the loss she's endured. I begin running my fingers along the length of the mark, softly caressing the bumps that make up the zipper-like scar adorning her beautiful olive skin.

I rest my forehead on the dark area and let the enormity of it all sink in. Lena sacrificed everything for me. She lost so much. My heart is pounding in my chest. Thoughts of what she went through alone cause guilt to stir within me. Although I'm not the cause of this scar, I am the reason why she suffered alone. She did it all for me and for my happiness. I let out a long breath to calm my erratic heartbeat.

When I look up and meet Lena's eyes, tears are streaming down the sides of her face. She lifts her right hand, resting it on my left arm. I grab her fingers, intertwining them with mine, placing them on her scar. Our fingers drag in unison from top to bottom and back up, tracing the dark lines along her skin.

If I know Lena, she thinks this scar has ruined her. But it hasn't. This scar has made her more beautiful; it reveals her strength and tells the story of a warrior who made it through battle and still knows how to love fiercely.

CHAPTER TWENTY-FIVE

No More Secrets

MARIALENA

MASSIMO IS CARESSING THE heinous scar that plagues my body, reminding me every day of what was taken from me, of what will never be. His gentleness is twisting me up inside, churning the emotions of what could've been. I place my hand on his arm, and he pulls it down, tangling my fingers with his so that we can explore the jagged line that mutilated my midsection and destroyed my body, ruined me.

In all senses of the phrase, I'm empty inside. I've felt so lonely for too long. My emotions bubble to the surface, and I cannot stop the tears from escaping.

He moves our hands and bends over, putting his lips to the zipper-like flesh, scattering kisses over it. "I'm sorry you suffered through it alone," he whispers softly, almost as if he didn't mean for me to hear him. My lips quiver at his words, and my eyes sting as the emotion stirs within me. I take a deep breath to ease my thundering heart.

Massimo lifts his eyes to mine; they're dark, moisture at their rims glowing with love and lust and understanding. Without breaking his gaze away, he stands and unbuckles his belt, removing his jeans. He still knows me so well.

He knows that I'm hurting right now, that despite our conversations and apologies, the loss I feel is profound. He is going to make love to me because his touch has the ability to tear down my barriers, to heal me, and help me understand that I'll be okay.

Massimo grabs his wallet from his pants and takes out a foil packet, tossing it onto the blanket. I watch as he tugs his shirt up and over his head and removes his tighty-whities, letting his beautiful cock spring free. It's as thick and beautiful as I remember, its tip glistening with his arousal. The anticipation of feeling him buried inside ignites a firestorm of desire.

He drops to his knees at my side to finish sliding my panties down, then moves, so he's straddling me.

His arm stretches out to grab the condom he tossed onto the blanket, and I rise from my position, swinging my legs back to kneel.

I reach for the foil packet, tugging it from his fingers, and toss it back onto the blanket. Massimo draws his head back, his eyes questioning me. I remove my blouse, letting it drop to the floor, and stand up, setting my feet astride him. He squeezes my curvy hips with his hands, the pressure sending a tingle up my spine and between my legs. His lips find my scar, and he presses gentle kisses along its length.

My head tips up, and I exhale, pushing my hands into his unruly mane. This is the moment I've dreamed of for years—to have Massimo make love to me again. I cannot let my emotions of the past, and all the loss I endured, continue to torment me as it has. I have to be present and let him love me as only he knows how to.

His fingers push at my entrance, rubbing circles, playing with my folds—readying me for him. His breathing is heavy, his breath burning the skin underneath it, and I mewl from the pleasure.

With my knees bent, I hold on to his shoulders to steady myself until I'm hovering over his cock, and he guides himself to my entrance. I lower myself onto him so he can fill me, his heat setting the fire within me ablaze as he impales me—filling me with love.

Massimo hisses as he's stretching me. His hands wander to my back and unsnap my bra, tossing it to the side, tightening his arms around my torso, our bodies as close as they can be. His breath is hot at my ear, sucking my earlobe between his teeth—whispering words of love and endearment.

Once he's fully seated inside of me, I adjust to accommodate him. For the first time, I feel full.

Full of love.

Full of understanding.

Full of Massimo.

His lips find my taut nipples, and I watch him through a veil of loose curls falling over my shoulders. Massimo raises his head and begins devouring my mouth, kissing me with fervor—our tongues twisting, turning, and tangling. His grip tightens at my hips, lifting me up and down—inch by delicious inch. I take everything he has to give—mine.

Despite the years, my body remembers him. With each thrust, it recalls what we once were, each outstroke a reminder of what we always should've been.

My pace is slow and measured—rise and fall—and I feel his love each time he plunges into me. I haven't been intimate with Massimo in over nine years, but I've never felt as close to him as I do right now. There are no more secrets between us, and for the first time,

I'm giving myself to him completely.

Tears stream from my eyes. He must taste them because he licks at them, first from the left cheek, then the right—taking my pain and sorrow as his. A pleasurable ache starts building within me, and my breath quickens.

Massimo must notice the change in me because he brushes kisses along my jawline before running his tongue up my neck, over my chin, and landing back on my mouth. Our tongues are pressing and stroking each other as I climb toward the peak of my arousal until it crashes into me, spiraling me through blinding pleasure.

My heart swells. Emotions churn. Love surfaces.

His hands move around to grasp my buttocks, and he lays me back, repositioning himself. I kiss his chin, drag my tongue along his jawline as he continues with his punishing strokes. I tug at his thick hair, kissing the sides of his mouth until I pull his bottom lip between mine, sucking and biting.

My hands move to his back, where I rake my fingernails from his waistline up. His pace quickens, and his head drops, his mouth landing at my ear. "It was always you, nobody but you," falls from his lips as he comes undone and fills me with everything he has and everything he is.

We lie still, embracing one another, Massimo seated within me. His nose at my throat is dragging in a back-and-forth motion.

He separates from me, jumps to his feet, and darts out of the living room, quickly returning with a small towel in hand and another blanket. He uses the small towel to clean me up, then tosses it to the side and lies down, pulling my back to his front, ensuring to cover us with the blanket.

We lie there, listen to the Goo Goo Dolls sing about better days, and appreciate that we're once again in each other's arms. Massimo pushes my curls to the side, kissing behind my ear and the nape of my neck while I'm dragging my fingers up and down his leg.

"My heart is whole again."

My heartbeat quickens at his declaration, and my skin prickles under his hot breath.

I want to look into his eyes, so I turn around and proclaim, "I've thought about this moment since the day I left you. I never thought I'd look into your eyes again."

"Neither did I. I was resigned to living a life without you," he admits.

We sit in silence, just staring at each other. Words linger in the air. He must be in his feelings, as I am.

"I always thought we were good together," I say,

resting my palm on his cheek. "I now realize we weren't because I always kept a part of me hidden away."

"You just realized this now?"

I nod. "Yes. I've never felt closer to you as I did just now, as you made love to me." He rewards me with a lopsided grin.

"It's how I'll always make love to you." His confession is one I never knew I needed to hear and one I don't have a response to. Instead, I kiss my index and middle fingers then place them on his lips.

He extends his hand, taking one of my ringlets into his fingers, and begins twirling. "I missed you, missed doing this with your hair. It always relaxed me."

"You always loved playing with my hair when we were in bed or lying on the couch together."

"Lena." His eyes are piercing, searching mine.

"Massimo."

"I forgive you. We still have a lot of healing to do, but the first step is forgiveness."

"Thank you."

"Don't ever do something like that to me again. No more hiding. No more lies. No more secrets. I promise that I'll always listen to everything you share with me and keep an open mind. Promise me that you won't shut me out again."

"I promise."

He kisses the tip of my nose.

"So this—" I gesture between the two of us "—is a thing again?" I ask.

"Is that what you want?"

I nod, feel my eyes stinging, fighting back the tears from the emotions coursing through me.

He grasps my hand and kisses my fingers before saying, "Me too. It's all I've ever wanted. I don't know what tomorrow holds but the best we can do is try and see where life takes us. Besides, you and I—we're meant to be, so I think we'll be okay."

My heart is thudding in my chest at his words.

"Does it hurt?" he asks as his right hand reaches down, touching the scar on my belly.

"Physically, no."

"Tell me about it."

"Most days I'm okay. I've mourned the loss of my uterus. Some days though, it sucker-punches me when I least expect it. Sometimes it's a random baby or kid walking down the street. Other times someone I know is announcing they're pregnant, and I want to be happy for them, but jealousy creeps in, and everything I lost comes rushing back. A stark and ugly reminder that I'll never be a mother, and it hurts like a motherfucker." His fingers continue touching the bumpy skin. His other hand moves the ringlets that lay across my face, pushing them behind my ear.

"I want you to know, even though my boys have their mom, you'll be a part of their lives. I have no doubt you'll love them with all of your heart." His words hurt yet also fill my heart because he wants us to try again and wants me to be a part of their lives. It makes all the suffering and damage I caused worth it because I know he loves being a father more than anything.

Tears escape from my eyes, and he swipes them away and begins kissing me again.

My phone is ringing, and it wakes me from sleep. I lift my head from the pillow and see Massimo sprawled on his back to my left, softly snoring. He looks at peace and as beautiful as he always has.

I pull the blankets back and go into the kitchen to dig for my phone in my pockabook, which has stopped ringing by the time I find it in my purse.

It was Natalia. The time on my phone reads 9:07 a.m. She must be calling because I have an 11:00 a.m. phone conference scheduled with a client, and I'm still not in the office. I press the green button to dial her back.

When she answers, I say, "Hi, Natalia. What's up?"

"Hi, Lena. I was just checking in because you're usually here before me, and I know you have an 11:00 a.m. conference call with the Acosta family."

"Yes, please reschedule it for this afternoon, anytime. I'll be in, but not until a little later."

"Okay, will do. See you soon."

"Bye." I hit the End button and drop my phone back into my bag before heading back to the bedroom, stopping in the bathroom on my way. When I approach the bed, Massimo is stirring awake.

"Hi, sleepyhead," I say, crawling onto the bed to sidle up next to him.

"Mmm, I could get used to this again." He smiles, his eyes still closed.

"I have to get going soon, but if you're gonna wake up, I may have time for one of your famous breakfasts and some of that crappy coffee you love to drink." I hint because my stomach is growling.

"I see how it is; you want me just for my cooking skills." He's laughing now. His eyes open, blinking away the sleep in them.

He kisses me and says, "Is it really you, or am I dreaming?"

"It's me. Let me show you I'm really here." I extend my hand down and grasp his morning wood.

We're in the kitchen, and Massimo is making bacon and eggs. He still remembers how I like mine—over medium. I pop a few bread pieces in the toaster oven and search for the butter in the fridge.

Once we're sitting at the counter eating, he asks, "When can I see you again?"

I shrug. "I have to work late tonight because I have a trial next week, and I'm prepping my client tomorrow most of the day. Maybe this weekend?"

"I have the boys this weekend, but we're going to Paulie's house Saturday night. They're having a dinner party, and our kids love hanging out. You should come."

The piece of bacon I'm about to bite into stops short of my mouth. "You want me to meet the boys already?"

"Yeah, why not?" He looks up from his dish as if I asked him the most asinine question.

"I don't know. I just thought you might want to take it slow."

He drops his fork, extending his hand out to rub his thumb across my beauty mark. "Lena, we're not dating for the first time. We know who we are and that we're good together, that we will be good together! Besides, at Paulie's house, there will be a lot of people around, people you know, so it's a good way for you to meet them, like a soft opening of sorts."

I nod. "Okay. If that's what you want, I'll follow your lead." And I bite into the bacon strip.

THREE DAYS LATER

Massimo and I decided it would be best for me to meet them at Paulie's house. Paulie got married a few years ago and he and his wife, Anna Maria, who I'll be meeting for the first time, bought a house in Stoneham. I asked Massimo to text me when he left so that I could arrive when he was already there. When I told Luci I was going, she was excited because she and Dom would be there too, which I'm glad about. Despite my knowing Massimo's whole crew, I didn't exactly leave on great terms with all of them. Other than the funeral, it's the first time I'll be seeing them in a social setting. Having Luci there is like having my wing-woman—an ally, so I don't feel awkward.

As I drive up 93 toward Stoneham, I have my radio tuned to Kiss 108. "This is Love" by will.i.am starts playing, and I crank up the volume. Once I find the address, I park my car on the street and pop the trunk to get the four bottles of wine I brought.

I ring the doorbell, and a woman with long, dark brown hair, wire-framed glasses, and a mole over her right upper lip opens the door. "Hi, you must be Lena. I'm Anna Maria. Please come in."

I step into the house, and she closes the door behind me. "Hi, Anna Maria. It's nice to meet you." She leans in and kisses me cheek to cheek.

"I've heard a lot about you. I'm glad to finally meet you."

I cringe at the words and fake a smile. She can probably see it written all over my face because it definitely doesn't reach my eyes. She must've heard horror stories about me.

"Thank you for having me." I follow her into the house, through a walkway, and into a large kitchen with a center island that opens up to a large family room, a long wooden dining table off to the right.

"Lena, I'm so glad you came." Luci gets up from the couch, where she's sitting next to Dom, and runs across the room. I place the wine bottles down on the counter and hug Luci when she reaches me.

"Hi, Luce, I'm so happy you're here," I whisper into her ear.

As I'm separating from her, I see Stella standing

with Massimo's boys in the far corner. She's glaring at me despite the boys talking to her. I wish Massimo had told me she'd be here because I probably wouldn't have come. I could kill him for putting me on the spot like this, but I need to own up to my mistakes, which is probably why he didn't say anything. I haven't had the chance to talk to her to apologize, to try to make amends. This isn't really the place for that to happen, but I also don't want it to be weird for anyone. I'll have to speak to her at some point.

Massimo sidles up to me. "Hi, babe," he says, kissing me on the cheek, letting his warm lips linger. "Thank you for coming."

"Hi," I say. I remove my coat and scarf, handing them to Massimo, which he takes and puts in the hallway together with my pockabook.

"Lena, good to see you again," Dom says, kissing me hello.

"Likewise, Dom. Love looks good on you," I respond.

"Seriously, Lena!" Luci exclaims, swatting my arm.

"What? It does," I tease.

"Lena, red or white?" asks Anna Maria from across the room, where she's holding a bottle of each in her hand.

"Red, please. Thank you."

"Lena, you look fucking great," Paulie exclaims, hugging me.

"Good to see you too, Paulie. Congrats on the wedding, the house. All of it. I'm so happy for you."

"It's great to have you back. Maybe now Massimo will stop being such an asshole," Paulie says, and laughs while patting Massimo on the back. "Hey, kids," yells Paulie, "come say hello." At that, four little people come running up to him, two of which are Massimo's boys. "This is my son Antonio and my daughter Alessia. This is our friend Lena."

"Hi," they both say in unison, and each kisses me before skipping back to where they were just playing.

"And these are my guys, Lucio and Leandro," Massimo chimes in, running his hands through Lucio's thick hair.

"Daddy, is this your friend we saw at the store?" Lucio asks.

"Yes, buddy, great memory."

"Hi, boys. It's nice to see you again." I squat down to their level, and they each come and kiss me before scurrying back to the other side where they were playing with Paulie's kids.

I stand and turn to Massimo, who hands me my wine glass. "You should've told me Stella was gonna be here," I whisper and sip at my wine.

"Nah, then you wouldn't have come. You need to squash that and make things right."

"You don't say!" I roll my eyes and walk away, crossing the room toward Stella, who's in the corner with the kids.

"Hi, Stella."

"Hi, Lena." Her arms are crossed.

"Can we go to the other room for a few minutes? I owe you an apology and would like to talk in private if that's okay." Without responding, she stands and leaves the room. I follow. We're walking through the hallway I just came through and into the front living room, where there's a formal sitting area.

We sit on the couch, and I look into Stella's eyes. "I'm sorry. I know those words may not mean a lot right now, may not do a lot to take the sting out of what I did. But I am. I never meant to hurt you."

"We were friends. You were gonna be my sister. You didn't just leave Massimo. You abandoned all of us. We were all left behind to clean up your fucking mess."

"I know I caused a lot of damage, wounded all of you."

"You don't know shit! You have no idea what it was like, and Massimo will never tell you. But I will.

He could barely get out of bed on some days. He cut himself off from all of his friends, barely ate, and was drinking a lot! I was the one who put him back together," she says, pointing to her chest, tears streaming down her cheeks. "Our mother and me, may she rest in peace. When I saw you were back, and he just let you back in, I was furious. I couldn't believe he was speaking to you!"

"You have every right to be. He's your brother, and you want to protect him."

"Damn straight."

I drop my eyes and fidget with my glasses. The silence is uncomfortable because I burned the bridge that connects us, and Stella is making sure I haven't forgotten it. The voices in the kitchen fill the pregnant silence between us.

"He told me, you know."

"About why I left?"

"Yes."

"I'm glad he did. If he hadn't, I would've. I wanted to tell him before I told anyone else. He deserved to know first. After that, I started to talk to those closest to me, to make amends for everything I put everyone through. I'm sorry that I'll never have the opportunity to apologize to your mother. I hope you can find it in your heart to forgive me someday."

"I get why you did it. I think you went about it the wrong way, but I understand. When Massimo told me, I even felt bad for you for all that you sacrificed and lost. The whole situation is so fucked up. And now we have Lucio and Leandro, and it's like I can't be mad because then they wouldn't be here. It's twisted because I want to be angry but can't be."

"Yes. You feel what I do, what Massimo feels, so I understand. Those boys are why I did it. I haven't seen him be their father, but I already know he's amazing with them."

"He is," she says. "They're the only thing that gave him life after you left. Even then, the Massimo I knew was never truly back. His light never shone as bright."

I grasp her hands in mine and say, "Thank you for sharing all of that with me. It means a lot."

"I accept your apology. I'm sure someday soon I'll come around again and forgive you too."

"I hope so."

"You only get to fuck up once, Lopez. Next time, you'll have to deal directly with me. Understood?" Her lips are in a straight line, her eyes squinting.

"Thank you, Stella. I promise, no more drama from me."

We both stand and embrace each other.

"You girls kiss and make up or what?" Massimo

asks. When Stella and I separate from one another, I see him standing at the entryway, arms crossed over his chest.

"Yes," Stella says. "But she knows I'll kick her ass next time if she even thinks about pulling any shit like that again." She kisses him on the cheek before leaving the room.

"You should've told me she was gonna be here," I repeat as he's approaching me.

"You would've made up all sorts of excuses not to come. Now it's done, and everything is good." He pulls me into him and kisses my temple. "I'm glad you're here. It's where you belong," he declares, and I squeeze my arms tighter around him.

"Yo, Dello, get your ass in here. Time to eat," Paulie yells from the other room.

He gives me one last kiss before turning to walk back to the dining room. Everyone is sitting at the table already. We settle into the two remaining empty seats, with Massimo sitting next to Leandro and Stella two seats down, on the other side of Lucio.

Anna Maria says, "Massimo, why don't you give the toast before we start eating."

Everyone raises their glasses, and Massimo looks at me and says, "To new beginnings."

We all repeat, "To new beginnings," and raise our

glasses before taking a drink.

EPILOGUE

MARIALENA

"WE'LL TAKE HOME THE gray and white girl in the second to last corral," I say to the young woman at the desk. Massimo and I are at the animal shelter to rescue a dog. I've wanted to rescue one since moving back to Boston, but I held off because I lived in the city. The female we're taking home is around three years old, and she came from a home with kids. The family that surrendered her couldn't keep her when the father of the family became severely ill. She's a small mixed breed Maltese Shih Tzu.

Late last year, we decided to finally move in together again. We dated for a little over a year before deciding it was time. Massimo had wanted to move in after just a few months of dating, but I was reluctant because of his boys. I wanted them to be okay with all the changes. It's hard enough having parents in two households.

We moved to a house in Newton Corner because Massimo has shared custody of the boys. They spend several nights each week with us and living in the city no longer made sense. Apartments in our price range aren't big enough, and the ones that are, are way too expensive. We now have more space, a yard, Massimo's drive to the boys' school isn't that far, and our drive into the city is short. Plus, my parents are less than a ten-minute drive from us, which is a bonus.

Once we complete the required paperwork, we're in Massimo's X6 driving home, and the dog is in the back seat in the pet carrier barking.

"The boys are gonna be excited when they meet her," I say.

"They're gonna flip out."

"We should wait to name her until they get to the house tomorrow; let them choose her name."

Massimo looks over at me, smiling. "Yeah, they'll love that. Thank you."

His hand extends across the center console, palm

facing up, and I curl my fingers into his and squeeze.

Massimo: I have the boys—be home in about 20.

Massimo picked up the boys from school. Lucio is in first grade, and Leandro is in kindergarten. Although I work from home a lot these days because I have a spacious home office, I don't pick the boys up often because Camila doesn't care for me. I've tried to be friendly with her, for the boys' sake, but it's not gone over well. Massimo has tried as well, but I told him it's not worth getting upset over; she'll come around in her own time. He's working on keeping his anger at bay when it comes to the whole situation.

Before closing the office door behind me, I power off the laptop to go into the kitchen, the dog following closely behind me, her tail wagging. Once there, I let the dog out into the backyard so the boys won't see her when they get here.

"We're home!" Feet pound the floor as they run through the house.

"Hi, guys, how was school today?"

"Hi, Lena," says Leandro, kissing me on the cheek.

"Lena, I'm hungry. Can we have a snack?" Lucio says.

Massimo saunters in behind them, carrying their backpacks. "Hi, babe." He leans in to swipe my lips; his are warm and wet. "Lucio, say hello, please," Massimo says.

"Sorry, Daddy, I forgot because I'm so hungry. Hi, Lena," he says, kissing me hello and hugging me. I squeeze him back.

"Thank you for that hug, Lucio. I needed that today."

"You're welcome. Now can we have a snack?"

I chuckle. "Yes, you can. You want a grilled cheese sandwich and some apple slices?"

"Can I have *dulce de leche* with my apple?" asks Leandro.

"Sure, I think I have some. Why don't you boys go wash your hands and put your stuff away while I make your snack?" The boys scurry out of the kitchen, and I can hear them running up the stairs.

"Babe, come here." Massimo wraps his arm around my thick waist, brushing kisses along my neck. "I missed you today."

"Missed me? I saw you this morning." I wrap my arms up around his neck

"I know, but I had to leave so early when I would've

rather stayed in bed."

"Rough life you have," I tease.

"I'll show you rough." He removes my glasses, placing them on the counter. He kisses me deeply, sucking on my lips and teasing them apart. Heat spreads over me, and I squeeze my legs together to quell the tingling sensation.

I hear the boys' voices and their feet as they begin their descent down the stairs. I quickly separate from Massimo, putting my glasses back on, and open the fridge to grab the cheese.

The boys eat their snacks, and when they finish cleaning up after themselves, Massimo takes them into the family room while I bring the dog in from the yard. I open the door, scooping her up into my arms.

"We have a dog?" Lucio squeals and they both jump up from where they're sitting.

"What's his name?" Leandro asks.

"She doesn't have a name yet. We were waiting for you guys to get home from school and name her," I say.

"It's a girl dog?" asks Leandro.

"Yes, buddy. You and your brother need to decide on a girl's name for her," Massimo tells them. I sit down on the couch next to Massimo, and the boys both crowd me, wanting to pet her.

"She's wicked soft. We can call her Fluffy!" Leandro says.

"That's a dumb name," Lucio says.

"Be nice," Massimo adds.

"What about Olivia? We can call her Livvy, for short?" I chime in.

"I like Livvy," Lucio says.

"Me too," adds Leandro.

"You both like Livvy?"

"Yes!" They scream in unison, jittering from excitement.

"Okay, Livvy it is." I pet her and run my hand over her soft hair before placing her on the floor. The boys follow her, both wanting to pet her, trying to pick her up, but Livvy keeps running away from them.

I stand to grab a few of the stuffed toys we bought for her, tossing them onto the floor so the boys can play with her.

Massimo tells them, "Guys, you have to be gentle with her. Make sure you don't get in her face. She needs to get to know you first, and then she'll be friends with you."

My phone rings, and I dash to the kitchen to grab it before I miss the call.

"Hello."

"Hi, this is Emily from the Crane Estate."

"Hi, Emily, this is Lena. What can I do for you?"

"We have to move the time of your appointment next week, from noon to 1:00 p.m., if that's okay."

Massimo and I are planning our wedding for this September, and we chose to have the ceremony and reception at the Crane Estate, a private property that overlooks Crane Beach—our favorite beach. We have an appointment scheduled for next week for a tasting. Massimo is dead set on hiring chefs he knows to prepare the food, but it would be way more expensive to do that. I convinced him to at least go to the tasting before he outright declines it. But if I know him, he's probably just going to keep me quiet.

"Yes, that's fine. Thank you for calling." I place my phone back onto the kitchen counter and return to the family room.

Massimo proposed to me earlier this year after we had settled into the house. This time, it was very different than the first time around. After a long day at work, I had arrived home and was feeling terrible because I had lost a removal hearing. As soon as I walked through the door, the boys were super excited to see me and asked me to go to the family room because they had a surprise for me. I was drained and had hoped to shower and relax, but that didn't happen.

FOUR MONTHS EARLIER

"Lena, Lena. Sit here, Daddy is upstairs, and he's coming now, but he told us we have to sit here and wait for him and that you're not allowed to go anywhere until he gets here," Lucio tells me excitedly as he grasps my hand and pulls me toward the couch.

"Wow. It must be very important if I'm not allowed to move. Can you give me any hints?"

"Nooo, Daddy said we couldn't say anything, that it's a big secret," Leandro responds.

"A big secret. Oh boy," I say.

"I'm going to get Daddy now that Lena is here," Leandro says.

"Okay, tell him that we're ready and that we didn't give away any secrets," Lucio chimes in. I chuckle at their enthusiasm.

What is going on here, and what is with all the secrecy? I'm so drained, and Massimo couldn't have picked a worse day for doing whatever he has planned. After losing the removal hearing, I had difficulty processing and discussing it with the client. There is a glimmer of hope with the appeals process, but it doesn't make today's loss any easier. I feel like getting up and telling Massimo that today isn't the day for surprises, but the boys are so eager, I can't bear to crush their excitement. Lucio is sitting next to me. He's jittery with anticipation. I hear Massimo and Leandro's voices and their footsteps on the stairs.

"Hi, babe," Massimo says, leaning in to kiss me.

"Hi. What's going on here?" I ask.

"Daddy, can we start?" Leandro asks.

"The boys have a surprise for you, and yes, boys, go ahead. I'll sit down next to Lena so you can start."

Lucio stands, and he sprints over to Leandro and whispers something in his ear. Massimo is sitting to my left and reaches for my hand, curling his fingers with mine. I look at him and whisper, "What are they doing?"

He shrugs. "I don't know. It's a surprise for me too."

He has that mischievous look, and I don't believe for one second that he has no idea what they're up to. When the boys are done whispering to each other, they separate, and both stand before us.

"Ready. One, two, three," Lucio says. In unison, they shout, "Lena, will you marry us?" Both boys start jumping up and down and then run over to Massimo, who hands Lucio a box. Together they open the box

and give it to me.

I glance over at Massimo, tears rimming my eyes. He reaches out, runs his thumb across my beauty mark, and mouths, "I love you."

"Lena, is the answer, yes?" Leandro squeals.

"Yes, boys, of course, I will. I love you with all my heart, and I want nothing more than to marry your dad."

"She said yes, Daddy! She said yes!" Lucio screams, and both boys start jumping up and down again.

Massimo takes the box from my hands, removes the ring from it, the same one he proposed with years ago, and slides it halfway up my finger. His dark brown eyes are soft and lock with mine. "You're my better half, and I want us to spend the rest of our days together. You make me whole. Will you be my Mrs.?"

"The answer is always yes," I whisper, my heart thundering in my chest. He finishes sliding the ring on and kisses me softly.

I rise from the couch and kneel on the floor. "Boys, come here. I want to hug you both because you've made me so happy with your surprise."

The boys both rush me, and I pull them into an embrace, one in each arm, squeezing them tightly. "I love you both so much. Thank you. Your surprise was the best one in the whole world."

Massimo kneels behind them and wraps his arms around them so that we're all huddled in a family hug. Tears are streaming down my cheeks. What started as a terrible day turned out to be a perfect night.

"Our appointment for the tasting next week was pushed back to 1:00 p.m. I'll call Luci later to let her know. Will you call Dom?"

Dom and Luci are attending the tasting with us to help us decide. We thought it best that someone come with us in case we can't make up our mind. Luci is my Maid of Honor, and although Rocco is Massimo's Best Man, Dom is coming with us because he'll help with the wine pairings. Besides, he and Luci are still an item, so we plan on going out that night after we finish at the Crane Estate.

"Yeah, I'll let him know."

"You want me to do homework with Lucio, and you can take Livvy and Leandro?"

"That works."

After the boys play with Livvy for a little while, Massimo and Leandro leave to take her for a walk, and Lucio and I sit at the dining room table to do his homework. He usually doesn't need much help and can finish on his own. As he's working through it, I catch up on some work emails.

When he finishes, Lucio says, "Lena, my teacher gave us this list today. It's for summer reading since school is almost over. Can we go to the library soon?" I take the sheet of paper he has in his hands.

"Yes, we have to return the books we borrowed last time. Tomorrow when you get back from school, we can go if you'd like."

"Yes, please. I love it when you take us to the library. It's one of my favorite things to do."

"Mine too, buddy."

MASSIMO

Lena is putting the boys to bed while I finish cleaning up from dinner.

When I reach the top of the stairs, I see the light in the boys' room still on and am ready to find out why they're still awake but see that Lena is with them. I quietly approach the door to watch them. The three of them are lying on the bottom bunk bed, a full-size mattress, with Lena in the middle. Lena is reading to them.

Lucio is tucked into Lena's side, and he's playing with her hair. Leandro has his head resting on Lena's chest with her rubbing his back. Since Lena and I moved back in together, they like it when she reads stories more than when I do it. So, whenever it's possible, Lena does the bedtime routine with them.

My heart swells when I see the way they are with her. I was worried about their relationship with her and that it would be strained or that their mother would poison them. Thankfully, neither of those things happened. It took them a few stays at the house to warm up to her, but it was amazing to see once they did. They're not her biological children, but she loves and dotes on them as if they are. When it comes to them, I'm the rule maker, and she's the rule breaker.

Lena catches me watching her, and a small grin creeps up while she's reading—animating the story as she does. Lucio is asking questions; his imagination is always so vivid during story time. And Lena indulges him, letting him tell his side stories for all the characters and going along with his storytelling.

By the time Lena comes into the bedroom, I'm already lying down and reading. After she finishes brushing her teeth, she places her glasses onto the nightstand before climbing into bed. She lies facing me, tugging the blanket up over her shoulder.

"The boys take long to fall asleep?" I ask, placing my book onto the nightstand.

"No. They fought it as always because they wanted me to read them another story, but they passed out."

"That's good."

"Tomorrow after school I'm taking them to the library. Try not to pick them up too late."

"Okay."

"You gonna finish what you started today?" she asks.

"What's that?" I respond, turning to face her.

"Come closer, and I'll remind you." She shimmies closer to meet me halfway. Her breath is hot and smells minty from the toothpaste. Her hand reaches for my face, resting on my cheek, and I brush my lips to hers.

"You were gonna show me how rough you were," she says in a breathy voice.

"Hmm. Let's see if I can remember."

"I love you, Mr. D."

"I love you more, Mrs. D.

THE END

To be informed of new releases, special offers, and upcoming projects, subscribe to Shelly's Newsletter: https://bit.ly/ShellyCruzNL

Visit my website: www.shellycruz.com

Email me: shellycruzwrites@gmail.com

Reader Group on Facebook: www.facebook.com/groups/shellycruzwrites

If you enjoyed this book, please consider leaving a review on the platform you purchased it from. As authors we truly appreciate reader feedback and reviews. You can also recommend it to friends and family, or mention it in reader discussion groups and social media platforms. Thank you so much for reading this story. Your support is truly appreciated and means SO MUCH!

A Note from the Author

This should be read after reading the book as it CONTAINS SPOILERS

I am forty-three years old and I've never been pregnant (and it's not for lack of trying).

You see, when I was eighteen I had still never had a menstrual cycle. So I did what most people would do and went to see an OB/Gyn. She only asked a couple of questions, she didn't order any tests, and she prescribed birth control. "Take birth control. That will regulate you and keep you from getting pregnant. You're eighteen and don't need to be having kids this young," she said in her flat voice.

I can still see and hear her if I close my eyes. For years I did as I was told and religiously took my birth control pill (almost) every night before bed. After all, she was a doctor and I had my whole life ahead of me to have kids, right? Maybe not.

At twenty-three I finally decided something was wrong with me. I had just started dating Alex (my husband), and I had been taking birth control for five years. I mean, there had been more than one occasion when I forgot to take the pill and I seriously thought it could be an oops moment. There were no oops to be had, which of course in hindsight I'm thankful for, but at that moment thinking something could be wrong with me made me feel broken. As an overthinker, I could not turn off the negative thoughts running through my head. I decided to stop taking birth control because I needed to see if I would menstruate on my own. I didn't.

For nearly one year I did not have a period. My hormones were all over the place, and I cannot forget to mention those stubborn wire hairs growing around my chin area that I obsessively tweezed every day. I felt bloated, moody, angry, sad, emotional, confused, and I was not feeling feminine in the slightest.

The Diagnosis

In early March 2003 (I was twenty-four) I saw a doctor at the University Health Center. He induced a period, ordered me to have all the tests (that the first doctor should have done) and in late April of that year, I finally got answers. I was diagnosed with Polycystic Ovarian Syndrome (PCOS), which is a hormonal disorder causing enlarged ovaries with small cysts on the outer edges as well as Primary Amenorrhea, which is the failure of menses to occur by age sixteen (and in my case I had yet to have a menstrual cycle without the help of meds).

"In over twenty years of practice, I have never

seen this combination. It's fascinating," the doctor told me with more enthusiasm than I would have liked to have heard. That doctor (an Endocrinologist) told me there was a high probability that I would never have children. The only words I heard were "never have children." Everything else sounded muffled. Those words may as well have been a punch to the gut. They knocked the wind right out of me and I was silenced by their heaviness. I felt like I was in *The Twilight Zone*. That day I called in sick to work and drove for hours in silence. No music. No company. No food. Just my thoughts and the open road.

It was news that I never shared. Not with my parents, not with my siblings, not with my friends. I put the secret in a box, wrapped chains around it, locked it up, and threw away the key. It weighed like a ton of bricks but damn I was good at carrying that weight. I always smiled, laughed, joked, hung out, lent an ear to all those who needed me, worked and studied like crazy. I was the person everyone could count on. No one suspected a thing. But behind closed doors, I felt shame. I cried in bed, in the shower, or when I would randomly see moms with their babies. I felt empty. I felt alone.

When I got my diagnosis, my relationship with Alex was becoming serious. I knew I had to tell him my secret. Not doing so would ruin everything and it wouldn't have been fair to keep it from him. I had no idea how I was going to do it. I was (and still am) never one to shy away from heavy conversations, after all they're part of life. But this? What would he say? How would he react? Would he leave me? This secret had me thinking and feeling things that are completely out of character for me.

I danced around the subject for weeks, waiting for the right moment, the right place, the right time. But let's be honest, there is no right moment to tell the man you love you probably can't have kids. So, one night over dinner as we ate our rice and beans I dropped the infertility-bomb. I opened up my secret box and told him everything. I felt so much lighter after saying it out loud to someone other than my reflection in the mirror.

His reaction was nothing that my mind had made it out to be. He hugged me, he told me he loved me no matter what, and he asked questions about it. Then he said, "The doctor didn't tell you that you cannot absolutely have children, he said you may not be able to. It's not the same thing. We will get help and we will have a baby." And just like that, he changed my perspective. His ability to see things from a different perspective and in a positive light when I cannot is one of the many things I love about him. From that day, I no longer had to face the struggles of infertility by myself.

Infertility

Over the next few years we sought help from my OB/GYN, an Endocrinologist (a doctor who specializes in glands and the hormones they make), and an Infertility Specialist. I underwent extensive testing, treatments, and took a lot of medication. Throughout this time, I still only had a menstrual cycle if I took meds to induce it. Despite all the things we tried, we never tried In Vitro Fertilization (IVF) because we couldn't afford it. I never got pregnant. My body wasn't cooperating. I was frustrated and angry. We gave up.

Because I couldn't get pregnant, I decided to focus on everything else in my life. If I just kept busy, bettered myself, volunteered, traveled, studied, and worked, then I wouldn't think about my body's inability to procreate. I loved doing all the things that kept me busy, but I still never addressed the underlying issue. I always told myself, there is still more we can attempt. There is still hope for us to have a baby. There is still time. I had to stop putting Band-Aids and blindfolds on what was wrong and make a decision once and for all. Years later we still want a baby and we have decided to try IVF.

In Vitro Fertilization

Last year Alex and I shared our struggle and decision to try IVF with our family and closest friends. It was the first time I really talked about my history with anyone other than Alex or doctors. The more I told my story, the more I wanted to share it. It's incredible how many people struggle in similar ways. But nobody talks about it. It's almost as if it's a taboo subject. I suffered in silence for many years not realizing that so many individuals around me were also suffering in silence.

In my forty-three years of life, I've had two spontaneous (aka natural) menstrual cycles. Because of that, I've felt ashamed, embarrassed, weak, not-woman-enough, out-of-control, like a failure (and many other things)—all because my body is broken and continues to betray me. After all, I often hear people say, or read an article that says, "Being a mother is the greatest accomplishment of a woman." When I hear and read those things, the only thing I interpret is that I am not a mother, therefore I am a failure.

I am at a point in my life where I make decisions that are the best for me (and my husband). If I want something, I buy it. If I want to experience something, I do it. If I want to travel somewhere, I go. But getting pregnant and having a baby is something I cannot control. And for this Type-A personality, that's a tough pill to fuckin' swallow. For years I kept silent and never shared my story because of the shame that coursed through my veins. I am no longer ashamed. I will no longer be silent.

This year we started the IVF process. I've had two Egg Retrievals and we have a good number of frozen embryos. We are now ready to move onto the next phase of transferring those embabies into my uterus in hopes that they'll stick and a baby will grow. If my story can help even one person out there, then my work here is done.

My lifelong struggle with infertility led me to create this fictional love story. It's a story I've thought about for a long time. When I started openly discussing my struggle, having so many private conversations with women about their similar journeys reinforced the fact that we need to discuss these issues more often. I talk about my struggle and my journey as much as possible in an effort to break the silence. Massimo and Lena's story is an extension of the journey I'm on—getting people to discuss infertility and the impact it has on people's lives.

Resources

If you are someone you know has PCOS, please visit: www.pcosaa.org

If you or someone you has Endometriosis, please visit: www.endofound.org

If you or someone you know suffers with Infertility, please visit: resolve.org

Acknowledgments

To my Alpha Readers: Janet Aznar, Jessica O'Connell, Kristie Puentes, and Akilah Harris—you ladies read this story as I was piecing it together, chapter by chapter. Thank you for your patience, guidance, and friendship. Your encouragement, feedback, constructive criticism, and support mean so much. I am truly grateful for each of you and this story is better because of your participation.

To my Beta Readers: Lisa DeMarco, Silvia Gonzalez, Nicole Reid, Shannel Rivera, Dawn Sousa Birch, and Jacob Cohen. Thank you for your honest opinions. You each provided feedback to help make this story authentic and real and it was crucial in making this work of fiction what it is. Jake, Massimo's voice is genuine and realistic because of your feedback. Thank you for helping me bring him to life. Your feedback was immensely helpful.

To everyone that helped me along the journey to make Nine Years Gone come together, my sincerest gratitude! **Murphy Rae** created a stunning cover from my jumbled visions and I couldn't have asked for a more beautiful cover; **Alyssa Garcia** with Uplifting Author Services made the interior of this book beautiful, and was so patient with me when I had a million questions; **Erica Russikoff**, my editor—I entrusted my book baby to you. Thank you for showing it the love that you did; **Virginia Tesi Carey** and **Lori Sabin**—your attention to detail is impeccable, thank you for proofreading with your fine-tuned eyes. **Kiki** and the entire team at **The Next Step PR**, thank you for all your support in helping me navigate my introduction to the author/writing world. **Christine Brae** and **A.L. Jackson**, both of you are two authors whose books I absolutely adore, and the words you've written have impacted me. You're both extremely talented, successful authors, and Boss ladies! That each of you took the time out of your busy schedules to read this story and provide me with your feedback is absolutely invaluable and there are not enough words to express my gratitude to each of you.

To my besties since day one, Jessica, Kristen, Lucia, and Melissa—you ladies give me life (and lots of ideas for my stories and characters) and I am thankful for each of you every day. My #RideOrDie sisters till the end of time.

A mi Mami, soy la mujer que soy por vos. Gracias por todo tu amor y todo tu apoyo. To my sisters and brothers, you all support me in all my endeavors and your encouragement pushes me to be a better person every day.

And last but not least, my husband Alex whose patience should be rewarded—it's not always easy being my other half. Gracias por tener tanta paciencia conmigo todos los días, pero especialmente mientras estaba escribiendo este libro. Te amo.

About the Author

Shelly Cruz is a lawyer who runs her own law firm in Miami, Florida. She was born and raised just outside of Boston, Massachusetts by a fierce Argentinian mom and super strict Puerto Rican dad. When she's not researching and writing legal documents, she enjoys expressing her creativity by writing fiction. She's a lover of love, romance, and relationships, which is why she writes wicked sexy romance. In her free time, Shelly loves reading, traveling, and riding on the back of her husband's Harley Davidson motorcycle while enjoying the open road.

Facebook: www.facebook.com/shellycruzwrites
Instagram: www.instagram.com/shellycruzwrites
Goodreads: www.goodreads.com/author/
show/20726422.Shelly_Cruz
Twitter: twitter.com/shellycwrites
Pinterest: www.pinterest.com/shellycruzwrites

Made in the USA
Columbia, SC
06 September 2022

66723920R00243